Virginia

Alan Smith

Stairwell Books

Published by Stairwell Books
161 Lowther Street
York, YO31 7LZ

www.stairwellbooks.co.uk
@stairwellbooks

ISBN: 978-1-939269-89-8

Layout: Alan Gillott
Printed and bound in the UK by Imprint Digital

The front cover is based on *Sunnyside* by David Gill. This is part of
a series of pictures of Earls Barton and the Nene Valley made by
the artist in 2014

For Amelie

Chapter 1

Virginia woke up in the house where she had been a child. She slept in the empty bed that her mother had left, in the clean white sheets that her mother had washed and ironed. There, when she opened her eyes, was the chest of four, deep drawers where her mother's underclothes and stockings, blouses and sweaters were folded into the smell of lavender from the garden. Virginia had opened the drawers when she was looking for sheets and pillow cases. Open and shut again on her mother's neat folding. The sweet rub of lavender was around her, now, lying wide awake with the muted, morning sun behind the curtains.

She had always worn her mother's clothes, raiding ruthlessly when she had lived here, at home, for the good, expensive clothes that her mother always bought. 'Quality lasts,' she would say, 'it's a dear do when you buy cheap stuff.' Virginia sat on the edge of the bed in the long, white nightie that had been her mother's. There was silken embroidery around its square neck and at the hem. Her mother had had it, always.

In the tiny, white bathroom she drank a glass of water and looked at herself in the square mirror over the sink. She saw her dark brown hair. It fell thickly in a wavy, heavy mass to the level of her jaw. With her splayed fingers she brushed it back from her face and held up her chin and looked into her own bright brown eyes that dared another word out of anyone.

She went into her old room at the back of the house where there was space for her. The nightie was long and got in the way. She pulled it off, over her head, and it felt odd to be naked in this room, doing this.

She stood up straight and found her balance, then stepped forward into her first stretch that pulled at her calf and the tendons behind her knee and down into her heel. She went through her whole routine, breathing, stretching, took her time, missed none of it out, getting herself ready. The softness of her flesh was a deceit; when she moved the hard line of muscle and sinew showed beneath it in curve and shadow.

She stood in the shower and thought about what she was going to do and how she would have to look. The sort of person who can do this, she thought, that sort of person. She listened to the hiss of the water breaking over her and thought about Dan.

She scooped out two fingertips of soft, vanilla scented shea. She put up her foot on the edge of the bath and spread out the slip smooth butter from knee to toe and onto her thigh rubbing gently with her fingers and harder with the heel of her hand into the long, relaxed muscle behind her thigh, one leg and then the other. With both hands she stroked the shea into her belly and buttocks, dipping again into the sticky jar, moving her hips against the movement of her hands. She rolled her shoulders under her palms and smoothed downwards over her stretched neck, over her breasts and finished, wiping her palms and fingertips along the edge of her ribcage, following the bone onto the edge and dip of muscle along her spine.

She put on her good, linen trousers that would not crease, they were jade and had a sheen that moved in the light, and a skimpy white tee shirt, that always made her mother's eyebrows lift, silky and clinging.

Virginia leaned forward into the big oval mirror on her mother's dressing table. Lancombe lipstick, perfumed and fruity on the edge of her tongue, almost transparent; gold-bronze grains on her eyelids; liner that quietened her eyes; blusher; black studs in her ears. She gave herself a long squirt of Calvin Klein, turned back to the mirror. Right, she thought, bloody right. She got up and took her jacket from the coat hanger that she had hooked on the door knob: a corn gold jacket tailored in raw, faded silk.

***

She sat in her car. Low white clouds rough-housed across the sky and great gaps of shining blue made the air she breathed hot and stale. The car behind her pulled away, she saw it in the mirror. A blonde woman in high heels and denim jeans walked past. There were two men with carrier bags, jaunty, bald and fat, brothers surely. They got into the car in front of her, smiled and backed away. She looked around at all the coming and going and it struck her, suddenly, that people dressed up a little when they came to the hospital. They had the look of people on holiday, that same sense of being out of the ordinary. She felt it herself, not ordinary; going to sit through a death and quite enjoying it. She got out of the car, not wanting the thought of that, and then, hidden in the sunshine, the cold wind caught her.

She walked past the open door that led to Dan's ward, putting him off for just a little longer. The corridor smelled like a new office block, a wide corridor running the length of the hospital, long and straight. She walked, sauntered along it, swinging her big, leather shoulder bag by its strap so that it brushed the plastic floor. She went past shiny potted plants and framed photographs of sepia Northampton and as she walked she read the signs, saying them to herself: Haematology, Patients with Samples, Urodynamics. She thought about that one, Urodynamics, what could that be then she asked herself?

A green electric truck, beeping and whining made her stand against the wall, a train of laundry bins. She looked across and saw the double doors. Theatres. There was the smell of fat, the steamy feel of gravy in the air. She strolled past Pathology, glanced into the bright, formicaed restaurant. She stopped and began the walk back. She put the strap over her shoulder and pushed her bag behind her arm and clicked her heels down the plastic street, past the reassuring, gruesome signs and stood still, looking into the ward where Dan lay, waiting to hurt her.

***

3

'I dreamed last night.'

'What about?'

But then he did not want to tell her, did not want all the effort of turning his pictures into words and, in any case, could not do it.

She stood, waiting for him, looking at the length of his body with its long, sharp bones. She could see the frizzy, grey hair on his chest where his pyjama jacket was folded open. He closed his eyes. The eyelids were suddenly there, reptilian, sliding on the roundness of the eye. She thought of her hand falling gently onto his breast, her white hand with its rings and the loose bracelets falling, pinching the nipple, softly. Not now.

He made pictures; all his life making pictures into big, serious things that stared back at him, stopping him dead with their completeness. He felt breath, felt something, on the bare skin of his chest, felt it in the hair, moving in amongst the hair, threading and parting, pushing its soft, wet snout. His pyjamas and the crumpled sheet beneath him pressed into his skin. He could see the sweat rubbing its way into the lines and crevices of his back.

'What about?' She said it so softly that he knew it was not for him. 'The first night I saw you I put my hand in your shirt and nipped you.' She was whispering, and made him angry with all these soft goodbyes.

He made the head of a boy, drawing quickly and picking up the face in watercolour and made him beautiful, then twisted the soft line of the nostril and rimmed it with blue, gorged the lower lip until it rolled with lust. He felt her hand on him, just touching, hardly touching. He saw her. She was sitting, half turned, on the bed. He had not felt her weight settle into the mattress. Away, he had been away, making and spoiling his boy.

'What did you dream?' she said. 'Tell me your dreams.' He picked his hand from the bed. She saw the thumb and forefinger feel each other out and fall onto the empty sheet. 'Tell me your dreams,' she said, mocking him.

'I dreamed about whisky.' He smiled at her, gave her his gummy, yellow smile and sent her away, remembering his hand, black ink under

4

the fingernails, bringing the half bottle out of his jacket pocket, pouring a tot for her into the metal cap. The thin, sharp metal edge on her lips, sipping as he big-swallowed and laughed his dirty, shouting laugh. The bastard.

'I dreamed about saving my empty stomach all afternoon and then going and having three big ones, one after another. "Large whisky. Large whisky,"' he said, ordering and seeing the barman in his plum waistcoat turn and push up the glass onto the optic, wait and push it up again. 'Never painted whisky,' he said, amazed. 'Never painted it. Why's that for God's sake?'

She took up his hand, bone white and pink. 'Tell me another,' she said, 'tell me another dream.'

'My eyes,' he said, 'are brilliant. The only things still going strong. Completely knackered, every other damned thing. I can't even shit. You know that something's not as it should be when you can't even shit. Something you take for granted that. I do anyway. What about you Ginny, do you take that for granted, shitting? I never thought you did. Not the taking for granted, the thing itself, the shitting. You were too lovely, too lovely to go around shitting all over the place.'

He had her laughing. 'You old bugger,' she said.

'Hair's okay,' he said. He took his hand from her and stroked his long, grey hair, grey streaked with ashy black. Good, heavy hair and his wrecked face. 'Hair and eyes,' he said. She watched his hand, one handed in his finger-threaded hair. He moved, just, his other hand, the left, looked down and pulled a mouth twisting face at the bloated vein and the tube sliding into him beneath a square of tight, pink plaster. 'Corset pink,' he said, 'flannel knicker pink.'

'Three things are okay then are they,' said Virginia, 'hair, eyes and your right hand?'

'My wanking hand.'

'Four things then.'

She made him smile.

***

5

She sat on the edge of the bed. Dan had only a single white sheet over him, it was turned down to his waist and he lay bare-chested, his pyjama jacket pulled right back so that it covered only his shoulders and his arms. She thought about his shoulders, how the bone stood up, right up, glistening beneath the skin. There was no flesh on him now. His wrists were frail tendons against the bluish mound of his pulse.

She put her hand on the thick, grey hair in the middle of his chest. He was lying there, sedately, a pile of pillows behind him. He gave her a smile, a smile ready to bite. She leaned forward and, as she kissed him, she felt her weight fall through her hand onto his chest and she held her body tautly so that kiss and hand barely touched him. She opened her eyes and there were his cool, blue eyes staring at her, watching.

She looked away and saw his mouth, his big strong teeth, yellow darkening to brown, dry lips now and big, soaked tongue.

'Sorry,' she said, 'did I hurt you?'

'All the time,' he said, still smiling. Smiling for himself. She patted his chest, gave it a soft blow with her fingertips. She smoothed the sheet, feeling the weave of the thread, watching the movements of her hand on the starched cloth.

'What's been happening?' she said, still not looking up at him.

'Which would you prefer?' he asked, 'drugged, undrugged, dream, morphine dream, fantasy, delusion, daydream or ordinary?'

'You choose.'

'The guy across the ward there,' Dan flicked his eyes and she turned and looked over her shoulder to see the empty bed. 'They gave him some dope for a pre-med for his operation. Something bloody silly, a bollock operation, something like that. Christ it hit him like a shovel. I had an hour of him singing to me, asking for requests. The bloody nurses went apeshit, said I was encouraging him. I got him through all of Oklahoma and most of South Pacific before he passed out. It was Bali Hi did for him. The high notes took the oxygen from his brain I reckon and donk, he was asleep.' Dan's chest jerked up and down,

6

laughing and grimacing, eyes closed. 'He'll not be singing when he gets back, poor bastard.'

She smiled and rubbed the soft skin of his belly. 'Belly button fluff,' she said. 'Don't they clean you out?' and she held up a pinch of grey stuff.

'What would you like next?' he asked her.

She shook her head, 'I don't know,' she said.

'What about an erotic fantasy?'

'Would I be in it, Dan?

'Not the one I have in mind. I could fit you into tonight's though and tell it to you tomorrow.'

She pursed her lips. 'Okay, I'd like that. What should I wear?'

'Leave that to me. Don't worry, I'll make sure that you wear something good. I'll not let you down.'

'Zips are better than buttons don't forget, for an erotic fantasy.'

Dan's eyes were closed and his ribs lifted, just, as he sipped the air. She sat back and watched him sleep.

'Velcro,' he said.

Chapter 2

When Virginia got the part that paid almost nothing in a play funded by Eastern Arts her agent sulked. Virginia took no notice, she was sick of being told what to do. We'll work on it together Dennis had said to her. He was a hairy six-footer running carelessly into his fifties. A big, dark man with lovely eyes who ran a small theatre in Bedford. 'Come on, come and do it,' he had said, 'I've got the dosh.'

She took the job and came back to live in her mother's house. A house stripped of possessions.

'This old thing,' her mother would say, holding up a vase, a book, a cushion, pots, pans, anything she could no longer put up with, the thing irritating her beyond bearing until she could throw it away, preferably smashed, into the bin. 'I don't like clutter.' Virginia had always saved what she could from her mother's geriatric minimalism. 'Cremate me,' she had demanded, not wanting the clutter of her own body, its growing uselessness irritating her. 'No damn good to anybody.' Muttering and prowling the house when her age and ricketiness goaded her to anger and then giggling, 'Silly old bugger,' when she saw Virginia laughing at her. 'I could do with a nice millionaire. I'd give him a good run. A nice big fat one. I could you know, a nice big wobbly one. I'd make the bugger wobble.' And then she had died. Just like that, bang, gone, emptying the house.

Virginia wasn't frightened of the house. The noises she heard in it never made her think of burglars or ghosts. Its sighs and clucking never startled her. She lay in bed and listened to it in the dark. When she got up in the night to pee she never put on the light, was never afraid of the other side of the door. She would sit on the toilet in the dark bathroom thinking about death. It was the only time and the only place that she did. She hoped that her mother's ghost would come and sit with her. Where, she wondered? She could sit on the edge of the bath in her dressing gown with her thick, grey hair wild from sleep and tell Virginia off for not finding her own millionaire. But she never did.

'That bugger,' her mother used to say, 'that dirty bugger. It's too late to warn you about him, isn't it, the dirty blue-eyed bugger.' Dan used to love to sit with her. 'Do you know he tells me mucky stories?' And she would pull a face and snigger and whoop with laughter.

The house was a hundred years old, perhaps a bit more. Her mother had been born in it, lived in it all her life. Virginia had trembled to tell her mother that she was off, leaving the house, the street, the village.

'You do what you want girl,' her mother had said. 'I always did, so you do the same.'

Whenever Virginia came back her mother was always there, making her assault upon the house.

'I've given young Michael that bed of yours, you hardly use it.' Giggling when she saw the daftness of it; but she liked the lovely space in an empty room just the room and the luxury of empty, wasted space.

So, Virginia stripped her bedless room of everything and painted it white. Threw the carpet and the underlay out of the window into the yard and left it.

'You shift it, you silly old bat,' she told her mother. Her mother, throwing her apron up over her head and shouting with laughter. Virginia got a man in from Wellingborough to sand the floorboards with a machine that made the house tremble. They were good oak boards and she made her mother help her varnish them. The two of them on their hands and knees, the room, like a drum, half echoing, her mother singing, *When They Begin The Begine.*

'You can't sleep on that,' said her mother, looking down at the futon.

9

'You lay a finger on it, you just lay a finger on it you bloody old ding bat,' said Virginia, laughing at her, wagging her finger. The room was bare, white, varnished. There was a raffia blind at the window. 'If you like,' said Virginia, 'we could do the whole house like this.' Her mother's lips disappeared and the spite in her eyes acknowledged defeat.

Virginia didn't mind that her mother was dead. Her timing had been perfect really. She was at the end of vigorous old age and was starting to fail. Bits of her crumbling and letting her down, her knees and then her back. 'This bloody eye, it's not right you know.' Now she was gone, and Virginia didn't mind at all. That'll be me, she thought and grinned at the garden, ready to have her mother's life. I could live here, she thought, an hour to London, I can get anywhere from here. The terrace of houses always seemed back to front to Virginia. The back doors opened up onto tiny, paved yards and then onto the narrow street. The fronts, bay windowed, looked southwards over the valley across the wide green flood plain of the Nene and up again, to the south, rising past Whiston and Cogenhoe, sending the eye from church to church all up and along the steady slope of the valley.

'They're going to flood it all you know,' Harry had told her. Harry, older than her mother and still digging and stamping around his garden. 'One bloody great sheet of water. It's the gravel they want, you see, for building and suchlike.'

'Terrible,' said Virginia.

'I don't give a bugger,' said Harry. 'I shan't see it. They can do what they bloody like.'

From the front door you went down into the garden, a long, narrow garden full of tall grass and brambles, buttercups and nettles. 'I can't manage it,' her mother had always said and never tried. I'll manage it, Virginia thought, now that I'm back.

Chapter 3

'Some kind of shady lawyer,' Richard told her. 'I met her at Dan's house.'

'What was she doing there?' She saw Richard smile.

'All sorts,' he said.

'Well, I hope she enjoyed what was left of him.'

'No, nothing like that, she was trying to buy pictures.'

'Sure.'

'She was. She was new in town and she heard about the house and the local werewolf, so she went round there.'

'Did she buy much?'

'Couple of things.'

'How did she pay?'

'Oh, come on, Virginia.'

'Is this her?' said Virginia, nodding at the door.

Sarah was in the suit she wore for work. She was a tall blonde with swimmer's shoulders. Virginia looked at Richard and pursed her lips

'You're Virginia,' said Sarah.

Virginia shook Sarah's hand and they smiled at each other. Sarah unbuttoned her jacket, 'Get the drinks in Richard,' she said. 'Don't just stand there with your mouth open. It's the lust,' she said to Virginia, 'he's a martyr to it.'

They made him buy a bottle of good wine and the bald, flat faced boy behind the bar said: 'I think you need a hand with these two mate.'

'Richard says you're a shady lawyer,' said Virginia.

'Does he?' And then she told Virginia about the ways she found out which people were worth suing. 'Who we should go after,' she said. 'No good suing paupers is it?' She laughed. 'People get really cross when the letters and writs start arriving.'

'Cross?' said Virginia.

'Should see them,' said Sarah. She had a drink and licked her lips. 'I make them jump up and down. And you,' she turned to Richard, pointing at him, ready for a row, 'what do you know about whisky?'

'Me?'

'There was whisky in Dan's glass, on his locker, just by his bed.'

'Really?'

Virginia lifted her feet from her shoes and onto the coldness of, the quarry tiles. There were a couple of fat men in smart suits, corporation fat, sitting at a table by the window. Virginia stared back at them. Through the window the sky was still blue and across the street was a shop window, jumbled full of toys. Red and yellow letters said: Fabulous Fun. The fat men were smiling at her and giggling.

'Another bottle of this,' Sarah said to the barman. 'And this time put it in an ice bucket. We want it to stay cold, don't we Richard?' She saw Virginia laughing at her. 'These,' she said, 'are not the first drinks of the day.' She was starting to sound a bit ponderous.

'I can see that,' said Virginia and she realised that she quite liked this Sarah, coming into the bar already half drunk and giving Richard some stick. She could see how it would have been with Dan.

'But this bastard, this little bastard, Richard here,' Sarah stared at the barman, who was wondering whether to give her a new bottle, 'he's been giving Dan, a dying man mark you, dying man, been giving him whisky.' She wiggled her glass at the barman, 'Come on you, get that poured.' Her accent had fallen apart and she was half way to Barnsley.

Virginia looked back to her fat men; they were staring at Sarah as if they couldn't believe their luck. Virginia made a shocked, false face at them and made them laugh. 'What are you two fat bastards laughing at?' said Sarah.

'Nothing,' they said together, laughing again and shaking their heads.

12

'I saw her,' said one of them, pointing at Virginia, 'on the telly not long since, in that series.'

'Get her kit off did she?'

'I was praying that she would. What sort of a writer has her in a play and doesn't put that in?'

'Well, Graham, I certainly would.'

'Her pal's not too difficult to look at either.'

They stared at Sarah. She was standing up straight, chest out, squaring her shoulders for a fight; pink to her ears with outrage, staring her angry, bright stare at Richard. He smiled and looked away. 'Don't smile,' she said, 'don't smile.' Then, shocked as the certainty hit her, 'You are one of them, aren't you, aren't you, one of the bastards who take him whisky in? You are, aren't you, you bloody are.'

'It's what he wants, Sarah,' Richard spoke softly and looked beyond her to Virginia. 'Tell her Ginny.'

'I don't want bloody Ginny to tell me anything. You can't take whisky into hospital. It'll kill him.'

Richard smiled, started to laugh, 'He doesn't need me to kill him, the job's done. He's glad of it.'

'What are you staring at?' said Virginia to the two fat men.

'Can't help it can we?' said Graham, politely. He shook his head, 'If you think that we're having lewd thoughts, well, you know what, you couldn't be more right. It's not our fault though. We're not going to apologise for it, are we Joe.'

Virginia smiled back, 'Bloody cheek.'

'I told you, Joe,' he said, 'I told you she was a belter. Look at that smile. I'm broken hearted.'

Richard leaned forward and put his hand under Sarah's jacket, stroked upwards with his thumb into the soft flesh and then the hard, upward curve of ribs beneath the skin.

'You can't do it Richard,' she said, hissing, 'it's wickedness.'

But he smiled at her. 'He's my friend,' he said. He leaned forward and kissed her angry face. 'So, I'll do whatever he wants. He's lying there, finished, and he can't do it himself.'

13

'Can't do what?'

Richard shrugged. 'Nip down to the shop for a bottle of scotch, so I do it for him.'

Sarah stood back so that he could not touch her. She picked up her drink and walked away, sat at one of the tables near the window. She stared into the street, her back turned, tense with anger. Richard leaned back, both elbows behind him on the bar, one foot up. He spoke to her across the space so that Virginia and the two men turned to listen.

'You can't go around with a face full of good intentions. How glib can you be? You don't know what to do, do you? So you fill your eyes up like a spaniel; let us all know how sensitive you are, what a decent sort of girl. Well, what good is that? Why do you want to stop him doing what he wants?'

'It's not much of a row this, is it?' said Joe.

'It'll not get going properly,' Graham said, 'until she joins in. Joins in properly. You know, hurls abuse at him and makes some unpleasant remarks about his sexual preferences.'

'You're right,' Joe nodded, 'that's exactly what this row needs.' He leaned forward and touched Virginia's arm. 'Who's Dan?' he asked her.

'Have you noticed,' Graham said, musing, 'how much better a row is, well, worse, if you see what I mean, when it's a couple of really good-looking people. It's not the same when a couple of ugly sods start screaming and weeping.'

Joe thought about it for a second. 'Well,' he said, 'You see, there's more facade to crumble. I mean, who'd want to knock down a block of flats if they could knock down Brighton Pavilion.'

'They are a bit Brighton Pavilion these two, aren't they?' said Graham.

'Why don't you two fuck off?' said Richard.

'Us? What have we done?' said Joe.

Sarah screeched back her chair and stood up, took two steps and poured the last of her drink over Graham's head, smacked the empty glass onto the table. The stem broke. She walked out into the street. Richard pushed himself away from the bar and followed her.

Graham sat still, letting the drink run down his face. 'When this sort of thing happens,' he said, 'you should never panic.'

Virginia reached forward with a tissue. 'You're going bald,' she said.

'Just pass me that bar towel will you?' said Graham.

***

She liked the look of them and let them take her over. They were smart, fat and prosperous. Joe was pale, a sickly Celtic white under straight, black hair. Graham was a square faced red man with blue eyes. They wore dark suits with big buttoned up jackets over their bellies. The three of them walked down the street towards the market square with its dirty canvas awnings flapping over the empty stalls. The last of the sun filled the street, got in their eyes and made them look down at themselves walking in step, Virginia in the middle, holding their arms, pulling them in closely. She liked the bigness of them, a couple of rugby players, hopelessly run down into flesh and fat, a couple of self-indulged glad-handers who liked their dinner.

'Well, I am pleased,' said Graham and when he smiled his face took on the gleam of pleasure and she could see him full of himself and she skipped up a quick, dancing step that made them shuffle and bounce to keep up with her. They jollied her into a bare, wooden floored restaurant. The waitress, a skinny rat-faced girl with red and white stripes across a big pneumatic bosom, lit a candle stub and smiled lovely teeth at them.

'You mustn't mind if they stare,' said Virginia to the girl. 'They're fat and old and harmless.'

'And here's me thinking that I'd copped off,' said the girl. 'Have you got a bit of a ménage going have you?' Her Liverpool voice, sudden and cheerful, pulled all their eyes up into hers.

'I just allow them to have fantasies about me,' said Virginia. 'It's enough for them.'

'Yeah,' said the waitress and bounced away, big footed in her trainers.

They sat facing her, both of them, filling the table in front of her with the shoulders of their jackets and the pinched knots in their ties.

'We're accountants,' said Graham.

'And speculators,' said Joe.

'Oh yes,' said Virginia.

'We've bought a racehorse.'

'Hey,' said Graham, 'will you open our new pub for us?'

'Course I will,' said Virginia.

Graham waved their first empty bottle at the waitress and she brought them a full one. They watched her quick struggle with the cork.

'Have a glass,' said Joe, 'you're not busy. What's your name?'

'Sadie,' she said, 'Just a quickie then,' and sat down with Virginia.

'She's on the telly,' said Joe, pointing.

'Hey that's good.' She looked blank. 'What do you do.'

Virginia told her.

'Hey, that's brilliant. Do you like it?'

'It's brilliant,' said Virginia and her heart lifted.

'Who'd you have to fuck to get that?' said Sadie, her eyes alight. Joe and Graham stared, dumb with delight. Virginia gave them a quick, dismissive look, leaned back in her seat and whispered into Sadie's ear. Sadie drew in her breath and bit her bottom lip, buck-toothed with surprise.

'You never,' she said.

Virginia nodded. 'For three weeks,' she said.

'What?' said Joe, 'what?'

***

Virginia slammed the door of the taxi and dropped her shoes onto the road. The driver had shouted at her to wake her up. Surly, self-righteous prick, she thought. She was a bit unsteady with sleep and wine and stood yawning in the narrow street, clenching her toes into the pavement and shivering. She watched the cab creep away, squeeze slowly past the parked cars and the overhanging lilac hedge. Its big, red brake lights came on and off in the darkness before the turn and then she was on her own. There was one street lamp and its light was half hidden in black leaves. She walked a couple of paces until next door's security light clicked on and a big white spread dazzled her. She sat on the wall and put her shoes on and found her key.

She stood at the old, white sink in the kitchen and let the tap run until the water was cold. She cupped the water in her hands and threw it up onto her face, dipping her head to meet it then wiped her face with her wet hands and flicked the water away. Her tee-shirt was wet and felt cold against her skin.

Dan's dying Mum, she thought. Lovely Dan. I know you liked him. He was a complete bugger though, wasn't he? He made me feel like I was his pal, do you know what I mean? First day I met him I got him into bed. I couldn't have him quick enough. And that's not like me, not a bit. I don't get carried away, not like that, but, Christ, I was itching to get my hands on him. Why's that then? I know he was terrible; I know he had a string of women. I only had him. Do you think that was stupid? I do, I think it was stupid. I only saw him on and off, when I was here. He'd never go anywhere, never move out of his old house. My stuff's still there, in my room. I had a room, he gave me a room. I told you about that didn't I? I know what you thought, so don't start on that again, just don't bloody start because I know it was a funny way of carrying on, but it suited both of us. Nearly seven years I've had him and I don't know why he's done this. He's done it on purpose, he has you know Mum. Why's he done that then? He keeps cracking jokes and watching them keeping him alive and taking the piss and trying to get the poor bloody nurses to tell him why they're bothering. They don't bloody know, poor sods. Why should they know? You don't need to know things like that. It's him that's missing the point isn't it? He's not all there is he Mum, asking things like that?

She stood at the sink with a head full of wine, having a cry and talking to her mother, talking to herself with her nice, village way of talking coming back, talking to her mother at the sink.

In the morning she felt bloated and her eyes were thick in her head. Don't do that again, watch out for those two, she thought. They had taken her to a shadowy, blue lit jazz club. Graham had danced with her, holding her hand so lightly that it was almost an effort for her to keep her hand in his. He danced slowly. Every time the band played a slow tune, *Do Nothing Till You Hear From Me, Diamonds For Your Furs,* he had taken her up and held her, barely touching her, and danced gently, led her round and round until she had wept.

'What's the matter?' He had been stricken. 'Dear God, what have I done?' She had picked up the tune again and made him dance and he had had the sense to shut up.

She stood in the bath and had a shower, gave herself a spiteful going over with her mother's loofa, turned the tap on cold and off again after a couple of seconds, thinking better of it. I'll go for a walk now, she thought, and then a big lunch will make me feel better.

She met Harry as she came out of the door. He stood solidly, feet apart, leaning back, giving her his hard stare and then letting his face fall apart into a smile.

'You'll have to forgive an old man stopping you in the street,' and he giggled, 'but I heard you were back. Are you stopping?'

She gave him a kiss on his grey bristles, 'Hello Harry,' she said. She had always thought of him as old, even when she was little, but she had always called him Harry, right from being a baby. She looked at him now, in his gardening kit, shirt undone so that she could see his vest. He's in his eighties, she thought and remembered him at her mother's funeral in the square, polished, Methodist Chapel, tall and upright in his dark suit and black homburg hat.

'Is it damp in the house?' he asked her. 'It must be.'

'I should have come round to see you,' said Virginia. 'I've only been here a couple of days, just to sleep really.'

Harry walked down the street with her and they looked into the tiny back yards and he told her who had left or died, who had moved in.

'I'm going to walk over the fields, Harry, blow last night away.'

'You'll get wet,' he said and they both looked at the sky.

18

'No,' she said, but it was dense with cloud and there was a thickness in the warm morning that made the hedges and trees heavy and blurred the far rise of the field slope. 'It'll be all right. Anyway, it'll not hurt me, it's only rain.'

She climbed up through the hedge, over the half rotten, overgrown stile, she could see the valley side falling away to her left, a shallow fall into the wide, bottom land a couple of miles away where the Nene lost itself in gravel pits and cuttings. Then she was in a big damp field, wide and green, full of sheep, clumps of them calling forlornly to each other. She could hear them eating. Their teeth were tearing at the grass, a neat rhythmic sound, chins lowered, chattering at the field. A ewe arched her back and two big lambs, big as her almost, pummelled into her udders, stubby tails wagging deliriously. Three trees marched the line of a vanished hedge and at the field bottom old farm buildings were falling into big clumps of elder bush. One of the sheep stood, startled, pointing like a dog. She could hear the thin hum of traffic on the dual carriageway that was stringing new trading estates and factories through the valley. Let it, she thought. She had never liked the valley with its wet, green flatness and the terrible half-perfumed smell from the sewage farm.

Chapter 4

That afternoon she sat and read to Dan. She had bought a thriller for him, *Get Shorty,* and she managed all the different accents: West Coast, East Coast, and gave herself a hell of a time trying to play all the characters and keep straight in her head whose voice was whose. She knew that Dan was staring at her, watching her face working away at the performance.

‘This is just showing off,’ he said.

‘That’s right.’

Before she could begin reading again he said, ‘I like America. I’ve always liked it, that slick, expensive veneer.’

‘You what?’ she was incredulous. ‘You haven’t been out of Northampton for years.’

He smiled. ‘I don’t want to go to America,’ he said. ‘What damn use would that be? You know what it would be, don’t you, if you went to New York or wherever? It’d be ordinary. Once you’d got over it being new, it’d be ordinary. I don’t want real reality,’ he waved at the book, ‘I want that reality, the reality you get on the telly. You know how bought cakes are always better than home made.’

‘You always liked my mother’s cakes.’

That made him smile again. ‘Yeah, they were good. But, still, they weren’t bought. They didn’t have that shine on them did they? They weren’t slick were they?’

‘You talk bollocks,’ smiling herself as she spoke.

‘I know I do,’ he said.

20

'Shut up then and let me read some more of this.'

He only lasted ten minutes, less than that, before he was asleep. She put the book down and touched his hand. There was nothing there, no strength in it. There were the long, tense fingers, the lines of bone and tendon and big veins crossing the white skin. She bent and kissed him and even through the nasty, clean smell of the hospital she had the taste of him on her lips. She touched the back of his hand with her tongue and wanted to get into the bed and feel the whole hard length of him against her. She wanted to get up in the middle of the night, like she used to, and get into his bed and feel his muscles slack with sleep and warmth. Go to your own room, he would tell her, go on bugger off. And she would slip her hand into his flannelette pyjamas, her head under the sheets in the lovely close smell of him.

She could hear his breath, now, a thin whistle against the slimy membrane of his palette. She pulled up a tissue and touched the white spittle from the corners of his mouth. 'I might as well go,' she said, whispering.

'No,' Dan said, without moving, without opening his eyes. She watched his chest moving, two, three times. 'Read a bit more.' He licked his lips and found more of his voice. 'Go on, read a bit more. Do all of the voices for me.'

That night they would come back to him when the ward was dark and he could see the night outside. The shapes came in at the window and after a while he could hold them there, framed. The big, loud mouthed bastard from New York, the gangster with the lantern jaw and big red lips, a juicy eyed murderer, he was there and Dan could hold him still and work on his face and give his neck a nasty razor rash with tiny beads of blood held, just held, under a filament of stinging skin.

Virginia looked up from the print and Richard was there, slim and pale, the soft skin of a child. He smiled at her, 'Terrific,' he said.

She shrugged, 'It's my job,' she said, pleased for his good opinion, the rare good review.

'I was passing,' Richard was speaking to Dan, 'thought there was time for a quick one before your supper.' He held up a bottle. 'Glenmorangie,' he said. He had two glasses in his other hand and put them on Dan's locker. 'You can keep the water glass,' he said to Dan and he poured three shots. They watched Dan wet his lips with the whisky; he held the glass out and Virginia took it from him and put it down.

'I've had a smashing row with Sarah,' Richard said, 'a blinder. She told me I was a murderer, coming in here and feeding you whisky. Did she think that I was damaging your health I asked her? Yes, she fucking well did, she said. She was screaming at me in the street, just like an opera. This was after we'd left you in the bar. Was that chap all right?'

'What chap?' said Dan.

'Sarah poured a drink on someone's head,' said Virginia.

'Great stuff,' said Dan and closed his eyes.

'But he was okay about it; he took me out for dinner after, he and his friend.'

'I wish I'd been with you,' Richard said. 'That mad cow kicked me, so sod it, I thought, and I kicked her back. She fell over. Well, I might have overdone it a bit, but then she just sat there weeping and screaming at me.'

'What did she say?' said Virginia.

'Oh, she was just swearing at me.' He looked fed up. 'You know, hawking up all the usual stuff, big phlegmy lumps of abuse.' He sat down on the bed. 'I'm glad you're here anyway, Ginny,' he said, and nodded at Dan. 'He doesn't run to much in the way of conversation, not these days. Look at him, he's nodded off again.'

'I'll be nodding off for good quite shortly,' said Dan in a breathy voice. 'Sorry I missed your row with Sarah, sounded good.' His eyes were still closed. They could see his mouth moving as if he were chewing; he worked his lips in and out until they were wet. 'Nice tits, Sarah,' he said. And then they could see that he was asleep.

'They might be his famous last words,' said Richard.

22

'Could do worse,' said Virginia.

Richard finished his drink, finished Dan's as well. 'I'll leave you to it,' he said.

'No, I'll come with you,' said Virginia.

At the desk Richard stopped to talk to the ward sister. 'He just had one sip,' he said and put the bottle and the glasses down in front of her. She was a nice-looking woman in her forties, a round pink face and short, blonde hair. She gave him a hard luck smile, turned and put the glasses and the bottle away in a metal locker.

'I'll maybe go and have one with him myself later on, a bit of a night cap,' she said.

Richard shook his head, raised his hand in goodbye and walked off.

'Bye', said Virginia and went after him. He looked a bit unsteady; the automatic doors jerking open made him jump and his head came up, startled. Outside he leaned against the wall. He took a couple of big breaths, hands clasped tightly in front of him. Then he cried and cried, like a child who knows that nothing is fair, hiccupping between breaths, covering his chin in snot. She waited for him.

'Bloody hell,' she said when he stopped.

'Yeah, all right,' Richard said. 'You got a hanky?' She fished in her bag for tissues and he wiped his face clean. 'Now you know, don't you?'

'Yes,' she said, 'I do. Now I know.'

He put his arm through hers and they walked along. 'Fancy a drink?' he asked.

Chapter 5

There were cars parked on both sides of the street. It was narrow anyway with its dark-bricked houses opening their doors straight onto the pavement. Virginia found a space and put her car into it, first time. She always did it first time, quick as she could, and it always cheered her up. Dan's house was at the end of the terrace; it had garden on two sides and he had let it grow wild. The hedge was tall and unkempt and almost hid the wooden gate.

'I'll do the garden for you,' she had said to Dan.

'Oh, will you?' he had said, halfway to stopping her. 'What will you do to it?'

She had just moved into her room. That would make it what, she thought, five, six years ago? 'We could make it like Giverny,' she said, smiling to herself, waiting for him to start shouting. 'You know, like Monet.'

'Bloody Monet,' Dan had said, softly. He had hunched his shoulders and leaned forward with his big forearms flat on the table, plumping up the muscle against his rolled shirt sleeves. 'Let's have some Jackson Pollock, shall we?'

It had taken her three weeks to get rid of the weeds and nettles. She had sprayed the lot, over and over, without bothering to save anything good. Dan had leaned in the doorway and watched her dig.

'Best to get the stones out,' he had told her.

'You could do that.'

'Me?' He had laughed at her. 'Me?'

He had waited until there was bare, turned earth. 'Smooth it out a bit,' he had told her.

'Smooth it out your bloody self,' she had said.

'I've been and bought these.' He held up a thick pile of seed packets. They were wild flowers, mostly ordinary things she was used to seeing in the hedges and scraps of woodland around Barton.

She stood, remembering all of this, just inside the garden gate, the tangled, clutching hedge up close behind her, falling in love with him again.

'Don't I get a say? I've done all the work here.'

'You can do what you like,' he had given her the big smile, the big, deceitful blue eyes, 'you know that.'

'It needs thinking about.'

'What does?' he had asked, sounding surprised at her.

'How we're going to set it out,' she persisted.

Dan had poured all the seeds into a saucepan and stirred them around with his fingers. 'Set it out my arse,' he had said and walked out into the new, bare garden scattering a pinch of seed here a pinch there, throwing it broadcast into the air so that the wind threw it around. He had poured the dregs from the saucepan into his big cupped hand and thrown them high over his head. 'All gone,' he had said.

There it all was, taking all the weight out of her legs so that she wavered backwards as if before a sudden push of air. The spiky hedge, the spindles of hawthorn, scratched into her hair. There were the two big lumps of stone, great big pieces of local ironstone, that Dan had trundled in from somewhere and an old stone fountain full of soil, pale green ferns trailing from it. There were dark centred, eye filling poppies, deep scarlet creased and silky, floating on the green. Hanging pockets, pink and violet, of columbine and foxglove; beneath them ragged yellow anemones and tiny, tight buttercups. The sunlight blurred them out of focus, turned their colours into air. There were slivers of colour for which she had no name: corn cockle and catchfly, hepatica, fumitory. Dan knew. There was nothing really at random, nothing without his transforming intention.

25

No-one had been in the house for weeks and the kitchen stank. Virginia brought in the big wheely bin from outside, struggling to get it over the step. Then she didn't have the heart to throw the mouldy plates away so she cleaned everything up instead. She sprayed the flies away and scrubbed everything clean: the plates they had used, the big knives and forks that Dan had liked. He's finished with these, she thought and wept over them. Crying away with the sink full of hot, soapy water, piling up the wet saucepans that Dan had cooked in for her, the big spoons he had licked and put in a bit more salt. She emptied the rotting fridge and washed it, washed the floor and wiped the table and the shelves and put all the kitchen away.

After that she went upstairs and emptied her room. There wasn't much: a few clothes, the duvet. She put them into bin bags and left them outside the door for one, quick, trip to the car and away; no going back again and again. She went through the house and shut all the doors and then, on the outside step, she locked up. At the gate she stopped to pick a poppy, thought better of it and threw it in the hedge.

Chapter 6

Dan wondered what to do, dreaming and forgetting, just a flicker of effort and he could focus on the nurse's clicking shoe, the bald man's newspaper, there across the shiny floor, opening and folding and reading. Stay with Virginia and let her come into his room and wake him up. Laying in wait for her while the room picked up colour from the early morning. She came in and he was asleep; he watched her feet fall silently on the thick rug. She folded back the duvet and lay against his back, her head held up on her open hand, over him. The weight in her elbow spiked the pillow. He slept on and he could see her, like that, watching him. She smiled and stopped smiling and pushed her falling hair away from her face. That's right, thought Dan, she has thick, dark hair that she sometimes deepens with henna so that it has shadowy reds and dark ochres in it. She put her fingers in his hair, black and grey, and lifted it and licked his ear, filling up his ear with her tongue so that he awoke underwater and opened his eyes. Then she came into the room so that he could not hear her, her bare feet thin with cold on the bare boards of the floor and then the rug under her pale, bony feet and she sat astride him as he slept so that with her and the duvet holding him it was difficult to turn over and see her pulling off her night dress and the white ripple of her ribs stretching upwards and the soft shiver of flesh as the white cloth ruffled her breast.

He woke up and saw the empty beds across the ward. He saw that the nurse was looking at him. She stood by the empty beds holding a stainless steel bowl.

'Where's Leo?' Dan asked.

'I've sent him for a walk,' she said. 'I've got to get him going again.'

'They only stuck the knife in him yesterday,' Dan said. Had he thought it? He didn't know. That gesture, that night gown coming up and off, over her head, thrown off like a waved flag. He had done that, that careless, airy gesture, throwing off modesty. Could have sold it twenty times that picture.

'I thought you said he was awake?' It was Leo's voice and Dan could see his big square face going up and over his bald head.

'I am awake, you bald bastard,' Dan said.

'He's fast asleep,' said Leo.

Dan could see the tube going into Leo; an opaque tube that curved out of his dressing gown and dripped into that clear, plastic bag. It was urine and blood. Look good that one would, thought Dan. Would the hospital buy it? They do buy paintings, don't they? Cheerful views of Victorian Northampton, cheerful green landscapes and skies. Blood and piss, look brilliant it would; hang it right at the entrance to the ward: Welcome. He started to do it, a big translucent close up of the pink tinged bag of piss held in the metal frame of the stainless trolley that Leo pulled around with him. All of the background was Leo's tartan dressing gown and his big knobby hand gripping the bright steel handle. Dan was laughing as he painted it, frighten the bastards to death this will.

'When I was painting, you know, I never drank. It never occurred to me.' Dan's eyes were open wide and the ward was bright from the sunlight in the window.

'Pity you stopped painting then, you gormless sod,' said Leo. He pulled his trolley full of piss up closer and sat on the edge of the bed.

'Always liked a bloody good binge though,' said Dan.

'Course you did,' said Leo.

Dan laughed. 'Then one binge led to another,' he said.

'And here you are,' said Leo.

Dan thought about the tube, about the moment when the eye, following the tube, turned away from the pucker of bruised flesh and

28

dark soaked stitching where the tube went into the living body. That'll be one for the canteen, he thought.

Leo sat in the square armchair at the side of Dan's bed. Dan watched him read the paper, watched the sour, down turned mouth in his bland, sardonic face. Nothing good then.

'Anything changed then, since yesterday's paper?' said Dan. Leo did not move. Did I say it, Dan thought? He stared at Leo. Leo looked at him. 'Did I just speak?' said Dan.

'No not a word.' Leo's jowls drooped even further.

'But I did just then?'

'Yes, loud and clear. Unless I'm taking the same drugs they're giving you, then it's anybody's guess what's going on.'

Dan thought about it. 'It's the opposite of repeating myself.'

'Well then, it must mean you're getting less old.' Leo had crumpled up the paper onto his knee. 'What was it that you didn't say?' he asked.

'I was wondering,' said Dan, 'if they're reporting a world changed for the better.'

'The gist of it,' Leo said, 'seems to be that the poor sods who were in the shit yesterday are still in the shit today and a whole lot of new poor sods have joined them.'

'So, I'm doing okay, comparatively speaking.'

'You certainly are: clean sheets, free drugs, and a nice young woman to wipe your arse.'

'I should quit while I'm ahead.'

'They say you're about to.'

Dan lay on his back, he turned his head away from Leo and stared at the ceiling and giggled. The skin beneath his grey stubble was smeared across his face. His lips felt gummy. 'Can you clean my mouth up Leo?'

Leo threw the paper onto the bed and got himself out of the chair, pushing his weight into the chair arms through the heels of his hands. He shuffled round, being careful with his tube and bag of piss. He wet a wad of tissues with mineral water and wiped Dan's lips. 'Open up a bit,' and he got right inside with a big, gentle finger. Then he wiped

Dan's face, found the bendy straws and gave him a drink. 'Swill it round a bit before you swallow,' he said.

'When I think of all the people I've had in my mouth,' said Dan. 'I never thought it was all going to culminate with a big ugly bastard like you.'

'Don't tell the wife,' said Leo.

'I should have done more portraits,' said Dan.

'What?'

'I used to do a few, every year, round about Christmas. Blokes would want their wives doing, you know, for a present. I'd take a few photos then put the image up on the canvas with a projector and draw round it. Money for old rope. I could knock one out in a day if I tried. I'll do you shall I?' And he went upstairs into the high, attic studio and opened the big, double glazed sky-lights to let in the sound of the moving air and started to stretch the canvas on its frame, taking his time so that he did not have to begin. He got Leo to sit and read the paper, but it got in the way, threw up the light awkwardly onto Leo's face so he got him a book, an old, brown-backed Penguin and went downstairs for breakfast and left him there, reading. Then he painted Ginny. Ginny stretched in the bath with the ends of her hair wet and breasts half floating in the steam, holding the brown book clear of the water. She had a glass of beer on the edge of the bath. She was pink from the hot water and there was the dark brown of the beer and the length of her arm out of the water, a twist of muscle and sharp turned elbow, holding up the old, dry book.

Leave her to it, he thought and poured himself a scotch. He stood in the kitchen doorway and watched the flowers in the garden throwing themselves into the air, sip-sipping at his scotch and thinking about the flowers coming and going and the frosts and the lovely sad weight of winter. Then he finished his scotch in a good big gulp so that he could feel it all the way down.

Chapter 7

The kitchen of her mother's house was on the north side and it was always cool. Through the window Virginia could see the blue sky and the narrow, tarmacked road that was black-bright with heat. She was in the soft air of the kitchen letting the cold tap run over her hands and forearms, over the pulse in her wrist. Dan could come in now and sit at the table, resting both his arms on the dark wood. He could have his shirt sleeves rolled up to his elbows, wearing his white shirt that was frayed at the collar points and we could have set him up to paint in the big front bedroom where the sun poured in all day or in the back where it didn't or any bloody where but in the bloody hospital.

She had thought about her mother that morning as she lay in bed, smiling at the bare room. Now that her Mother was dead she could let the room fill with junk, fill up the house if she liked. It was starting already: books and newspapers, vases, flowers, old shoes. I'll clear out the kitchen, she thought, but there was nothing to do once she had thrown out the senna pods and bicarbonate of soda, half a bag of spoiled flour. Her mother's cupboards were scrubbed clean, no mess, no dark corners. The fridge and washing machine shone. There was the new micro-wave her mother had bought just before she died. Course I can work it, she had told Virginia, I'm old, not stupid. She could work the video too, thought Virginia. In the bookcase, specially bought, there was a tape of every bit of television that Virginia had ever done, even the adverts. That would have to go, the bookcase and the bloody tapes, thought Virginia, sick of crying whenever she saw them.

Now she thought about Dan doing this to her, sipping his way through a bottle a day of whatever it was and then going out for a few pints and a few more belts of scotch in the pub. The pictures had stopped, and the sketch book, and he had really got into the drink, holding the drunkenness together and sneering, laughing that sore throat drinker's laugh and lighting another cigarette and laughing at himself falling apart. The bastard, she thought, the bastard, handing me this one to go over for the rest of my life.

Harry knocked on the window, came walking down the backyard and rapped his knuckles on the window as he went past it on his way to the door.

'Are you there?' he called through the open doorway.

'Come in Harry,' she said. She turned off the tap and began drying her hands and arms on a thin cotton towel, soaking it. 'I'm just cooling myself off.' She smiled at his whiskery white face, pink from the sun. 'Sit down, I'll make some coffee.'

'Have you been having a weep?' Harry said. He had his face on one side, bright eyes staring at her. She nodded.

'Just a little one,' she said.

'Well, you will. So, don't you worry about that, duck. You could worry if you weren't weeping. If you've got a bit of heart in you, you can't avoid it.' He sat down. 'You don't mind my saying that do you?'

'I don't, Harry,' she said, 'I don't.' And she wept a bit more into the wet tea-cloth.

'Am I going to get this coffee or what then?' Harry asked, pretending to be rough with her.

She sniffed and wiped her nose on the back of her wrist. 'You'll want biscuits as well, I suppose?' pretending back.

'If you've got some,' said Harry. He leaned forward, and rested his big forearms on the table. 'It feels a bit better now, this house does, now that you're living in it. It let all the cold in when your mum popped off.'

32

She sat with him and let him go on about the ordinary business of dying. 'You get a bit more callous about it as you get older,' he said. 'Well, callous might be the wrong word, but it's not so bothering as when you're a kid. Not for me it's not anyway. You've got to expect it when you're in your eighties haven't you?'

'I don't think Mum minded at all,' said Virginia.

'Course she didn't,' said Harry, cheerfully, 'didn't give a bugger.'

***

'Do you get any sense out of him?' Virginia stood at the foot of the bed, watching Dan sleeping.

Leo put down his newspaper, 'Yes and no,' he said.

'I don't,' said Virginia. 'He's done this on purpose you know. She pointed at Dan's paper grey face, 'Smart move, hey?'

'It must be galling,' said Leo. The dryness of his tone caught her up in a quick flare of anger and she turned into his big, serious face, bigger with sadness just for an instant before he spoke again. 'You can see it can't you?' he said. 'I can. I bloody can. There you are doing your stuff, painting away or in my case going into court with some tosser and trying to get him off, and then suddenly, click, your light goes out. Then you think, dear me, why am I doing all this? Especially you might think, why am I doing this over and over again? Nothing dramatic you know, not a case of shooting yourself or stepping out of a high window, just some pulse that should beat that doesn't beat. I can imagine that, can't you? The value draining out of everything, no way of choosing to do x rather than y. So, you put the telly on and have a drink and when people bollock you for it, it strikes you as funny.'

She stood and listened, waiting for him to finish. 'What are you talking about,' she said, disgustedly. '"Light goes out," "Pulse doesn't beat," what sort of damned rubbish is this? I don't want to hear a plea in mitigation for this selfish sod. I want him kicked up the arse. But he's put himself beyond that hasn't he? That's the point of all this, you know, to show us all how singular, how remarkable he is. Well he isn't, he bloody isn't; he's cruel and selfish and too bloody lazy to live. All

33

he's done here is to show how ordinary he is; what a bloody ordinary, spineless creep, just giving in, packing in, when he felt a bit fed up.'

Leo sighed, and it stopped her.

'I'm sorry,' she said, not sounding it. 'I don't know why I'm unloading on you. I don't even know your name.'

'Leo,' Leo said. He held out his hand and she stepped round from the end of the bed to shake it.

'Virginia Moore,' she said.

'So he's been telling me.'

'Just think of him as one of the tossers you try to get off,' said Virginia. 'He wasn't like that, but he is now.'

Leo smiled. 'He makes me laugh,' he said.

'He makes me fucking sick,' said Virginia. 'I'll push off before he wakes up. Not in the mood for him. Sorry about all this Leo.' She turned to walk away, turned back. 'Sorry,' she said, 'sorry for being such a shit. How are you? Are you going to be okay?'

'Me?' he said, surprised, 'I'm all right. A couple of weeks and I'll be off on holiday.'

'See?' she said, 'see?'

***

She could not stay away. She came back in the evening and sat with him. There was no substance to the lick of his body under the white sheet. She sat and stared at his hands and listened to the liquid rattle of his breath. She remembered his hands on her body, their bigness, the broad palms shaping her flesh, the first flutter of panic under the strength of them, wanting and not wanting to evade him.

'I went to the house,' she said, 'and cleaned up the kitchen. It was crawling, but it's okay now, I cleaned it all up.' He stared. 'The house is full of pictures, Dan. What are you going to do with them all?

'There's some lovely stuff there. Are they the ones you didn't want to sell?' Her voice fell, 'Might as well sell them now love, you won't be seeing them again.'

34

His breath whistled in his teeth as if he were forcing himself rid of it. He licked his lips. Virginia touched his right hand, felt, under the tips of her fingers, the soft ridges of veins, the long white tendons. She knew, and then did not, that Dan was old and wrecked. It came in and out of focus as memory vied for her attention with what she saw. She would be just back from somewhere, weeks away in London or touring or the two wasted months in Los Angeles and Dan would get her to set the table and pour his drinks and listen to her stories. There he would be making a curry. Why did he think that curry was so exotic, she wondered? Dan's treat, make you a curry, love, he would say. The waitresses were better looking than me, she had told him.

'You're good looking,' he said, matter of fact, not bothering to look at her.

'Not American good-looking Dan, not orthodontist, plastic surgeon, pumped up, peachy glowing good looking.'

'You're too old for that.'

'Thanks pal,' she said. She sat drinking wine and watched Dan get his lump of crumbly Lebanese Gold out of the kitchen cupboard, reaching up so that his loose cuff fell back onto the hard, white flesh of his arm. He broke a piece of the lump onto the chopping board, powdered it with the big, broad bladed knife and scraped it into the curry.

'Ready,' he said and grinned at her.

Silly bastard. She looked now at the wraith of him. No more marijuana curry, no more love in front of the fire with his paintings stacked around the walls and his big hands black with ink and yellow coal flame licking into his careless, dissolute eyes.

He opened his eyes and she caught the first seconds of panic in them. Then, his calm glance at the ceiling before he turned his head, cold, mocking, taking his time with her.

Chapter 8

'I knew you'd do it,' Graham said, and sipped his Guinness.

Virginia pulled away a big flake of white flesh from her fish and wiped it around her plate until it was sloppy with parsley sauce. Graham watched. Watched the moist flicker of her lips before she opened her mouth, then her teeth and tongue tip. He watched her chew.

'I think I'm in love,' he said.

'Tough shit,' said Virginia.

'A quick shag would do.'

'No,' said Virginia and gave him a big smile.

'Ah well,' said Graham, 'it's only manners to ask. Wouldn't want you to feel that the magic had faded.'

She ate more of her fish. Graham sat behind his empty plate, watching her, staring.

'Tell you what,' she said, 'ask me again in a year.'

Graham reached into his jacket pocket and took out a flat, electronic diary. He picked at it with a metal pen. 'Let me get that in the diary. I'm on a promise am I?'

'No you're not, you bugger. But you can ask, can't you, who knows?'

'Why not now?' Graham said. The joke was over.

'Not now, Graham. Things are getting me down right now.' She had stopped eating, stopped smiling. 'In a year though, everything will be okay again. A year should do it.'

'What's up?' he asked. She looked up at him and saw his pink, veiny face frowning at her. He sat back in his big body, pouting with worry.

She shook her head, 'No,' she said.

'Anyway,' Graham said, 'you're in the diary.' He flicked it open again and pretended to read. 'Ask Virginia about a shag.'

'Are we having pudding?' said Virginia.

He pointed at her. 'You'll put weight on,' he warned. 'There aren't many fat lady parts and if you do get fat I'll take you out of the diary.'

'I don't get fat. I can eat anything: sugar, chips, Big Macs any damn thing. Naturally slim and gorgeous I suppose. It's just something I have to live with.'

'I'm not,' said Graham, glumly.

'Yes you are love,' said Virginia. She looked down at her plate, caught out by a quick burst of affection for him. She gobbled up the rest of her fish and wiped the plate clean with a bit of bread.

'Treacle sponge?' Graham asked her.

She nodded, then said, 'Come on then, what should I do? I've never opened anything before.'

'Well,' he said, 'we'll invite lots of people: press, photographers, telly if we can.'

She jumped in. 'I can do that, I can get somebody from the telly.' And then she saw him trying not to laugh. 'You sod, you bloody sod. That's what you want me for isn't it?'

'No. It's not, honest,' beaming the lie at her.

'You sod,' laughing back into his fat, red laughter over the treacle sponge and the custard. There were chocolate ripples in the custard and she dipped her finger in and licked. 'I love custard,' she said.

***

She met Richard outside Dan's ward. 'What's wrong?' she said, thinking suddenly, He's dead.

Richard shrugged, 'Just lounging about,' he said, 'trying to make my mind up to go in.'

She took his arm and pulled him up close to her. 'Don't be soft,' she said. 'It's no good being soft with that bugger in there.' Their faces were close and suddenly he dipped into her and kissed her cheek.

'You're pissed,' he said, shocked at the acrid edge to her breath.

'I might be. It's possible,' said Virginia. 'Come on, in we go.'

He let her pull him in. She stopped at the nurse's desk and whispered, 'Get the bottle.'

They stood at Dan's bedside and she took the Glenmorangie from Richard and held it up. 'We've come for a drink, so bloody wake up.'

Dan was staring at them. 'I'm awake.'

Virginia sat in the chair at Dan's bedside. He turned his head on the pillow so that he could see her. She poured an inch of whisky into his water glass. 'Cheers,' she said and drank half of it.

'She's pissed,' said Dan.

'That's what I told her,' said Richard, 'but I think that she already knew.'

'I was looking at Richard,' said Virginia, 'when I came in just now. He's a bit of all right Richard is, don't you think so?' They both looked at Richard. 'Thin,' said Virginia, 'tough looking little bugger, shiny dark hair and a nice mouth. Not drifting off are you?' she said to Dan. 'Not going off into a little death dream are we, not being half a ghosty? Good, you shit, you shit bag. I want to tell you about my dinner. My dinner I've just had with a fat accountant who likes Guinness and treacle sponge and leg-over and a bit of a laugh. Not like you, you death watch bastard.' She had another go at the whisky. 'By God it's an easy drink this is. You never liked a bit of flesh did you, not really liked it did you, hey, did you?' And she saw that Dan's eyes were closed. 'See, Richard, see?' she said, whispering the confidence to him. 'He was a watcher, that's all he was. A worker out, a brainful of ideas and nothing,' she ran out of words, 'nothing, nothing in his belly.'

Richard stood, stony faced, he put his hand on her shoulder. She shook her head and rested her cheek against him, felt his hand stroking her neck. 'No,' he said, softly, 'no.'

Chapter 9

Virginia flicked down the indicator and turned out of the traffic into the stillness. There they were again, the big, Victorian houses and the tall black railings of the old garden in the centre of the square. She turned off the engine, but stayed in the car with her eyes closed. No more drinking, she thought, no more feeling like this in the morning.

Behind the houses, on one side of the square, the university had built into the enormous back gardens and made a jumble of red brick teaching rooms, a canteen and studios. It was early and everywhere was empty and still.

She sat in the shabby room, a dance studio with exercise bars and a smeared mirror, and waited. There was a piano, a scatter of chairs against the end wall, a couple of blue crash mats on the floor. Lines of sunlight came in through narrow slatted blinds. She sat and listened to the big, empty space.

She heard the outer doors open and shut. There were footsteps, the last few seconds on her own, the door pulled outwards and there was Dennis. He was heavy, big footed, rubber soles squeaking on the grey lino. He wore a loose black tee shirt, black jeans. He saw her and his heavy, threatening face, sallow skin and black hair scowled past her and quickly around the room. She looked up at him, staring until she got the big grin creasing into his face and he dropped his briefcase, bang, onto the floor.

'Look what the techy's done for me,' he said. He was waving a compact disc at her. 'It amazes me.' She could see it did. 'The things they can do. All the stuff for the play: music, sounds, all on the one disc, wallop, no problem.' He held it up for her and made its perfect, silver flatness shimmer in the sunshine

Virginia liked his dark skin and the darker, simian hair, the big biceps soft with flesh. He turned away before she could say a word to him, a little swagger, pleased with the cleverness of doing things. She watched him walk the room, setting out the few things that they would need. He picked up one of the stage blocks and walked around the room holding it in front of him, straining backwards to balance its weight, making up his mind. He banged it down, banged down a bit of business into the room, went back for another, half a dozen paces and back and back again, setting out the space.

She sat up straight on her hard chair, hands in her lap, feeling the tension soften out of her shoulders, watching him, his arms tightly folded, hugging himself and muttering, 'Come on, come on, you lazy buggers.' He looked up, smiling, and turned to her, 'They've been shopping for costumes; God knows what they'll come up with.' She managed a smile, still thinking about shouting at Dan, the shit bag. She was lost in him, the old white stink of his whiskery skin that was nothing like him.

Then there was the noise of the three of them laughing and shouting into the room, tumbling over each other's words. Claire, a white blonde street kid, thin ratty face and brittle eyes. 'Been shopping, yeah, we've been shopping all weekend,' she said. 'These two gits are a total embarrassment.' Paul pushed past her, roughing her up smiling all over his big, smooth face. His long black hair and close clipped beard made him a stubby, mafia dwarf. 'You big rough bastard,' said Claire.

'It's just terrible,' John told her, 'doesn't know his own strength.' John, bald and big nosed, built like a sleek middleweight, held up a white plastic bag, held it wide open between his hands. 'Come on, come and see.'

'Why are they an embarrassment?' Dennis asked, laughing at Claire.

'She's so sensitive,' said Paul.

40

'It wasn't bargaining you did with that poor woman. It was a charity shop for God's sake.' She gave John a push. 'You seduced the poor old thing, sold yourself.'

'Not for second hand clothes I wouldn't. How cheap do you think I am?'

'John, you'd do it for a string vest,' Claire told him.

John dropped the bag and pulled out a man's jacket. 'Come on Virginia,' he said, 'don't sit there being all pensive, get this on.'

She jumped up, 'Alright alright,' jumped into their mood. 'That's not mine,' she said, but she took the jacket anyway and put it on and flopped around in it. She wrapped it around herself, she could almost double it, then held it wide open like wings for Claire to fly into and she wrapped the coat around both of them and they danced four legged round the room, stamping and screeching. Virginia stopped, suddenly, and held out the coat for Claire to step away.

'Just showing off,' said John. 'If the director were half a man he'd stop this sort of thing in rehearsals.'

Virginia threw the coat at him. She knelt, scrabbling in the plastic bag. 'Come on, come on, let's see what you've got.'

Claire was fiddling with a brown, flimsy scarf, trying it this way and that about her shoulders. Virginia got up and took Claire's hands and held them away, wide, and looked at her. When she let go, the hands stayed there, in the air, placed. Virginia took the scarf and arranged it, smoothing it, pinching up the folds of it, feeling the line of collar bone under her finger tips, their faces close, serious. 'Yes, yes, that's it,' said Virginia, 'like that, so that you can move.'

'Go on the lot of you,' Dennis was booming at them clapping his hands as though they were kids, 'over there by the wall.' They lined up so that he could see the clothes. 'It's all in our colour range,' he said and they stood there, like children, being watched and picked over. 'Just be still, still.' She froze, trembling with the effort, the tension of it.

***

41

They wandered off into their own, serious, selves, doing their own familiar routines of stretching and twisting, breathing and humming, prowling the room. Virginia loved to watch Paul warm up. She watched him change himself, watched the change in the shaped lip and the line of his eye, the swagger insinuating into his walk, shoulders flexing and muscles bowing out the arms. She followed him, changing, doing what he did, a child in a playground game. He made something military, a threat, in his barefoot tread, march, prowl around the floor. As he moved he began to sing some nonsense, his quiet, chorister's tenor rising into a big whoof of noise and falling. He skipped a dance step into his walk, twisting, dodging on the ball of his foot, this way and back. Then, stretching the line of his back, reaching high up into his neck and up to the high skull tip, the strength for it coming up from the hard hollow of his stomach, feeling it under his ribs, the strength of it pushing him up, erect. And she was nowhere.

Claire held up her hand, offering the back of her hand to the air in front of Virginia. Standing close to each other poised like fencers. Virginia touched the hand, the tendon under the pad of her finger. They moved, moving together, hand and finger tip, drawing out the line of arm and shoulder. Twisting together, stretching and dipping, opening inside thigh and belly to each other, almost brushing, touching. Virginia closed her eyes her face moving with Claire's. Claire's eyes were closed, Virginia knew, so that there was only the touch of their hands. The sliver of space between them flickered. Eyes still shut, Virginia felt Claire's hand twisting over itself, away from her and felt her hand taken, held gently in Claire's soft palms, pulled, with that thrill of being embraced, into Claire's breast. Their eyes opened into each other's, laughing, tricked into this new intimacy.

They had to fight. Dennis took them over and over it. Virginia stood over Claire, prissy and full of herself. Claire wailed and sneered, pressed her face into Virginia locked their bodies together and they fell and rolled into each other scrabbling and spitting. They broke suddenly, listened to Dennis's comment and worried away at how to place this hand, where the legs should go, how to save their elbows.

Claire lost her line, took the prompt and howled it out, 'Fuck it, fuck it,' in frustration. Dennis took them back again. She rolled and felt the squash of Claire's breast into her back, threw her off and felt the spiky hands scrabbling at her dress in pinched handfuls. Dennis stopped them and they lay on the floor, still.

'It starts,' said Dennis, 'after the longer speech where you can be in a position to kick her.' The room was quiet and empty, only their calm voices.

'If I get her down to there,' Virginia said.

'And kick her,' said Dennis.

Virginia stroked Claire's back, somehow sorry for the kick. 'I only kick the floor,' she said, smiling.

Claire nodded, laughed at her. 'I know,' she said, 'I know that.'

Virginia looked down at her, Claire, half lying, her white face staring upwards twisting her open throat.

'I don't know how to do this,' said Virginia.

Again and again they did it, picking up the same word and movement. Again. 'How's that?' said Virginia. Again, to get it right, make it as it should be, with none of the fast and loose contingency of the ordinary, natural world. Dennis made her worry about this person she was making up.

'She does this all the time does she?' he asked her.

Virginia paused. 'Yes, she's done this before.'

'Why's that then? What's she up to?'

Virginia paused again, wondering why. 'It's so that she can be established. So that she can make herself real.' Virginia did not feel real.

Dennis kept on at her. 'She does this with everyone then?' He gave Virginia a picture she could form up into words and she got her eyes into his as she spoke.

'Yes,' she said, 'she's pretty much a bag with everyone.'

Dennis held out his hands affirming what she said, 'To make herself real.' They thought about making her real. Dan was there and the poor deserted garden and the poor house and the hospital and the white bed sheets and Dan's too big hands and his clean pink nails.

That's what Dan's up to, Virginia thought, dying, to make himself real. She shrugged off the thought, feeling silly with the neat cleverness of it. But still, now, she saw him as a single threaded plot. That's what the bastard's up to, she thought. She rehearsed what Dan was doing, put it together, pointing up the detail of this or that, arranging inch by inch what should be seen. There was no uncertainty when she made things in this way, not the hopeless tangle of second by second, day to day realities. She felt miserable, thinking of Dan, making, coldly, an artefact of himself.

Dennis stepped away from her. Claire got up from the floor.

'Let's break till two fifteen,' said Dennis.

They walked away, a sudden walking away from their space. Claire walked to the piano where she had sandwiches, cake and crisps. She had a line up of packets and cellophane and cups on the top of the piano.

'We need to go shopping,' said Paul.

'These jeans, look at them,' Claire said. 'Don't they pick up the muck. Look, it's all down this leg.' She brushed the white dust with the flat of her hand.

Virginia sat and watched them slipping into their shoes, rummaging in bags, drinking the morning's cold tea. She wanted to get going on the play again, not sit here waiting for Dan to start up once more in her head. She knew that he would and that she would have to keep on being angry, at least until he was dead. She wished that he would get on, quickly, and be dead. How do I feel about that? she thought. Okay, she told herself, not bad at all. Be dead. Hurry up.

They were not acting now and it was easy to be themselves. After all the morning striving to make invented things look easily, fluidly real, Virginia watched their ordinary movements and was convinced by them. How simple ordinariness was, how unthought, unthinkable, an unmade world of disingenuous, unmade intent. Unless you're that bastard, Virginia thought.

44

The morning had left her raw. Better to have had a few rows; a bit of spite dribbling through rehearsals would have been just fine. I'm okay with rows, she thought. I wouldn't be feeling like this if I'd just told Dennis to fuck off.

It was warm and sunny, the street was full of trees. In the sandwich shop everyone was plump and pleasant and a nice old man held open the door for her and smiled. She ate the sandwich as she walked. She gobbled it down and turned back for another. She made them all laugh in the shop. She put her head on one side, smiled, made herself blush, shook her head. 'I can't help it,' she said and laughed back. When she was outside she walked off crying. This isn't right, Virginia thought, this isn't right, weeping in the street and then, as she was doing it, thinking, what does this look like, am I doing it right, and then going back to the tears that she couldn't stop anyway. She thought about the telly where there wasn't the time to mess about with theories and self-examination you just had time to get to know what to do and then it was done and you rushed into the next bit. She was too young to have done Rep but she had heard people talk about it with a kind of yearning: learning one play, rehearsing a second, performing a third, all in the same day. Where would Lee Strasbourg have been in that regime, she wondered? And fucking Kierkegaard. They wanted her to turn her insides out and call it art. Dennis as well. I'll bet Dennis still reads all that shit, she thought. That fucking fucking shit, feeling the anger right down to her feet, stamping along the street, holding her sandwich, weeping.

They started again. Dennis pulled them out of their warming up. 'Come on, come on, we have to sing. We need to get the singing right.' Virginia liked the singing; it made them kinder, made them stand away from the cruelties of the play. She started singing from where she sat on the floor with her back against the wall and her legs splayed out in front of her on the cold lino. Singing Dan away from her, filling herself with noise. She started off with nursery rhymes and Claire crawled over and sat with her and sent her lovely, easy voice up and over Virginia's. The three men stood in the middle of the room singing around Claire's lead. 'We need to do the Fauré,' Dennis called at them. He turned to Paul. 'Don't be frightened of it,' he said. 'You're telling yourself you can't sing; of course you can sing.' Virginia and Claire stood on either side of Paul and held his hands for the singing. He missed his note and they stood closer to him, trying to rub their singing into him. Virginia squeezed his hand and pulled it up against her breast; she could feel herself singing against his forearm. Dennis came and put his arm around him and walked him away around and back, they touched hands and began again.

'When do I breathe?'

They stood close to him. Claire, sharp with anxiety, watched him, her fingers pointing at her mouth, showing him, mouth open wide, filling up the sound. John gestured him up, all his body, hands, shoulders lifting him and Claire's lovely smile quick in her eyes as he got it.

'You're happy?' said John, a real question. Paul nodded.

'We should make it a part of the warm up,' said Dennis.

'Before each performance,' said John.

'In the interval,' Virginia said.

'So that he's happy,' said Dennis.

Virginia stood close to them. What shit people talk about actors, she thought, what shit they talk. Claire took Paul away to sit with her on the floor. She sat facing him, up close between his legs and made him sing. 'La la it through,' she told him, 'just to get the note,' slapping her hand, slap down flat on his thigh.

He had a big grin on his face. 'I'll just sing the bits I'm sure of shall I and keep quiet for the rest?'

Chapter 10

It was nearly seven when they finished, and Virginia drove home in the low dazzling sunshine. She took her time, maundered along and when she remembered to look in the mirror there was the big white face of a lorry close up behind her. She made herself go faster until she was in the clear again. The hedges had been left to grow big and they took the sun out of her eyes; big trees left to grow so that it was like driving through a forest. Then, suddenly, there was the huge space of the fields, low stone walls and then the traffic signs. She slowed for the sudden narrow turns of the next village, the tall, shady houses of pale stone. At the far end of the village, just before the awkward bridge and the flat fields, there was a pub. It was built into a crooked terrace of Georgian houses and she had to park on the street.

It was an old pub, but everything was polished and neatly in place so that it did not look old at all. There were half a dozen men at the bar. They looked shiny and cheerful, washed and brushed after a day's work, in their clean shirts, drinking beer and talking about rugby. She stood at the bar and listened. They switched to racing and then television and what a mucky bloody film last night's had been; bloody disgusting.

'George, come on you lazy bugger,' one of them shouted. He turned and gave Virginia a smile. 'You've got a woman here on her last bloody legs for thirst.'

She sat up at the bar ready for a drink and read the menu.

'Are you going to risk it?'

She looked up and smiled. The man who had spoken was leaning forward over his pint glass. 'Do you think I should?' she asked.

'You'll need to be hungry.' He was a big, round faced man with grey hair.

'I am,' she said. 'Go on give George another shout for me.'

They all started shouting, 'Oy, come on then George, George get yourself in here. George, George.'

'What the bloody hell's going on.' George was fat and ponderous in a soft, pink pullover.

'Get your skates on, there's another victim here for you,' said the grey-haired man.

George gave her her drink and took his time telling her about the menu. While she waited and while she ate they nosed their way into her business: was she local; did she work round here; her accent wasn't local? Yes it is, she told them, of course it is. Posh local then, they told her back. So she gave them a bit of her best Barton.

'What other accents can you do then?'

'Bloody cheek,' she said, and she looked and laughed at the man who had spoken and she made him blush. He was a big blond man with a peaches and cream complexion and he stood there, bursting out of his shirt and blushing at her.

He took a step towards her and said, quietly, 'You're on the television, aren't you?' She could smell him: cologne and the smell of the iron on his shirt. She leaned towards him, almost touched him, almost felt her hand on his arm.

'Shush,' she told him, her voice down to a whisper.

'I say,' he said, whispering back. Standing even nearer to her, speaking even more softly, he said, 'Why, is it a secret? You can't be on the telly in secret can you? I mean it's the telly, everybody can see you.' He had a lovely, ingenuous, Royal Garden Party voice. She was drawn into secrecy with him. Looking into his eyes and then away. She caught the laughter in herself.

'Shut up about it for God's sake or you'll get this lot started.'

'Oh right, yes,' he said and stood back, guiltily.

Virginia finished her drink. 'Right,' she said, 'I'll be off then.' The group of men said goodbye to her and watched her out of the door.

'See you again,' George said.

She stood on the pavement, going through her bag for the keys. She had it open on the roof of the car pulling a jumble of stuff out of it.

'Not lost your keys, have you?' The big blond stood in the doorway of the pub, smiling his pink smile at her. He stepped onto the pavement and she stared at him, breathing in, wincing with relief that he had followed her.

'No, got them,' and she held them up to show him.

'Sorry I nearly dropped you in it,' he said.

'What?' Still staring.

'In there,' he pointed back at the pub. 'You know, nearly gave the game away about you being on the telly.'

She smiled back. 'Oh, don't worry about that.'

He saw her smiling and he shuffled away and then seemed to pull himself together and make himself speak. 'I'm not a fan or anything like that,' he said. 'I mean I wasn't going to make a nuisance of myself. I just noticed that it was you on that make-up ad. As far as I was concerned you were just some woman in the bar. Well, you were weren't you?'

'Thanks,' she said.

'Anyway, you can come back anytime, no need to worry. I shan't say a word.' He looked away and then gave a quick, sheepish glance back at her.

Virginia laughed at him. 'Thanks,' she said again. 'Thanks, I shall. It's a nice pub.'

'They call me Hank,' he said.

She laughed out loud at him. 'Dear God, why do they call you that.'

'I don't know,' he said, standing up straight into her laughter. 'It started at prep school, when I was little you know, Well, I was never little, even as a baby I was a bit of a giant. Perhaps that was it? It sounds like a big person's name doesn't it?'

She held out her hand, 'They call me Virginia,' she said.

49

He took her hand and she gripped back hard against the weight of it.

'I'd offer you a drink,' Hank said, 'but it would just cause talk. You know, if we went back in there.'

'I don't mind.' She leaned against the car ready to talk to him for as long as he liked.

'But anyway,' he said. 'I've got to be off. My daughter you see, she cooks for me in the evening. Well, this evening. She'll flay me if I'm late.' He stepped back from her, 'What about tomorrow, I always pop in for a beer after work?' He smiled and brushed his fringe across his forehead.

Virginia let her face fall. She knew how to do this. She had been at this all afternoon and she thought, and then she didn't need to think at all, to do this and then that 'So that's it is it? You're just going off and leaving me to it.'

'You've eaten haven't you. I mean you're very welcome, but you had something in the pub.'

'Only a snack.'

'You had the pie and chips.'

'Oh for God's sake invite me.'

He couldn't get the grin off his face and swayed from side to side holding his arms stiffly with embarrassment. He gave each fist a little shake. 'Well, yes, all right. It's just up the road.'

'Get in,' Virginia told him.

As he was putting on his safety belt he said: 'You're awfully good at picking chaps up aren't you?'

***

'Your daughter's nice,' said Virginia.

'Yes, I know.' Hank said. 'She's terrific isn't she?'

'What about her mother?'

'No,' said Hank, 'she wasn't terrific.'

'Tell me about her.' Virginia said.

50

'No,' said Hank, 'perhaps not.' They stood in the cobbled courtyard of the farm. 'I should have turned off the lights,' he said, 'then we could have seen the sky.'

She looked at him, standing there in his shirtsleeves, hands in his trouser pockets, looking up and around at the old stone buildings.

'Is she alive?' said Virginia.

'Yes.'

'Divorced?'

'Years ago.'

'Oh good,' she said, the words out before she had thought them.

He shuffled a bit, head down. 'Been here for absolute years. Graveyard's full of us. Not a direct line. I can't see a direct line holding out like that, but the family name's there so I suppose it's cousins and so on. We go back forever, until the records peter out in fact.'

'What name?' she asked.

'Strong,' he said. It set her off laughing and she grabbed his arm and hugged it and gave a big open-mouthed laugh.

'Absolutely bloody perfect,' she said and then stopped herself, hand to mouth. 'Oh God that's rude isn't it. But look, you are aren't you, I mean, strong?'

'It's a jolly good job I'm not sensitive, isn't it.' Her hand was still on his arm and he patted it. 'You don't have much in the way of discretion do you?'

'No,' she said. 'I'm a bit pushy I am.'

'That's all right. Come and push me around again.'

She kissed him. Half turned, reached up into his face and kissed him, hard and quick, on the mouth. He didn't move, just stood there, unsurprised and let her kiss him. What am I doing this for, she thought. What am I doing? 'Right,' she said, 'I'm off.'

He watched her get in the car and as she was starting the engine he bent to the window and said, 'Will you be passing tomorrow?'

'Everyday for a while.'

'Don't go in the Public Bar. I'll be in the Lounge.'

Chapter 11

She drove home and sat on her own at the kitchen table with the script and Dennis's notes. She sat, quietly, going over them and drinking one glass of wine and not letting herself drive into town to let Dan rough her up. Let him sit with Leo or Richard, let the bastards tip toe round him brim spilling with whatever it was they felt for him. She wanted him dead so that she could have him back again, the big fleshy man she'd had to begin with.

Every morning, day after day, Virginia drove into the sunshine. Just outside Barton there was a straight, new road through metallic fields of still, green wheat. She braked downhill at the tail of a long line of cars queuing at the roundabout and then she was on the old, slow road into Bedford through the honey stone villages and humped bridges. In front of her on the far, open slope of pasture there was a glowing shape of linseed blue. Hank's village slowed her right down into third, second gear in the blind turn of the street. When she tried to conjure him up in her mind she had only a few, snatched impressions of him. There she was, not knowing what he looked like. Of course you do, she told herself, but she didn't. He was a blond, but the rest of it had gone and all that she had was the feel of his arm, the hard flesh that had shocked her. When she had taken hold of his arm she had felt his warm skin and had held on to him, wanting to press her mouth against him, into the soft inside of his biceps and the moist pit of his arm and breath him in.

She was on the lookout for Hank, but there was no one about on the dusty pavements and she was soon out into the sunshine that flickered through the overgrown hedges and hurt her eyes. She settled down behind a lorry, dawdled along and made herself late.

She was last in and they had already unpacked themselves against one wall of the room. Every morning they made a messy, shambling camp, a scatter of chairs, back packs, carrier bags and clothes. Claire was already eating cake and there was a growing spread of crisp packets and biscuits. Paul and John were sitting on the floor drinking coffee from thin plastic cups. There were spilled rings of it and wet brown tissues and crumbs. There were handkerchiefs and socks, trainers, sweaters, mineral water and dirty plates, coats and sweaters, chiffon scarves, sunglasses, cans and bottles, watches, mobile phones and rumpled photocopied scripts. Virginia pulled off her sweater and threw it on a pile.

'How do you do it so quickly?' she said to Claire. 'Look at it.'

Claire was winding a scarf around her hair. She looked up as Virginia spoke and said, abruptly: 'How's this then?' Her hair slipped free and she started again.

'You need a mirror,' said Virginia.

Claire shook her head. 'I have to do it on stage.' She tied it.

'Learn it with the mirror,' said Virginia.

Claire held out her arms, 'How does it look.'

'It's good.' Virginia backed away, she picked up one foot and then the other to take off her shoes and then walked away, barefoot, to begin.

She walked quickly feeling the whole length of her foot, bare on the cold floor and put a swagger into her shoulders, head up and skipped a step into her walk. She sat, straight backed, on the floor making herself still for an instant. She thought only about herself, about her back and the muscles in her stomach and how her breath felt below her ribs. She lay on her back and did slow stretches, her hands touched, stretching, and she felt the tight pain of it at the tops of her biceps and through her armpits and the mesh of muscle, flesh and rib. She sat up, straight

53

backed, hands on thighs. Then stood, stood still, finding a balance. Slowly, she let her head fall and followed, slowly, down, letting her hands pull down the weight until she palmed the cold, plastic floor. She closed her hands and let her knuckles trail the floor, bent double, hair falling, and she shook her hands right then left, open mouthed, letting the movement sing up the air from her, bubbling up nonsense. She liked making the noise and stood up straight, throwing it across the floor and into the wall. She beat her breast bone, Tarzan-beating a rhythm, humming and walking so that her jaw and head vibrated with the noise.

She walked softly around the room, around Paul who lay on his back twisting left and then right. She watched him do a dozen, quick, half sit ups and lie back flat and drown her with a room vibrating hum that he let fall into a sudden swooping melody. She saw the muscle of his arms and thighs slack against the hard flat floor. She watched him, big shouldered, doing press ups, sudden and surprising, hurting himself with them and standing up breathless and then poised and still and then into a strong, harsh stretch with the noise starting up again, a babble of consonant noise and one big-mouthed, yawning sigh.

Virginia turned so that she could stare at him, squaring up to him like a boxer, balanced, staring. She felt her weight falling plumb straight into the thickness of her foot, toes wiggling, shoulders just forward so that she felt their weight and the strength in her arms resting lightly against her body, hands touching modestly, like a fighter ready to twist, pull back, punch.

***

Claire danced.

'What do you want me down to, in the strippy bit? Down to basic or to the bra?' She danced, pulling her hair loose, pulling down the zipper on her woolly jumper.

John stood up and walked one two steps into her, putting his hands on her waist, showing her the dance. 'Like this,' he said and stopped her. His fingers touched her hips, showing her her hips. 'Does she have to be in time?' he asked Dennis, 'like a cabaret dancer would be?' Dennis shook his head. John danced with her, down to her bra, getting her eyes into his. 'Come on,' he said, 'again with the hair.' He stood away from her and watched her. 'You've blocked it in your head, where you're going, haven't you?'

They made her sexual, these shrewd observers, this ordinary girl, this girl they have watched in the street, with the twins crying in the supermarket. How would she be sexy? How would she make this clumsy try at falsifying herself. They watched this girl that Claire was making and suggest this and that to make her awkward and absurd. 'What if I did it like this?' Claire said. 'Like this,' showing them.

They all smiled. Done it. Made it.

***

They were late finishing and the streets were empty. The sun was in her eyes until she turned over the railway bridge and then had to brake as the leaf green bend came too quickly. She was speeding for him, knew she was and felt a fool, making the ordinary road fly past. She did not like the thought of him waiting for her. She had him in her mind, sitting there in the empty pub lounge fretting that she would not come. She felt a fool, this putting of herself into his hands. She knew that she was going to do it, that it was done. Well, sod it then, she thought and thought about how big, how gigantic he was. The way he sat with his hands in front of him. Hands like dinner plates her mother would have said. Leaning forward with his hands curled round each other. His finger nails were manicured, she thought, just realising it.

She stopped outside the pub, ready to drive off again, but rushed out of the car without her jacket, two steps over the pavement.

He was reading the paper. He looked up at her, not smiling, surprised.

'I like your glasses,' she said. She wanted him to smile.

'Just for reading.' He took them off and waved them at her. 'Getting old,' he said.

She sat down on the stool across the table from him. He was fiddling with the slender, half moon glasses. 'You have them manicured,' she said and tapped the back of his hand with her forefinger. He turned over his hand and she saw the soft flesh of his palm. 'I'd have thought a farmer would have hard hands.' She was sitting primly, straight-backed on the stool. He was looking at his hands, showing them to her.

'No,' he said, 'not really, not nowadays. It's all machines and anyway the guys do all the rough stuff.'

'You're the brains behind it all are you?'

'My word yes,' he said, 'that's me all right,' and he smiled at her.

'Would you like a drink?' she asked him.

'No,' he said, 'not really.'

'Give the landlord a shout, will you?' said Virginia.

He shook his head. 'No, no let's not get into all that. Let me show you around, while it's still light. Round the village. I'll get the keys for the church, it's a lovely building.'

'Where are they then?'

'Well, I've got them here actually.' He patted his jacket pocket. 'Church Warden you see.'

Virginia blinked at him. 'You're not in the choir I hope,' and saw him smile. 'Oh God you are, aren't you?'

'Always have been,' he said. 'Apart from when I was away in the army.'

'Salvation?' she asked.

'Royal Anglian Regiment,' he told her. 'We think of it as the county regiment still. Bit out of date now, I suppose, but my father and his father and so on all went in.' He folded up his glasses and put them in the top pocket of his jacket.

'You look a real gent,' Virginia said.

'I am a real gent,' he told her. He stared at her as if he were trying to remember her. He stood and offered her his hand and she let just a little of her weight into it as she got up.

He held open the door for her and as she brushed past him she felt him move away keeping a polite, tense distance. They stood on the pavement, looking away from each other.

'Which way?' she asked.

He looked beyond her, across the road to the old houses. 'We can go into the lane. Over there. It goes up the hill to the church. He pointed, half-heartedly, as if expecting her to turn him down and she felt stranded as his shyness made her shy. She stepped up to him, sudden and clumsy, and took hold of the loose material of his coat sleeve and shook his arm.

'Come on then,' she said. 'Come on, don't be soft.' She could feel the rough tweed in her palm. 'What's the matter?'

'Yes,' he said, 'across the road then. It's really nice; a good, square Norman tower, a nice, tough looking little church.'

There was a broad, green path up to the church and she made him hold her hand to pull her up the steep bits. 'Hold my hand,' she said to him and reached towards him, appealing and impatient and made him grip hard to keep the weight of her hand in his.

'Stop pretending,' he said.

'Pretending what?'

The church was in the middle of fields. Over the low stone wall there was a dripping hillside of pasture and then a huge, heavy field of yellow flowering rape.

Virginia stood up straight, stretching after the climb. 'How come the church isn't in the village?'

Hank turned to look at the church as if he were trying to weigh it up. 'I've always thought that it must have been to start with,' he said, 'and then the village moved, probably because of disease, maybe some early enclosures. It's lovely though isn't it to walk away from people into open space, like this, without all the rooves and walls and windows pressing in on you; just the tower going off and up into the sky. Not that it goes terribly far.'

'Doesn't anyone know?'

He shook his head. 'No, they don't and if they do they can jolly well keep it to themselves. I don't want to be silted up with knowing everything. Never understood people wanting to know about everything. What good can it do? Such a simple thing this is: fields, sky, church. It's not a hobby you know.'

'What isn't?' she said. His serious face made her quiet in front of him. She still held his hand, awkward now herself. He saw it and smiled.

'Here's a Strong,' he said and pointed to a gravestone. 'Seventeen thirty-six. It's all a bit difficult, you can see how the stones are weathered. The Jacobean ones, look, those with the death's heads, I'm pretty sure that they're Strongs as well. It all tallies with the church records and what family stuff there is.'

'There are sheep,' said Virginia, 'look.' She was pointing over the wall of the churchyard.

'Can be a terrible nuisance,' said Hank. 'Just imagine in early summer when there are lots of them baa-ing away like billy-oh, drowning out evensong. Still, quite biblical in its way.' He took from his pocket a big, brown metal key and held it up for her to look at. 'We'll catch the sun nicely now, you'll see.'

Inside the church the low, evening light threw the colours from the windows into the stone and the dark, polished wood.

'All the usual curios,' said Hank, 'memorials and so on. I think that you can easily overdo that sort of thing, though, don't you?' He was standing a couple of steps into the church looking upwards and around as if he were surprised to see it all still there. 'I never really feel comfortable with the idea of a church being a bit of social history. Although, people seem to like that sort of thing nowadays.'

Virginia sat down in a pew near to the back of the church. The hassock left no room for her feet. There was a black, scuffed hymn book on the ledge in front of her. She watched Hank walk forward towards the altar, strolling, stopping to rub his palm on the shiny, rounded back of a pew. The weight of empty air, shaped and heavy above her, bowed her head. There was the coloured, evening light and in front of her, luxurious against the wood and stone, was the sumptuous green cloth of the altar and its sombre, shining ornaments.

Hank sat down beside her. 'What do you think?' he asked, softly. She nodded, not looking at him, her mouth tight against her teeth. He whispered, 'What are you doing?'

She turned slightly towards him. 'Saying a prayer,' she said.

'Thought so,' said Hank. 'I do that myself. Never give it a thought in the ordinary way of things, then it seems the natural thing to do in here. Can't manage it in other people's churches, though. I suppose in theory it should be all the same, somehow it isn't.' He sat quietly beside her with his hands on his thighs and after a while she could feel his breathing. She thought he was asleep and turned to look at him.

'You do that a lot do you?' he whispered, 'say your prayers?'

Virginia shook her head, 'No,' she said, whispering back, 'not for years and years. I'm saying a prayer for my friend.'

Hank's face was close to hers. 'What for? This friend's in trouble I suppose?'

Virginia nodded. 'Can I tell you?' she said.

'No,' he said, 'not in here. If you tell me in here I've had it haven't I?'

***

'Tell me here,' said Hank. They sat in Virginia's car, parked in Hank's farmyard. The old, stone buildings were all around them going darker than the sky. She told him about Dan. She told him a part of it, Dan's part. Then she lied. Panicky, convincing lies that pushed back, into a time long past, her room in Dan's house and loving him.

'Why not just do it?' said Hank. 'Why not just shoot himself?' Virginia shook her head. 'Not off his chump is he?' Hank asked.

'Anything but,' she said. 'You'd think that it was all perfectly normal, you know, some poor man dying in the way that people do. So, you sit there and have a bit of a chat. It wouldn't be so bad if it was, was some dreadful disease that was killing him, but it isn't. It's him, he's doing it, he's the dreadful disease, the bastard.' Hank was staring at her. She

59

stared back. 'I couldn't keep it up. I went and got pissed and then gave him a bollocking.' She smiled. 'Showed myself up; had a real screech at him.'

'Good,' said Hank. The way she swore made him want to laugh.

'Haven't been back since. I'm fed up of the whole thing.'

'Of course you are.'

'I'm just going to do my play. I'm going to do that.'

'You can't though can you,' Hank said. 'Don't be silly, you can't just turn your back.' Virginia turned away from him. 'You'll feel rotten about it when he's dead. You'll regret it; you'll think badly about yourself and it'll go on and on.' He waited for her to speak, but she didn't. 'Are you hungry?' he asked.

She got out and slammed the door so that the car shook. She waited for Hank to get out and then turned on him. 'Don't you tell me that. Don't you tell me what to do.' Hank folded his arms on the roof of the car and leaned on them. He made a sad face at her and kept quiet. 'Invite me in,' she said.

'Would you like to come in?' said Hank. 'There are only leftovers in the fridge, but you're very welcome.'

'What leftovers?'

'A bit of beef, I think, and some leftovers we could fry up.'

The old stone doorway was out of proportion, too wide for its height and the heavy, dark-stained door needed an effort against its weight to push it open. There was a cold white room with the washing machine, drier and freezer; there were boots and wellingtons on the floor and half a wall of rough coats.

'Go through to the kitchen,' Hank said. 'I'll have a root around and see what there is.'

Virginia sat at the table in the middle of the enormous kitchen. The ceiling felt low and close and the last light of the evening lost itself, softly, in the room.

'You okay?' said Hank. He was holding a big, white plate in one hand and pointing at it with the other. 'I'd forgotten what a lump it was. Do you want the light on?'

'No, it's lovely,' said Virginia. 'I like your table.'

'It's good isn't it?' It's always been here as far as I can remember.' He put down the beef in front of her. 'I'd offer you a beer, but you're driving.'

'I can have one.'

'Best not you know.'

He gave her a tonic water and she watched him cut the beef into thin, red slices and then make a salad dressing. 'I'll grate some carrot into this shall I, with a bit of shallot and garlic? Will that be okay? There's horseradish, but it's bought I'm afraid.' She nodded at him. 'Then there's last night's apple tart,' he said.

Chapter 12

She left early, well before ten, Hank stood in the yard, hands in his pockets, watching her go. She drove through the dark countryside and, because her head was full of Hank and his leftover dinner and his church and his noisy, innocent sheep, she went past her turn for home and kept on the main road into Northampton. She was suddenly in the big street lights and then the white illumination of the hospital. Dan's ward was quiet; the only light was by the nurses' station. Virginia went and leaned on the counter.

'Is he asleep?' she asked, softly.

'Oh, Jesus you made me jump.' It was the blonde-haired nurse. She held her hand spread against the bosom of her white apron as if to calm her heart.

'You're late, aren't you?' said Virginia.

'Doing a double,' said the nurse. 'There's no staff to be had, especially not nights.'

Virginia half turned and pointed into the darkness of the ward. 'Is he asleep?'

'Should be,' said the nurse, 'he's doped up to the bloody gills.' She laughed and drew Virginia into the laughter. 'Fancy a belt of his scotch?'

Virginia was laughing and nodding. 'Yes, why not?' she said.

'Come round here then,' said the nurse, 'sit down here out of the way.'

They sat sipping Dan's good whisky from thick water tumblers.

'How long do you think he'll last?' said Virginia.

'Not long.' The nurse looked tired; the soft, yellow light caught every shadow in her face. Beyond them there was the dark vagueness of the ward.

'Is it always quiet like this?'

'It is when Sister Morphine's on duty,' said the nurse.

'She works here a lot does she?

'A trusted colleague.' She looked straight at Virginia. 'I bloody well hope somebody has the sense to top me up with it if I end up in here. Too bloody right I do.'

'How long is not long?' asked Virginia.

'Go and check now if you like.'

'Short as that?'

'Could have been yesterday.'

'Can I go and have a look at him?'

'Of course you can, duck.' The nurse put down her glass and took Virginia's from her. 'There's no need to feel bad about the other night you know. You were right to bollock him. Being at death's door doesn't buy him any special treatment. Not in my book. He's still got to shape up. There's never any excuse for being a shit is there?' She went with Virginia to Dan's bed. 'If you wake anybody up you can bloody well get them back to sleep again.' They tip-toed, whispering, past soft sleeping beds.

Virginia whispered back, 'I wouldn't know how.'

'Quick blow job,' whispered the nurse and they both started, couldn't stop, giggling. They stood over Dan's white face, listening to his gummy breath, hands over their mouths to stop the laughter. They put their arms around each other, cheeks touching, laughing quietly into each other's faces.

'I shouldn't hold this last piece of nonsense against him,' said Virginia, 'he was lovely.'

'Yeah,' said the nurse, 'I bet he was a bit of a laugh wasn't he?'

'Do you know what he did once?' They huddled together like conspirators in the dark.

'What?' said the nurse. 'What did he do?'

***

Virginia sat in the quiet ward. She sat in the big square hospital arm chair by Dan's bed and listened to him breathing in the dark. He'll stop, she thought, he'll stop soon. Not tonight though love, not tonight. Don't stop while I'm sitting here will you? I don't want that. I don't want you dead. I don't you know. That's why I get mad. When I came home I thought that you'd be there in the house and I could sneak in and wait for you. I had a little plan where I was going to sneak in and get into bed and wait for you coming in and then knock on the floor. Then you'd come up and I was going to get a real grip on you. I was by God, I was going to ravish you, ravish you, you old bugger. There was nobody there, you know, everywhere was cold and stinking. Why didn't you phone me, why didn't you come and see me? You should have. Bloody Richard never said. I bet he knew.

Chapter 13

In the morning she drove across the valley to see Richard. It was a close, damp morning, flecks of rain in the air. There was a steep road out of Barton that dropped onto the river and then the canal in the sodden, reedy fields. Harry was right they were tearing up the valley and there were the vast, new lakes like mercury in the muted light. She was glad to get out of it and twist up the old lane to Richard's house. There was a tiny, ironstone village, just a few elegant houses and a church, a big church with a turreted tower. She drove up the long, awkward drive to the house past green fields that seemed always to be empty, then a ramshackle of brick outhouses, old stables and Richard's back door. There were the four stone steps and the door that was too big. She picked up the black, cast iron knocker and made it bang through the house and then she banged it again to get herself in the right mood for him.

'Didn't know if you'd be up,' she said when he opened the door.

'Up and working,' he said. He leaned forward to kiss her, but she pulled away from him. 'What's the matter?' he asked and she could hear that he was afraid.

'They reckon Dan's not going to last the day.' She was trying to be hard faced and failing.

Richard turned and walked down the hallway into the house. She followed him into the big, double bayed room that looked over the valley. There were two levels of terraced lawn with stone balustrades and urns. Below them the valley was blurred with cloud.

'What a bugger,' he said.

'I went and sat with him last night,' said Virginia. She was standing, looking out of the window. When she was in Richard's house she always looked out across the valley and picked out Barton church and then tried to find the terrace where her mother's house was. The first time that she had been here, she and Richard had stood looking for her house.

'Left of the church tower and down a bit,' and Dan had pretended to see the colour of the curtains.

Imagining him playing about like that made her angry again. 'He was okay when I went away. I haven't been away long, have I, only a few months and then I come back and all this has happened.' She heard Richard sit down and when she turned away from the window she saw him in the armchair, staring at her. 'Did it never enter your fucking head,' she said to him, 'to tell me what was happening?'

'No, no it didn't,' said Richard. Virginia didn't say anything; she hadn't the heart to be angry. 'He didn't say, "Don't tell Ginny," of course he didn't. Telling you or not telling you never occurred to either of us. Why should it? You don't have to go around telling people things. It's not compulsory, you know, even if there are a lot of fools who think it should be. Some of us don't like babbling away about how we feel and who we really are and all that weak-kneed bullshit. We just get on with it. If Dan wanted to drink himself into the grave, why shouldn't he? As a matter of fact, I thought he was behaving like a twat and I told him, but it's not up to me how he behaves is it? It's up to him.'

'What about me?' Virginia said, quietly.

'This is what he wanted,' said Richard, 'this is what he's got.'

'You don't like it though do you,' she spoke even more softly.

'Like it? Of course I don't like it. How can I like it?'

'If you'd told me we could have stopped him.'

'You could have tried, but not me. What would 'we' have done, gone and smarmed him up as if he were some demented kid, counselled him out of it? I can see that happening, can't you?' He was

66

sitting up straight, sick with anger, 'Listen Ginny, anybody who can be bloody well soft soaped into being good can't be much, can they?'

'I'd like to have known,' she said, miserably.

'For you, not for him,' said Richard.

Why not for me, Virginia thought, why not? It would have been a damn sight better than stumbling into this. 'You didn't think about me then?' she said.

'Think what about you?'

'How I was going to feel.'

'You buggered off. You did what you wanted to do.' He sat back in the chair and waited for her, but she wouldn't speak. 'Why the bloody hell shouldn't you? Good for you. That's what we all do if we've any sense. Nothing else is any damn good. And when we've done that, done what we want, it's no good whining about things. Dan doesn't, so don't you.'

'And don't you,' said Virginia.

'I don't.'

'Not bloody half,' she told him. Then she shut up, sorry for him. He stared at her.

'I wish I hadn't stayed away.'

'Why did you then?'

'I was working. Dan never called me, never rang up after I'd been on the telly to say that I'd been terrific, never rang me back when I called him. So I let it drift.' She stood, wishing that there was somewhere to put the blame. 'How are you anyway?' she asked him.

'Pretty crap.'

'It's what you deserve,' she said. She came away from the window and bent and stroked his head and kissed him.

'All this time,' said Richard, 'I've known him all this time and now that's it, he's going to die, this morning or this afternoon. Known him since I was a kid.'

'I know.'

'He taught me at the college.'

'I know.'

'Nobody else would have me, I was such a little twat.' Virginia sat on the soft arm of the chair with her arm across Richard's back. She let her weight fall against him. 'He told me I was good and then he sneered at me, showed me up in front of people for being a waste of time, a lazy bastard. He set about me once you know. I mean, he really did. He gave me a pasting. I was black and blue. No exaggeration. I thought he'd broken my ribs. Bloody hell Ginny, I had black eyes, big puffy lips. He kicked me, the bastard.'

Virginia was laughing, 'What did you do?'

'I started turning up for all his classes, that's what I did. Never missed after that, I was bloody terrified.' She laughed again. 'It was no joke Ginny, I was only a little thin kid and there he was a big bull of a guy. He'd found me in the pub, the White Elephant, and he dragged me down the street to the college. When he'd calmed down a bit he said: "You, you're going to get your work done or I'll break your fucking neck." He was really serious. He always was about work.'

'Until he stopped,' said Virginia. 'It all got completely out of hand, drove him mad, out of his mind.'

'What? What did?'

'Art did. Bloody Art. All that looking and looking and then trying to make things stand still, stand up, alert, as if they were all conscious of themselves and drinking in everyone's attention. He did too much of it; he should have gone to watch football or gardened. Even when you had a shag with him you knew he was paying far too much attention to what was going on. I had to stop him, you know, stop him painting me. I knew he was watching me, you know, in bed with him.'

'I know.'

'You what?'

'I know. I've seen some of the sketches.'

'Bastard.'

'Didn't know it was you though.' He smiled, 'I mean, how could I tell?'

'Where are they, these sketches?'

'And pictures.'

'Pictures?'

'Still in the house.'

'You couldn't trust him, could you? "No, alright love, I won't, I promise I won't. Promise," that's what he said. Bastard, lying bastard.'

'Is it you?'

'Course it's me.'

'Could be quite a few people.'

'No, it's me. I knew he was watching me. Getting me down just right. That's what he used to say, isn't it, "Look. Just look at things,"? Well, serve him fucking right; drove himself fucking potty, didn't he? Didn't he?'

'What are you on about?'

'You, you gormless sod. You just carry on being a lazy useless little twat and then you'll be happy. That's what I'm going to do, I am. This play…'

'Thought you liked it.'

'This play, come and see it, we're on in Bedford, I've gone in for it just like Dan. Just like him. I let him in, see? Started thinking he was something special, what he did, what he did was special. But, that's it. All I've done is, is, I don't know, but I'm stopping, see? Next thing I do is a musical, with a happy ending. With a chorus of happy fucking children, a fucking stage full in fucking frills and fucking ribbons.'

Chapter 14

Virginia was awake as soon as the sun came into the room. She had left the curtains open so that the light would pull her awake. She lay in her mother's bed that was too high and too soft for her and wished that she could drive to Bedford and get on with the rehearsal. She wished that she was going to drive through Hank's village and try to spot him on the empty street and then get into the traffic jam and then get on with work.

Across the valley there were shadows of clouds on the fields; she watched the dark drift of them. Below her the sun was getting into the swollen, summer gardens all along the terrace.

She did her warm up, still thinking about work; did the stretches and the singing and thought about Harry waking up next door and hearing her whooping and soaring. She did Paul's exercises: press-ups and then onto the balls of her feet, breathing, making herself feel strong, ten more press-ups until her wrists and elbows hurt. She shook herself loose and breathed quietly.

Still in her pyjamas she sat outside on the step and drank her tea, looking at the garden. It was still the mess that her mother had neglected, but it was full of insects and butterflies and a sun-picked sheen of pollen dust. 'It is,' she thought, 'it's teeming.'

'Was that you singing?'

She looked up and there was Harry at the garden wall to her left, close to her. It was a low, brick wall and he leaned on it so that he could bend closer.

'I thought I'd snuffed it in the night and it was angels I could hear.'

'Oh, don't do that Harry. Not you as well you, silly old bugger.'

'What have I said girl? Don't cry for God's sake.' He was panicking, starting to wobble from side to side.

She pulled down a handful of the sleeve of her pyjama jacket and wiped her cheeks and then her nose. 'It's my pal,' she said, 'my pal Dan.'

'What, your painter feller?'

'He's bloody died on me, the rotten bastard.'

Harry heaved himself up onto the wall and started to climb over it.

'Don't, you old fool,' she said, 'you'll fall.'

But he had his leg across the top of the wall and rolled over and onto his knees. He was grinning, pleased with himself.

'Don't cry duck,' he said.

'I'm not crying. It's just the thought of it that sets me off now and again.'

'Well, you'll be a bit raw still from your mother going.' He was still on his knees, kneeling straight up in front of her.

'I've got to make all the arrangements. There's nobody else to do it, nobody to trust anyway.'

'No problem that.' Harry put his hands on her knees. She felt the weight of him and saw that his breath was coming quickly.

'I told you didn't I?' she said, relieved that she could nag him. 'You can't be climbing walls when you're a thousand years old.'

'I climbed that bugger.'

'Yes and it's knackered you.'

'Be quiet will you.' He flashed his false teeth at her again. 'It's a piece of bloody cake, just ring the undertaker up and tell him to sort it all out. Then you give him as much money as he can stagger off with and it's done.'

Virginia sat there nodding at him. 'Shall I give you a hand up?'

'You'd better or I shall be stuck here.'

She stood up and took hold of his forearms, still thick with muscle, and she staggered as he put his weight into her hands. 'My bloody knees,' he said, hissing. He was dressed in his gardening rags.

'You're in tatters,' Virginia told him, 'you look like an old dosser. There's no need for it.' She turned back into the house and left him holding onto the doorjamb, wincing with the effort of straightening up.

'I'll make some fresh tea,' she shouted back at him.

He sat and had his breakfast with her, toast and a couple of fried eggs.

'Now then,' he said, 'ring that feller up that we had for your mother. They did a good job.' He looked up and saw that she had her mouth full. 'It's usually about a week you have to wait. Unless of course you're lucky and they have a cancellation.'

She stopped chewing, 'A cancellation?' she said. 'What do you mean, a cancellation?' Harry looked puzzled and then he started to giggle.

He sat drinking his tea in the kitchen and watched her wash up. 'Will you have a do?'

'What?'

'A bit of a drink after the funeral?'

***

When she was finished with the undertaker she rang Graham. His secretary tried to put her off. 'Don't put me off, don't tell me he's busy. I'm busy. Just get him on the phone will you?' She stopped, amazed at herself. Then Graham said he was busy.

'Oh come on Graham, you can spare half an hour.'

'I can, I can spare half an hour, but you'll have me out for the afternoon, you know you will.'

'No I shan't.' She was feeling better already, imagining his big face heavy with lust. No, not lust, she thought, guile.

'Why so keen on me all of a sudden?' he was asking and she could hear the chirp in his voice and knew that he would come. 'Why so keen on me?'

'You cheer me up,' she said, smiling, 'you know you do.'

'That's what you need is it?'

'A little,' she said, the smile gone, thinking about traipsing around with all the paperwork of Dan's death and then going to the undertaker's.

'I'll see you in that pub,' Graham said, 'the big place opposite the Guildhall. What's it called, Pig and Dildo?'

'Rat and Parrot.'

'I knew it was some bloody silly name.' He was hurrying her off the phone.

'Oneish?' she asked.

'Don't be late,' he said and rang off.

***

Graham leaned on the bar so that it held up the squash of his belly.

'You sounded busy, on the phone,' Virginia said.

'There's the opening coming up. Got to get it right.' He waved at the barmaid and she skipped along from the other end of the shiny bar and stood in front of him, young and beaming. 'Pint of Guinness,' he said.

'Come and sit down,' said Virginia.

'And a ginger beer and one for yourself,' said Graham. The three of them watched his Guinness settle.

'Dan died,' Virginia said. She said it without thinking, the words would not wait.

'You're okay, are you Virginia?' said Graham. The barmaid topped up the glass, a quick, soft squirt into the white mousse, and left them to it. Virginia watched her serve a small, dark man. Graham picked up his glass and drank the top inch. 'Come on,' he said, 'over there in the corner.' He stood by the table while Virginia took off her raincoat. 'Give it here,' he said and he spread it over a chair to dry and then he watched her sit. 'You're the best sitter I've ever seen.'

'You what?'

'Best sitter. You sit beautifully, with your back dead straight, head up and waiting for the next thing to happen.'

'Sit down yourself, you fool.'

'I look crap when I sit with you.'

'I'll look gorgeous for both of us. Now sit down for heaven's sake.' She watched ready to tease him back. 'Now then, stop twisting yourself round and put the base of your spine against the back of the seat, head up, shoulders back and, bingo, there you are.'

'Bingo my bum. Do I look like you? No I don't. I look like a big fat ugly bastard.'

'Which is already a vast improvement,' she said and made him smile.

'How are you doing?' he said.

'Not bad, Graham, not bad.'

'Have you eaten? You ought to eat. Hang on for just one minute and I'll get you some grub. Something stodgy, give you a bit of ballast.' She watched him do his usual windmill waving at the waiter.

'Look sharp, old lad, can you?' he said. 'We're starving.'

She wished that Graham would come to the funeral, she could do with him.

'I'm not going to a funeral for a chap I don't know,' he told her.

'Oh come on,' Virginia said, miserably, 'it'll be good.'

'Good? How can it be good, you silly girl?'

'Come to the party at least.'

'Party?'

'Wake then. Look, I don't want it to be morbid, Graham. I'll never get through it if there's a lot of weeping and carrying on.'

'Listen,' Graham said, 'I've been talking to Joe about your mate.' He leaned over the table, soft voiced, 'He reckons, and so do I too, that he's going to take quite a battering from the tax man.'

Virginia was taken aback, 'You what? That's the least of his worries. Where he is right now he'll be having to explain quite a bit more than tax evasion.' She tried to laugh, but it started her crying.

'Sorry. Sorry,' said Graham.

'No it's all right. Go on, tell me.'

74

'You ought to empty the house. Well not empty.'

'Why me.'

'If he's got a lot of unsold stuff in there, I mean you said he was good didn't you, his stuff sold, you said.'

'My God yes. People were fighting to buy it. When he could be arsed to do anything.'

'You listen to me Virginia; it will all go into his estate and then the inland revenue will take a big depressing bite out of it. So, you ought to hide it.'

'It's not mine.'

'It could be.'

'You're a hard-faced bastard you are, Graham. Do you know that?'

He reached out and took her hands in his. 'Only about money. Only money. You've got to be.'

She walked Graham back to his office, past the quiet, white houses on Derngate, her arm in his.

'Do you really think we ought to?' she asked him. 'Isn't it stealing?'

'Who would you be stealing from?' He spoke to her as if she were a slow child. 'Who's going to inherit all this stuff?'

'Nobody. Nobody I know of anyway,' said Virginia. They were standing on the gravelled front of the tall house where Graham worked. 'It's a bit sad that,' said Graham. He took her hand in both of his. 'Listen then, are there any pictures of you or anything connected with you? Virginia nodded. 'Take those, it's only natural that he'd give them to you.'

'Richard could do that as well,' she said, turning the idea over, speaking half to herself.

'Tell him if you must, but just remember the first rule for successful crime is that you do everything on your own and never tell anyone anything.'

'It's not crime though is it?'

'It's close.'

She kissed him. 'Good old Graham. You will come to the do won't you?'

75

'Of course I shall.' He paused, just a little uneasy. 'Listen, do you want me to come to the house and go through the pictures with you? Better do it fairly sharpish, you know. Before the funeral if you can. It might be a bit grim on your own.'

Virginia nodded. 'Yes.' She said. 'Yes, thanks Graham,' and she kissed him again.

Chapter 15

A line of people stood on Dan's garden path. They all had a drink in their hands and every time the gate in the overgrown hedge clicked open they turned to look. A squat man with a red beard stood in the gateway and looked towards the house; a ripple of heads nodded at him. There were two women behind him waiting to push their way forward.

The garden was full of flowers. There was no breath of air. The French windows were wide open and Dan's front room was filled with people talking and laughing and the noise of them came into the garden. Virginia was glad of the noise. She stood on her own, on the threshold, looking into the room. She watched Sarah. Sarah was wearing a tight, black suit and garish, red lipstick. Her long, blonde hair was drawn back, softly from her face and held in a plait, loosely, with a dark ribbon folded in. Graham was with her, listening to what she said. He looked like an alderman, a big, fat man with a lovely balding haircut and smooth pink face. Sarah sneered, ready to weep or spit. They stood close together in the crowd where people smiled into each others' faces and had another drink. A smart-looking bunch they were in the arcane clutter of Dan's house. A house full of hanging plants and swathes of old, dry grasses and thistles, bottles and gothic candlesticks, jars, pots, knives and plates, a rolling pin stuck in a brown earthenware jar, coloured biscuit tins, a pile of clean laundry going dusty in a corner. The dresser was full of jumble sale painted plates. A room where nothing mattered that made you careful not to touch a thing. There was a child's paper parasol in the dead, summer fireplace.

Virginia walked through the room, across the foot of the staircase to the kitchen. There was Richard pointing his pale face at the air, making anyone think again about talking to him. Virginia watched him; he leaned back against the draining board, sipped whisky from a tumbler, one of Dan's good ones Virginia saw. He put the glass down, half twisting behind himself to place it amongst the jumble of tins and pots, the white kettle, the biscuit barrel. Virginia smiled at him. Between them was the kitchen table, full of bottles, wine, gin, whisky and clean glasses and a big white salad bowl of melting ice. A creamy fat woman pushed through the crowd and put a bottle of malt on the table. She had on a white summer dress that showed her strong, fluid arms and breasts. She grinned at Virginia and gave her a kiss.

'Who's this?' said Richard, nastily.

'God knows,' Virginia laughed back at the woman. 'Another one of the many. Like me.'

'Wasn't he a bugger?' said the woman. She had a glass of whisky in her hand and pushed towards the door holding it over her head like a trophy, brushing her bosom across the back of someone's dark suit.

'Why am I like this about it?' said Virginia. 'Why can't I be like her?'

Richard nodded at the table, 'If we drink this lot you will be.'

Virginia smiled at him again. He folded his arms across his chest and sighed and took a big breath as if he were about to run away or dive from some great height. Virginia made herself smile and made the smile stay there on her face so that she was sick of herself. She poured herself a big glass of the malt. 'Just one then,' she said. She edged round the table and stood with Richard.

'Where's the body?' he asked her.

'You what?'

'Where's the body? You know, Dan.'

'Yes, I know whose bloody body. There's no need to get snotty.' Virginia took hold of his lapel. 'Don't turn nasty,' she said, 'don't turn nasty on me, Richard, I'm not in the mood for it.'

Richard said nothing; he stood there, ignoring the weight of her fist. He drank some more whisky, put the glass down beside him on the worktop.

She spoke gently: 'Behave, lovey, come on, shape up and get me through this.'

'They're all here aren't they?' Richard said. He smiled at her. 'I'm glad. It used to be like this, didn't it?'

'Every bloody deadbeat in town,' said Virginia, smiling back and then making herself not smile. Richard reached across the electric hob, tore two sheets from the kitchen roll for her and took her glass. She wiped her face, turned to him, close to his chest, a secret. She lay her head against him. 'Help me round this lot up when the hearse gets here. I want this to be quick. Quicker the better.'

'Don't tell them, let them stay,' Richard spoke softly bending to her ear.

'They'll want to come,' said Virginia.

'Will they buggery. Let them stay. We'll go, just the two of us.' He could feel her shaking her head. 'Stand up straight.' When she did he said, 'You look lovely.'

'I dressed up for this,' she told him.

'Everybody has,' he said, managing a laugh. 'Have you seen Sarah?'

'Not for a while.'

'She's with your mate Graham somewhere. She's wearing a sort of tight black suit, a bit silky. The lapels on the jacket start buttoning somewhere near her belly button and she's obviously naked underneath. Poor bloody Graham, you've lost him, he's hypnotised.'

Virginia turned and leaned against the sink. She looked around the crammed kitchen. 'All this stuff,' she said. They looked at it together. There were two big paintings of Dan's brick street on the walls. 'I thought that you and Sarah were together?'

'Now and again,' said Richard.

Virginia picked up her whisky glass and took a big drink, struggled to get it down. 'It's a bit depressing isn't it, "now and again". I suppose I was a bit of "now and again" with Dan. I should have made more of it shouldn't I? You know, moved in properly, made him marry me or something.'

'You'd have had to catch him at the right moment.'

'Or get pregnant,' said Virginia, enjoying the thought of it, 'had twins.'

'He'd have been good at that,' said Richard.

'What?'

'Being a father.'

It took the words away from her, gave a sickening sense of the past coming to an end, all things ending and Dan ending and not being here at his party in his house that belonged to no-one now.

'Would he?' she said.

'See the way he sorted me out? Once he'd taken me on he was always there. Even my bloody mother liked him.'

'Yes.' She was thinking of her own mother making tea for Dan and sitting him at the kitchen table to drink it so that she could listen to him while she baked or washed up or fried him a bacon sandwich.

'Return of the Harlot,' said Richard. Virginia looked up and saw Sarah sidling towards them through the people and the clutter. She had Graham in tow, holding his chubby hand.

'By God,' said Virginia, 'you're right about that jacket.'

'It's a tribute,' said Sarah, 'Dan would have liked it.'

'He'd have been in it,' said Virginia.

'Actually,' said Sarah, looking pleased, 'it's quite difficult to stay in it myself. But Graham likes it, don't you Graham?'

'Can't get enough of it,' said Graham. 'The hearse is outside.'

'Guest of honour,' said Richard.

'Oh fuck,' said Virginia, she was trembling. 'Get them quiet Graham,' she said, 'go on shout at them, you can shout, and then I'll tell them what we're going to do.'

***

'This is nice,' said Richard, coldly.

'I told you they'd all want to come.' Virginia held his arm tightly. 'Are you going to say something?'

'Such as what?'

Only the two of them had come right up to the grave. The others stood amongst the grave stones, a thin fan of people, turned, focused on Dan held swaying above the earth by the tight, black ribbons of the undertaker's men. Virginia could see it was an effort for them to get him slowly into the grave, not let him go crashing down, bouncing, splitting the polished wood.

'This plastic stuff,' said Richard. He rubbed his foot on it.

'Astroturf,' said Virginia.

'What?'

'Astroturf. It's Astroturf.'

The undertaker's men stood up straight. They were winding the dark ribbons around their hands until the sinuous, fluttering lengths were tightly rolled. They stood with their hands clasped in front of them.

'Is that all right?' one of them said, still looking round for the vicar.

'Oh yes,' said Virginia. 'Fine, yes.'

'All gone,' said Richard.

'Right then,' said the man, awkwardly.

'Right then,' said Richard, sneering at him. They watched the men walk away through the old graves, past Dan's friends.

'Silly sods,' said Virginia.

'You'd think they'd never buried anyone before,' said Richard. He turned to the two workmen waiting with their shovels. 'Come on then you two, get shovelling.'

'Stop it Richard.'

'Stop what?'

'Shush, just be quiet,' she said. They heard the earth falling. 'Just be quiet.'

***

Virginia fell asleep in an armchair in the front room. It was an old fashioned, faded chair that held her upright and let her in and out of sleep so that Dan's party came to her in noisy snatches that made her dream. She gave up hoping that they would go and went and slept in the armchair and when she awoke there was the dream of them, a sickly dream of getting them out of the house over and over again. Then there was the empty room and the still house. The curtains were open and she could see the orange lit street. She got up and went to the window; her car was still there. The room didn't look too bad, she thought, nothing smashed, nothing spilled that she could see. In the kitchen it was better than usual. Rows of clean, wet glasses filled the table, clean plates and cups stacked on the draining board and worktops. There was a black bin bag folded shut in the corner.

She switched on the kettle and found the coffee pot. I'll take the coffee pot, she thought. It was Dan's old, shiny metal pot. There were no insides to it, he just spooned coffee in and poured hot water over it so that there were always bits in the coffee. That'll be nice to remember him, thought Virginia and it cheered her up.

The door opened and made her jump out of remembering, 'Oh dear God,' she said and pressed her hand against her breast.

'Sorry,' Richard said. He was leaning in around the door; she could see his white skin. 'We stayed on the sofa upstairs. Just wanted to check you were okay.' Virginia nodded at him. 'What time is it?' he asked her.

'Coming up to five,' she said. 'Is it Sarah up there?'

'Of course it's Sarah,' he said. 'What do you take me for?'

'I know you,' she said.

He came into the kitchen. He only had on his underpants and she saw him shivering. He sat at the table and pushed the glasses away so that he had space to rest his arms on the table.

'It was a good day really,' he said.

'Wasn't it,' she said. She stirred the coffee as she spoke, stood with her back to him waiting for the grounds to settle, one hand holding onto the handle of the pot. 'I'm going to take some things and then I'm finished here,' she said. 'I'm not coming back and I'm having nothing more to do with arrangements or problems or anything to do with Dan.'

'What things?'

'I'm taking all the pictures and drawings of me and anything else I fancy. I'll do it with you so that you can stop me if there's anything that you want.'

'Yeah, okay.'

Virginia turned over two clean mugs on the draining board and poured them half full of coffee. 'If we don't,' she said, 'the tax man or whoever will have the lot.'

'Yeah.' He touched his white skin, touched the nipple with his fingertips.

She put his coffee in front of him, 'Graham told me.'

'Yeah,' said Richard, 'he's been on at me about it.'

'Has he?' She sat down, not wanting Richard's quick, possessive spite.

'Yeah, when you were asleep. What's his game then?'

'He's just being nice.'

'Is he? Well, I should watch him. He's a bit keen, Ginny, I'm telling you, he is. Said he'd come round this morning. None of his bloody business is it?'

'We'll do it now then, if you like. You and me, before anyone else has a chance to interfere.'

Richard looked down into his coffee. 'There's Sarah,' he said. 'There are one or two fairly extraordinary pictures of her that she would prefer to have herself.'

'Dear God.'

Richard looked up, smiling. 'Actually they're good pictures. Not the sort of thing for the dining room wall, but bloody good.'

She couldn't help but smile. 'Did he have an affair with Sarah then?'

He didn't rise to her. 'Affair?' he said, 'what sort of a word is affair? This is Dan we're talking about here.'

'Oh all right then, did he give her one, shag her, slip her a length or whatever it is that you want to call it?'

Richard sipped his coffee. He looked down into the cup again. 'Nobody's saying and me, well, I'm trying not to ask.'

'Not like Dan to miss her out,' said Virginia, enjoying the malice of it. 'Not if she was lolloping around the studio all trussed and ready.'

'What about you?' he said.

'Portraits,' she said. 'The only advice my mother gave me when I started acting: keep your clothes on. She was dead right and I always do.'

'I'll go and get mine on, shall I, and then we can have a good root round.'

She followed Richard up the stairs, followed his white legs and straight back. 'I'll start with the drawings,' she whispered.

'I'm not asleep,' Sarah shouted.

Up in the attic room Dan had two big map chests of dark wood. It was a long room that ran the length of the house with one big sash window that let in the first light and the noise of early traffic. This high, at the top of the house, she could see a big, feather pale sky above the town. Virginia sat on a backless swivel chair and began looking for herself. There were drawers full of sketches; pen and ink, pencil, charcoal, water colours that she had never seen, years and years of work, loose sheets and thick, spiral bound pads. A lot of the sheets were dated and she worked out where she might be in the chest. She was all together, in one drawer. There were not many, a dozen or so big sheets of white paper and there she was, having a drink, laughing, sitting at a cluttered table. There was only one that took her by surprise. She was asleep, half under the duvet, her hair on the pillow, her shoulders were bare and her arm crooked against her face.

She didn't want them; didn't want them hurting her with this particular empty misery every time she looked at them. She took them out of the drawer and laid them, one by one, flat on the floor looking at them in turn, carefully, and wondered how she should carry them. Sell them, she thought and blow the money. Serve the bastard right. How much? She would see what her agent had to say. He'd find a use for them, the bloody spiv. She stood up straight and wiped her eyes.

She should have been in bed with Dan now, still asleep in the early morning. Then she could have read and listened to the radio and listened to him creaking about on the loose floorboards as he worked and she could have shouted to him and he could have sworn at her for interrupting. She left them there on the floor and went to look for Richard.

He was in the low creaking room over the garage. One of the rooms where Dan had worked. As he stepped back she could see the floorboards shifting under the square of dirty, floral carpet. There were stands of paintings, leaning racked against each other along the walls. Richard had five paintings turned around, facing into the room and he was staring at them. He was holding his hands against his cheeks as if he were holding his face together and looking at the cheerful, lewd colours of the pictures. 'I think this must have been his Don't Give a Bugger Period,' he called.

Virginia stepped through the doorway hearing in his tone that he had found something he wanted. 'I remember these,' said Richard. He waved one hand at the paintings as if he were making an introduction.

'The pictures or the girls?' Virginia went and stood with him.

'No, not the girls,' said Richard, 'Never met them, worse luck. I suppose they could be grandmothers by now. He had them on the walls downstairs when I first started to come round here. Thought he'd sold them years ago.'

'Do you know,' said Virginia, 'I was a bit shocked when I first saw them.'

'Jealous,' said Richard.

Virginia nodded. 'What a sod he was. Fancy painting people like that.'

'They love it,' said Richard, very matter of fact.

'Do they?' Virginia was intrigued.

'I'm telling you. You'd be surprised how keen lots of women are, girls especially, to get their clothes off.'

'Are they?'

'It's true. And once they're off they'll do any damn thing at all. It's as if it's a great relief to have done it. You know what a relief it is when you tell a secret, betray someone, what a burden lifted? That's what it's like.'

'That's a terrible thing to say.'

'True though.'

'How do you know what people feel?'

'Trust me, I'm an artist.'

He left her looking at them and started on another stack of canvases. He bent and pulled them forward one by one and let their weight rest against his legs. 'Come and see,' he said. 'These are you aren't they?'

'Yes they are,' she said 'They are, I remember them.'

'They're lovely,' said Richard. He pushed the stack of them backwards and then began to take them one by one and set them out against the wall, leaned one against a straight backed wooden chair, one against the table leg, one against the easel until there was a semi-circle of pictures for them to see.

'I want them,' Virginia said. 'All of them.'

Chapter 16

'You're getting fat, Dennis,' she said. She put both her hands flat against the sides of his belly and pressed into the soft flesh. 'You're a fat git that's what you are.'

'Cheeky old tart.'

'You never used to be a fatty.' She rubbed her hands against him and made his belly wobble. 'You used to be all muscley.'

'Well, it's a good job you're still gorgeous then, isn't it?'

'Fat's all right, honest it is,' she said, falsely. 'People find it sensuous you know.'

He pretended to scowl at her. 'Listen, he said, 'we've done to the very death all the things that you're not in.'

'I'm sorry Dennis,' said Virginia, 'I know how tight things are.'

'Not a problem, really.' He put his hand on her shoulder, she stepped forward into him and he had his arms around her. She could smell him, the clean laundry smell of his tee shirt. She sniffed up the tears and stepped back.

'So, I'm afraid it's going to be a full day for you.'

'Good,' she said. She walked away, down to the end of the studio to the jumble of chairs. She sat and took off her trainers and socks, crossed her legs one way and then the other, rubbing her feet, massaging her toes with the ball of her thumb.

She did her stretches and then walked slowly around the room and then more quickly, wanting to run. As she moved she began to sing the first few notes of the requiem, the Faure that they sang at the end of the play. She raised her head and let out the mournful, soaring sound through her open mouth. She knew that Claire and Paul and John had come into the room and were watching her. They were taking their coats and shoes and socks off and watching her, wondering about her, fresh from her troubles. She kept on until they were closed into themselves, in their own stretches and movement and sounds, and went and sat quietly to wait for them.

Dennis sat with his notebook open across his knees and watched Virginia and Paul. Virginia knew that the scene was disgusting. She knew it and Dennis had them do it over and over again, this bit, that bit, backwards and forwards, creating the ugly thing. Virginia didn't care what the girl might be feeling. She knew that if you hit someone like that then they would fall down and she thought about how that would look. What would you do if someone did that to you; how would it look? She went through the scene with Paul. He swung his fist at her and she dropped away from him onto the floor. She knew what to do when he kicked her and then, when he left her on her own, she counted, six, seven seconds and moved her legs slowly and then, slowly, counting, thought about how to take her weight on her arms, stretching, to show the audience her face. 'How did it look?' she asked.

'Okay,' said Dennis, 'not bad.'

Then they tried to do the whole scene, concentrating on their notes and each of the changes and making each tiny thing just as they had agreed that it must be. Virginia stopped and said: 'I'm not getting enough of this. I'm listening to him and losing what I do.' She was kneeling, looking up at Dennis; she let her weight fall back onto Paul. He put his arms around her neck and she could feel the shape of them held gently against her and his hand on the flesh of her arm. There was a silence; no-one knew what to do.

'Paul, look directly at her,' said Dennis, 'and see what happens.'

They began again. Then the man's arms were around her and she could feel the tense shape of them. He was haranguing her, a venomous weight forcing her to her knees. He knelt behind her, forced her head towards the ground. She twisted and said the words

88

into his face. His hand was on the stretch of her neck and on her throat on her thigh and her belly. His words and their ugliness made her scream her words at him and into the hard, dark body and then she knew that he had stopped. She went on beyond him, beyond the artifice and the room split with silence.

'We'd better stop there,' said Dennis.

Virginia was sitting on the floor, crying. 'That poor girl,' she said, suddenly present, 'that poor girl.' Paul sat down behind her again and put both his arms round her, his face close to hers.

'It can get to you,' said Dennis, 'I know it can. Doing it again and again like that. It makes it.'

'Bastard, bastard.'

'It looked good though.'

'Bastard. I don't give a fuck what it looked like.'

'Seriously, it did.'

There she was with all of it running through her head and knowing now how it would have been. This was what Dan had done, she knew it was. It was what he had been doing when he said; 'Look, look at it.' This was what he did in the time he would spend looking and watching and letting his eye make and remake until he had a flower, a dog, someone's foot, more real than flowers and dogs and feet could be. More real than when you glanced at them in the ordinary world. And then Dan was sick of it. She was sick of it herself, the specialness of art.

They went through it again, changing movement, position, timing. They went over it until she was moving with Paul, his arm, his fist and she wasn't thinking, how does this look; she was doing it and feeling all the things that her body did. Paul held her softly and she took up her face from the floor and felt his cheek against her back, just touching. They sat up together in one movement. She put her face up into the light and leaned back into his embrace, folded her arms onto his across her breast.

'Well,' she said, 'that fucking got it.' She sat there, becoming herself again.

John had walked across the room, she heard the soles of his feet on the cold floor, and put his arms around Paul and rubbed his shoulders. 'Don't cry Ginny, don't cry.'

'Can we do that again?' said Virginia.

'Right now?' said Dennis. He sounded doubtful.

'Yes,' she said, 'yes. Just let me go and have a pee.'

Paul let his arms fall away. They both got up. He took a step backwards and started to tap dance, slapping and stamping his bare feet. As she went out she heard Dennis say, 'Don't move your arms so much when you dance.'

They got over it quickly, analysing, laughing: do this, do that, hands behind your back, turn here, do that, that works better, I'll just come straight in shall I?

'Yes, that's better,' said Dennis.

'That's your cue to come in,' said Virginia.

'Shall we walk it through and mark it?' said Dennis.

'Yes.'

And they did, lost in the technical detail of this and that. They practised the embrace, the snarl and where to turn away. 'When he puts his hand on her dress, take his hand, hold it like that and bring it between you.' Dennis watched them do it. 'Yes, that's nice in profile.' They did it over and over, creating the ugliness, until its power to hurt them bled away and they were worn out with it. They stood, heads down, writing their notes, mumbling, agreeing, pacing it out, words and movements. 'That's fine, yes, that's fine,' going over it again, backwards and forwards. Paul looked up, nodding and they were all nodding and smiling at each other. Big smile. Okay.

They had a quiet afternoon. They sang and walked their brief procession at the play's ending. They sang the haunting stillness of the Faure out into the room and afterwards the air about them held the quietness. Claire lay on her back, yawning, rolling, while John and Virginia walked their scene over and over again. Dennis spoke to them as they did it and they whispered back.

'Right, come on then,' said Virginia, speaking out, loudly, into the room.

'Are you sure?' said Dennis.

'Yes, yes,' said John. He walked away, turned, stood waiting for Virginia to begin. She stared at him, watched him lean back, arms outstretched, palms flat on the wall. He pushed forward, touched his mouth and nose and hugged himself. Virginia felt his body in his hands, holding himself in. He stepped forward, one foot, springing up into a step.

She began. Hardly knowing it, she began. She remembered it all and remembered and did it at the same instant, watching herself and thinking about all of it all at the same time.

They went through the last twenty minutes of the play and at the end, after the singing, there was quietness that went on into the air of the room. They stood, amazed, and the air in the room looked back at them, amazed.

'Well,' said Dennis, 'we should think about that. I'll tell you what I think, shall I? Give you some notes?'

They nodded at him, all right, yes. They sat, quietly, taking Dennis's notes. Virginia wrote on her script, nodding, knowing that this was not the last word. She stopped and thought about what she was doing, making it twist and turn into sense.

'If you're in love then you do surrender control,' said John. 'It's a state of grace.' His words sat Claire up straight.

'Well, I know what I think about that.' And what she said pushed John's eyebrows up and Virginia waited, delighted, for the row.

'Strange that,' said John, starting to laugh.

'You tell us about that in the morning,' Dennis said. 'Think about it.'

Chapter 17

Virginia thought about Hank. As soon as she was out of town and driving home through the empty evening she thought about him. She thought about him waiting for her day after day and then giving it up and walking home in the first soft darkness of the summer night. He'd better be there, she thought. He'd better be there, waiting for me. Then she thought about rehearsing the play: it was there in her head, turning and turning, showing itself to her so that she knew all the ways of making it look like this and like this. It never stops, she thought, smiling, touching her face, her hair, we never stop, it stays with us. When they have another conversation, do something else, the thought of the play stays with them and they go back to it. Like Dan, the liar, the maker of his own world. She has him there, in her mind, and uses him for her sense of what an illusion is. She turns him here and there, quickening herself against him. She hoped that Hank would be in the lounge bar of the pub reading the newspaper and wondering if she will come through the door. And so she makes him up doing that. If he were not there then she would go to his house and knock on the door and he would open it and stand in his shirtsleeves, the cuffs folded back from his hands with the light behind him so that it fell on her and lit her for him and the shadow line moved over her when he moved. She would stand up close to him, step up to him and touch his shoulder and wait for his hand on her.

He was standing on the pavement outside the pub talking to the grey haired man. She drove past them and then stopped the car a few yards down the road. She walked back to them.

'Hello gorgeous,' she said and stood up on her toes to kiss his cheek.

'Right then,' said the grey-haired man, 'I'll see you tomorrow. Gorgeous.' He grinned at Virginia and went into the pub.

'Oh good Lord,' said Hank, 'I'm finished. I shall have to sell up and leave.'

'It's a test,' said Virginia, 'a knightly ordeal. There'll be lots more.'

'When?'

'Oh, I'll keep thinking them up.'

'It will end with me punching someone.'

'Good, I've always wanted to have men fighting over me.' She had her arm in his. 'Where are we going?' She saw him hesitate. 'What?'

'Well,' said Hank, 'I was going to watch the football on the telly.'

'Come on then,' she said, pulling him forwards. 'I like it best when they fight, don't you?'

'Rugby's best for fighting,' he said.

'Or Ice Hockey,' said Virginia.

Virginia sat on the settee watching a high, long-shot of the stadium and listening to the urgent team news. She put back her head and shouted, 'Come on Hank it's starting.' There he was, in the doorway, with a shiny meat dish full of sandwiches. 'What's in the sandwiches?' she asked him.

'Couple of minutes yet,' he said. He put the dish on the coffee table. Virginia leaned forward and peeled back a piece of bread. 'Pheasant,' said Hank.

'What's that?' she said, pointing.

'Chestnut stuffing.'

'Is it real?'

'Of course it's real, my daughter makes it.'

'Where is she?'

'She's gone off with her mates from the university.'

'What university?'

'Just be quiet will you. Look they've started. I'll get the tea.'

He came back with a tray of cups and plates and pots of mustard and gherkins. 'Right,' he said and sat down beside her, handed her a plate and poured the tea. 'Who are you cheering for?'

There were four goals and Hank never moved. When they had eaten the sandwiches she had picked up his arm and put it over her shoulders and leaned against him. 'Don't you play hard to get with me,' he said. She was asleep well before half time and woke up for the last ten minutes of the game. She turned more closely into him and brought her feet up onto the settee.

'Sorry,' she said.

'What for?' He didn't move. She took his free hand and held it. 'You have a bit of a sleep if you want one,' he said.

'Rotten company though, aren't I?

'No,' he said, 'not a bit.'

She sat up. 'Was it a good game?' she asked.

'Terrific,' said Hank.

'The bit I saw looked good.' She turned to him and saw that he was still sitting with his arm open as if ready for her to fall back into him again. 'I've got to go. I must Hank. I shall have to work now. There's stuff I've got to do now, ready for tomorrow.'

'It's cool babe,' Hank said, quietly.

'What?' She was giggling. 'You what?' hardly getting the words out for laughing.

'My daughter used to say it.' He was beaming at her, a great big cherub, pleased to have her laughing.

'Did she? When was that?'

'When she was thirteen, I think.'

Virginia picked up his hand and patted it, 'I've got to go, though, really.'

'That's all right.' Hank got up. She saw him standing by her, looking awkward. She waited for him to touch her but he didn't. She held his hand, made awkward, now, herself.

'Have I got everything?'

'Your bag's in the kitchen,' he said.

Outside it was palely dark. 'I left off the yard lights so that we could see the stars, but the moon's shining away up there so she's put them out for us.'

Virginia opened the car door and threw her bag in. 'Same tomorrow?' she said.

'I'll pick you up in Bedford if you like, we could go out.'

'I can't go out, Hank. There's too much to do. Really.'

He stood still, waiting for her to go. 'We'll do the same again, shall we?' he said.

'Give me a kiss then,' she said. But he stood there, his face falling.

'I kiss you,' she said, pretending to accuse him. She smiled at him, wondering if he was doing this on purpose. No, she thought, no he's not.

'Yes, I know you do,' he said.

'Kiss me tomorrow,' said Virginia. She got into the car and drove off.

Chapter 18

Hank sat her down at the kitchen table. He had pushed all the mess of newspapers, books and old post to one end. He had the other half covered with a white linen cloth. The silverware shone. 'Well, of course,' he said. 'I polished it especially, and the candelabra.' Six candles, stuck out of true, in the deep silver shine. 'Looks good, doesn't it?' There were beautiful, white plates and crystal. 'I thought of shutting the curtains to get the benefit of the candlelight, but it seemed a bit silly.'

He fed her slivers of smoked venison and she said: 'Is there more?'

'It's only chicken,' he said, 'but I really like it with ginger and lemon.' He stood at the stove with his shirt cuffs turned back. 'Bit more white wine,' he said and he made the pan seethe and steam. 'You can't have any to drink though, you poor thing.' He poured himself a glass of the wine and, standing up very straight, drank half of it. 'Just a drop then,' he said and poured an inch of wine into her glass. 'Very good,' he said, 'Alsace, Riesling, very dry.'

She smiled and smiled with not a word to say.

'What's the matter, what have I done,' he paused, '"my sweet angel-devil" ?'

She laughed out loud, 'Oh God it's poetry, you're doing poetry for me.'

'Know where it's from?' He wasn't a bit put out and she carried on laughing in his face.

'No, I don't,' she said, 'go on then, where's it from, tell me?'

He waved his glass at her, 'Not telling you.'

'You're pissed, aren't you?'

'How did you tell? Something I said, was it, that gave the game away?' He stood over the table holding a shiny, steel frying pan. 'There's nowhere to put it.' He stood, trying to make up his mind. Virginia reached out, stretched, for a newspaper, folded it and put it on the tablecloth.

'There,' she said.

'No style at all some people,' said Hank.

He watched her eat.

'What are you doing?' she said, 'eat yours.'

'If I eat mine I can't watch you properly.' He was sitting back in his chair making no effort to hide that he was looking at what she did. 'I like the way you eat; you look really hungry.'

'I am really hungry, but I'm not eating if you don't.'

He smiled at her. 'Oh, go on,' he said.

'No, I'm not,' she said. She kept hold of her knife and fork, ready to attack him with them.

'I'm too tired to eat. I've been cooking all afternoon.'

'No, you haven't, you've just fried some chicken and put a few bits in with it. Bloody eat.'

He scuffed his chair squarely to the table and started. 'I can still see you,' he said. 'Anyway, I thought you'd be used to being looked at.'

'No,' she said, 'no, not a bit. It's not like that.'

Hank was well into his chicken, 'Oh it must be, surely.' He spoke and chewed. 'Up you get and do your stuff in front of hundreds of people. I mean, you must notice them watching what you're up to.'

'No. Well, yes, I suppose so. But it's not like real life, whatever that is.'

'You what?'

'Real life,' she said again, caught by the edge of surprise in his voice.

'This is real life,' he said. 'You can't be in any doubt, can you? Don't be silly.'

'Real life seems a bit funny at the moment.'

'You've stopped eating,' said Hank.

'You stopped me.' She looked down at her plate again and cut a piece of chicken. 'The ginger's good,' she said.

'There are big bits and thin bits,' said Hank. 'I do it deliberately.'

'Do you?' She saw him waiting to be asked. 'Go on then, why's that?'

'The only parts of life that aren't real are the made up parts,' he said, forgetting about his ginger.

'But people make things up all the time.'

'No no, it's the things that are made up that aren't real; the business of making them up, well, that's real enough.'

'But what if you live out the things you make up?'

'Then you're a fool. That's obvious enough isn't it?'

I do it all the time, she thought. 'Is this real life?' she said, dead serious.

'Yes,' he said.

She looked at the table cloth and waved her knife at the plates and glasses. 'But didn't you make all this up in advance: having me here, setting the table with all these lovely things. Isn't that what a plan is, living out all the made up stuff?'

She knew she had irked him. 'Nothing about this is made up,' he said, flatly. 'Nothing about this between you and me is unreal. This has happened to me.'

'Oh yes?' Virginia smiled at him, put down her knife and fork and smiled right into his face. 'What is it, all this that has happened to you? Come on, out with it.'

'Eat your dinner,' said Hank.

She could see him smiling as he ate, laughing almost. She kept quiet. She ate some chicken, found a piece of ginger that filled her mouth. She watched him. He kept on looking up, catching her eye, looking away and looking as if he knew something.

'Anyway, how's your pal?'

'What pal?'

'What's his name, Dan?'

She saw the happiness fall away from Hank and she thought, It's the look on my face that's done that. 'He died,' she said.

'You thought he would.'

She was thinking: I never told you. Why didn't I tell you? How could I sit here not telling you? She breathed in, but the sigh trembled in her stomach. 'Oh God,' she said, 'I'm crying onto your tablecloth.'

'No problem,' said Hank. He sat still, not moving towards her, not touching her, waiting for her to calm down.

She slapped the table with the flat of her palm. 'Bugger,' she said, 'bugger. I'm all snotty and red now.'

'You carry it off really well,' said Hank.

'I'll tell you about Dan,' she said.

'It doesn't matter. I never knew the guy.'

'We had the funeral on Friday and I was really glad to be rid of him and I just felt a shit about it. Then we went through his pictures, I told you didn't I that he was a painter, and there I was and I remembered how brilliant he was. Brilliant. I keep on feeling a shit, feeling glad to be shut of him.'

'Are you still glad?' said Hank.

'Yes, yes I bloody am.'

'Good,' said Hank. He said it quietly, his face placid and serious. Virginia stared at him, not knowing what to say to his "good", not knowing what he meant.

Chapter 19

Virginia sat up in her mother's bed with her notes propped up against her knees. She was thinking about the way in which Paul moved around her and what she had done as he moved. She should move with him, follow him physically, step out after him. She wanted to follow him and step up to him and spit back. Not this woman here she thought. She closed the notes carefully so that she did not lose her markers and the loose pages of what she had written.

She sang the first notes of the Faure and stopped, thinking suddenly of Harry a couple of bricks away, imagining, his big, white, whiskery face sitting up in bed in his vest and striped pyjamas. Mustn't frighten Harry, she thought.

She turned off the light and wondered what she would dream about. Her head was full of the play and she did not want that mixed up with Hank. It would mix up with Dan, she thought, Dan and his pictures and the thin, mean sliver of himself that he had left with her. She felt awkward about her stolen hoard of pictures. What do I do with them, she thought, I don't want them. What made me want them when I was loading them into the car? I can't hang them up around the house, some morbid, never ending tribute to the bugger. I wonder what they're worth? Should be right at the top of the market now that he's just dead. Wonder if the News of The World would buy his story? There must be enough in it for the News of The World. I could be in The News of The World, she thought. I'd have to be if I sold the story to them. Worth thousands I bet and thousands for the pictures as well.

I wonder what he did with all the photos; there must be hundreds of them somewhere? I'll have to get the pictures out of here before Hank sees them; not much of a welcome for him, seeing a dead lover's paintings of me all over the place. Graham will sell them for me. He can keep me out of it.

She wanted to think that Dan had kept the pictures because they were of her, but there were so many that he had kept. Perhaps that was why he had stopped, seeing them all piling up against his walls and thinking that he had done enough, done too much and that it was all a jabber of repetition. She fell asleep and dreamed, but when the alarm sounded she had no idea of what the dreams had been about.

The telephone rang while she was drinking her tea in the kitchen.

'Got you,' said Graham.

'I'm hardly here,' she said. Why do you want me anyway?'

'Will you be there, definitely, for my opening?'

'I think so. When is it?'

'I told you.'

'Did you?'

'Yes I did, I told you.'

'Well, tell me again.'

'It's tomorrow night, Virginia, tomorrow night.'

'All right, Graham, don't get shirty.'

'But you will be there, won't you?'

'What time?'

'What time? What do you mean, "What time"?'

'I can be there for half seven.'

'Don't forget, will you? Will you? I've got you on the adverts. You've got to be there.'

'I said I would be.'

***

'We should have had the funeral here,' said Richard. He stood in the middle of the din, hands in pockets, head on one side. 'Graham might be a crook, but this is all right isn't it?'

'He's not a crook,' said Virginia.

They stopped a waitress. 'It's you,' said Virginia.

'That's what I thought,' said Sadie. 'Have you seen this costume, have you?' She turned round and bent over so that the short, black skirt rode up over her stocking tops.

'Terrific,' said Richard.

'It shows my arse.'

'It's wonderful.'

Sadie turned back to them and held out her tray of champagne glasses. 'Bloody French Maid kit. I don't know what things are coming to, honest.' Richard drained a glass and took another. 'Whose your friend?' Sadie said to Virginia.

'Richard,' said Virginia, 'this is Sadie.'

Sadie smiled her beautiful, tooth-filled smile at him.

'You're so beautiful,' said Richard. He was on his fourth glass now, working his way through her tray.

'He's a bit of a bullshitter then is he Virginia?'

'Not usually,' said Virginia, 'but I think he's after you.'

'Is that right then?' Sadie said to Richard. She took the empty glass from him and handed him a full one.

'Well,' he said, 'well yes, I suppose it is, if you're asking.'

She gave him a second glass in his empty hand. 'Drink that,' she said, 'and I'll think about it.' She turned away from them and pushed her way towards the bar.

'You simpering deceiver,' said Virginia. 'I'm going to warn her about you.'

'That will do me nothing but good,' said Richard. Then, as a voice fell and soared into the room, 'Look,' he said, 'look.'

'It's Marilyn,' said Virginia.

In the spotlight, the blonde hair and black sequinned dress.

'She's gorgeous, isn't she?' said Graham, suddenly standing between them and staring at the shimmering stage. They stood and listened to *Every Time I Say Goodbye*.

'Are they all going to be like this, the songs?' Virginia said. She put her arm through Graham's and pulled him close so that she could speak quietly.

'Why?' he said.

'Well, listen to it; I'm going off in a corner somewhere for a sob.'

'No, it's okay, no need for that. She'll do all those Marilyn songs, you know, *I Wanna Be Loved By You,* that sort of thing.'

'Thank God for that.' She looked round, nodding, exaggerating her approval. 'It's a nice place Graham.'

Graham puffed himself up. 'It was the old cinema, a little flea-pit, closed down for years. A terrible waste.'

'You look like George Melly,' said Richard.

'Good suit isn't it?' Graham smoothed his hand over his dark, double breasted front.

'Love the shoes,' said Virginia.

Sadie came back with a tray of fresh drinks. 'Hiya big man,' she said to Graham.

'Listen Scouse,' Graham told her, 'don't stand around here talking to us, go and get the drinks served.'

'I'm serving them,' she said, indignant. 'Look.' Richard took two more full glasses, drank one off, put down the empty on Sadie's tray, took another full one.

'What do you want me to do,' asked Virginia.

Richard spread his arms wide so that the champagne flutes were out of the way and leaned forward to kiss Sadie over her tray. She pushed her face towards him and he kissed her pout.

'Don't do anything,' said Graham. 'I've got a couple of people primed to point you out. So, that will set everybody off, pointing and whispering at you.'

'Have they started?'

'Why else do you think I'm standing here, putting up with Maggie bloody May's antics and still managing to smile. Will you bugger off?' he said to Sadie. 'Go on bugger off and give somebody else a drink will you? How many have you had?' he said to Richard.

'Fifteen,' said Richard. He drained his left-hand glass and swapped it for a full one. 'Sixteen.'

Virginia took another glass for herself, took one for Graham and gave it to him. 'Come on sweetie,' she said, 'leave these two sots.' She took him by the hand and pulled him away from the tray of drinks. 'Come on.' She wanted to be near the stage so that she could see clearly the singer's face and look at how she stood in her dress, see the sweat on her make up. 'We'll get her to sing to us,' she said to Graham. 'Go on, go to the bar and get some champagne for her.' She pushed him. 'Go on, it's bloody hard work when you're performing; she'll be ready for a drink. And the pianist. Go on.' She pushed him again.

Virginia stood on her own with the light from the stage edging up to her. She stood up straight, sipping her drink, listening to the shining song in the pale bright light of the stage. Marilyn was singing *Love Me Tender*, but nothing like Elvis. She made it a rougher song, getting a bit of Billie Holiday into it somehow.

Graham was back. She felt him touch her arm and when she turned to him he said: 'What's the matter?' she shook her head. He had Sadie's tray of drinks. 'Let her finish,' he said, 'and then get up there with this.' She took the tray. 'Give her a drink and then just turn and smile at me.'

In the brightness of the stage Virginia said: 'This is lovely; the songs are lovely,' and the singer smiled a creamy blonde smile at her and said:

'I'm bloody parched.'

Virginia turned, holding the tray one handed, fingers splayed under it, and laughed out into three, four, five camera flashes. She saw, at Graham's side, a bald man crouching under a big square video camera. She turned, offered the pianist a drink and left the tray of full glasses on his piano.

'Will that do you?' she said to Graham. He kissed her and leaned back, arms wide, beaming at the camera and made her laugh.

They stood at the bar. Graham had pushed his way into a space and they leaned together in the noise.

'Time to go,' she said.

'Surely not,' said Graham, 'surely not?'

'I've got work to do. Just a couple of hours, but I want an early bed.'

Graham touched her arm. She felt his hand half closed at her elbow, a single caress of her forearm, his hand on the back of her hand. She smiled. 'Ten minutes and I'm off.' She saw his face and turned her hand into his soft hand. 'It's all right for you, but tomorrow morning first thing I'll be up and doing.' She took her hand away and pointed, hard, into his chest, as if they were quarrelling. 'Two days we've got and then we're opening. You don't know what it's going to be like for us. It's not a question of lounging around in an office and fiddling the books like you do all day.'

'Can I come?'

'Where to?'

'The first night.'

'Of course you can; anybody can. Richard's going to be there, and Sarah.'

'Not a good idea then.'

She was surprised, 'Why isn't it?' and then she laughed, her mouth open in delight. 'You've been after Sarah, haven't you?'

Graham looked away, into the crowded room, looked back, failing not to smile. 'I'm on the rebound,' he said. 'You know how it is when a middle-aged man gets rejected. Is it my fault that you broke my heart?'

'So, you got straight back into the saddle?' said Virginia.

'So to speak,' said Graham.

'You sod, you unscrupulous sod.'

'What? What have I done?'

He had her laughing. 'You're still trying to give me a little pull as well aren't you? You are, you're trying it on with me.' She had let his hand go and was tapping the bar with her forefinger.

'Well,' he said, careless, smiling. 'I've got my confidence back now haven't I?'

***

Her mother's house felt warm and still when she stepped in through the kitchen door. Virginia listened for a few moments to the heaviness of the air and let the door stand open to let out all the shut in weight of the day's sun. She thought about the insects in the outside darkness and found the kettle in the shadows made by the street lights. The gas flame clicked alight and fiercely blue. She leaned in the doorway waiting for the kettle to whistle and tried to think about the play, but the singer came back to her. *Every Time We Say Goodbye,* what a damned, damned thing to sing in her big throaty voice as though she meant it. Those stupid words, cliché tripping against platitude and turning her heart over.

The paintings upstairs went back to her first sight of Dan.

'Loved the chocolate advert,' he had said to her. He had come up to her at the bar, stood at her side, leaning forward to catch the barman's eye, glancing at her when he spoke.

'Did you?' she said, snapping back at his dry tone.

'Lovely frock, just caught the shape of your shoulders.' He spoke without looking at her.

'I'm before him,' she said to the barman.

'What do you want?' said Dan, laughing at her bad temper.

'Large scotch,' she said, thinking, who's this then, already liking the look of him.

'And a large scotch. Yeah, lovely shoulders.'

She poured water into her drink, sipped it and listened to him talk about her shoulders and then sing the chocolate advert song to her, nodding and jigging his head to its silliness. 'Yeah,' he said, 'piece of work to be proud of that was.'

'Thanks for the drink,' she told him. Clever bastard, she thought, annoyed, and then laughing at herself. He turned away from her, holding two full pint glasses up in front of him, shuffling awkwardly through the press.

Go on, spill it, she thought and then thought about herself in the chocolate advert in that gingham, milkmaid's frock. Can't still be on can it? It was over a year ago.

'Is that one mine?'

She turned to him. He was pointing at a pint of beer on the cluttered bar. 'I don't know,' she said and then, when she heard herself sulking, she picked it up and gave it to him. 'There you are; drink it and shut up about chocolate adverts.'

'It was your shoulders.'

'Oh yes?'

'It was.' And he touched her shoulder, ran his two fingers along the line of her collar bone, over the roundness of her shoulder, onto her upper arm. 'Gorgeous,' he said. She had stood there and let him touch her.

Now, back early from Graham's do, when she should have looked at her notes and the bits of scribble on her script, when she should have done her stretches and gone early to bed, she went into the back bedroom, her old room that she had scraped bare, and looked at the pictures. They were on the floor, leaning, stacked, against the walls so that she could walk past them one by one or stand, as she did now, in the middle of the floor turning round and round again, slowly.

I would prefer the money, she thought, to doing this over and over again and I know that I shall, this profitless, stale maundering about in the past. Graham can sell them. Then, stopped and saw herself, her flesh and bone making shadow and colour in Dan's picture of her in the pub. We were never there, she thought and thought of him making up the picture from sketches and photographs and making her the centre of all that light. Spending weeks on her, getting her right, starting again, getting her just right.

'I'm a painter,' he had said to her that first night in the pub, standing at the bar, sipping his brimful pint glass. She sipped her whisky and said nothing, but she had a good look at him: lovely big hands and he had touched her right from the first without, almost, a word between them and it had never entered her head to stop him, to turn away. He waited for her to have her good look: a big, greying man in a good, dark suit; white shirt, three buttons open and she could see the hair on his body and felt like slipping her hand in there onto the soft muscle.

His mouth, flesh red and wet with beer, smiling and showing his smoker's teeth.

The painting she was looking at, there she was sitting in a pub, was her portrait, catching her living halfway through some gesture, an artificial thing she had never done. Dan making her up for the sake of the picture, for a story of her sitting at a polished table of beer glasses slavered with froth, cigarette packets, bottles, thin stemmed wine glasses.

I have to get rid of them all, she thought, or this will never be over with. I could spend my life coming into this room to look at these pictures. He could have me for the rest of my life and he's not going to do it, the bastard. I'm sick of him reeling me in, the casual bastard. All he was interested in was painting pictures and then standing around being a painter, living his painter's life in his painter's house with all that arty fucking clutter. What sort of a doe-eyed camp follower has he made me look like. Liar, the liar. She turned out the light and slammed the door behind her.

Chapter 20

The waiter came and she stopped what she was going to say. He was a creamy skinned, blond boy. 'Another bloody blond,' said Virginia and made Sarah laugh. 'I'll have the mussels then,' said Virginia, 'for a start. Then, I'll have the sausage and mash.' She looked up at Sarah, 'What? What are you smiling at?'

'Bit of a legend,' said Sarah and she sat up straight and laughed into Virginia's hostility. 'For the eating. Dan was always going on about it, how you could pack it away.'

'Oh, he did, did he? Spend a lot of time talking about me, did you?' trying to get some spite into her voice.

'Oh, come on Virginia, don't be snotty with me.' Sarah's voice softened, 'The poor thing's dead now.'

'Poor thing my arse,' said Virginia. She poured her glass half full and took a big swallow. 'God, that's cold. Makes your teeth ache.' She looked around the high-ceilinged restaurant. 'This used to be a furniture shop,' she said. 'It's nice though, the way they've done it out.' She poured wine into Sarah's glass. 'I'm not snotty,' she said. 'He just pisses me off, that's all. Everything about him. Everything.' She took a good look at Sarah, like a man might, appraising, not bothering to hide it.

'What do I look like,' said Sarah and Virginia saw that she was ready for a row and smiled at her.

'Lovely. You look lovely. I can just see Dan gobbling you up like strawberry cream,' and she smiled at her again.

'Don't resent it,' said Sarah, angry.

Virginia caught the bright edge of her tone, 'I don't,' she said. And then she looked away across the room and said: 'If he could be alive I'd give him to you. I'd do anything to have him alive and out of the ground. Absurd, don't you think, to need him dead to be able to think like that?'

'Who ordered mussels?' said the waiter. He reached around Virginia, put in front of her a deep white plate piled with slick black shells. He put it down with a quick clatter. 'Be careful with that, it's hot.'

She turned her head, looking at the biceps and then up to the wrestler's shoulders. 'Stop now,' she said.

'Sorry?'

'In ten years time you'll look like Bluto.' She reached up and poked his biceps and made him laugh.

'What? Who's Bluto?' He looked at Sarah, 'Who's Bluto?'

'Well,' said Sarah, 'I think you're lovely.'

'I think you're lovely,' said the waiter. He looked at Virginia, making a serious face for her, 'and I think that you're lovely too.'

'Oh piss off will you,' and she made him laugh again.

Virginia ate with her fingers, scooped the flesh from the shells with her tongue. She paused for a mouthful of wine. 'Wonderful,' she said. She wiped her plate, soaked up the creamy sauce with her bread. She had the shells stacked neatly, one inside another.

'I should have had that,' Sarah said.

'Should have told you,' said Virginia. Then, pretending that the thought had just occurred to her, she said: 'Are you shagging Graham?'

'Stand on the table and shout, I would.'

She put her hand to her mouth, laughing. 'Sorry, sorry. It's just that he's such a trier.'

'Well,' said Sarah, 'I certainly wasn't going to...'

'Oh God, you are, aren't you?' Virginia put both fishy hands over her face and pretended to be surprised.

'Be quiet, will you?'

'What did you do?'

'You cow, you cheeky cow,' said Sarah, but she was laughing now. Virginia waved at the waiter. She waved the empty bottle at him and reminded herself of Graham. Sarah picked the last slivers of duck from her salad. 'Such an ugly man,' she said, watching for Virginia's reaction, 'and big. Never done that before, never had to manage such a great big thing.' She was pretending to talk to herself and Virginia let her, dying to hear. 'I let him run through his whole middle-aged seducer's routine.'

'The sod didn't do that for me.'

'You what?'

'He just asked me.'

'He asked me. I simpered a bit, sort of shocked and fascinated. Gave him the big eyes.' She looked up and gave Virginia the big eyes and made her snigger. 'But I'll tell you what, I was just a breath away from saying yes to him. Just the excitement of it. I mean what a thing to do.'

'And then you did it.'

'No I didn't. I let him go through the whole fandango. Kept it up for a few days. Then…'

'Yes?'

'Then I went back to his house with him. Have you been there?' Virginia shook her head, willing her on. 'It's massive, massive. He shows me round. We got to the swimming pool. Yeah, a great big pool; not a penny dip thing, a big proper pool. I walked away from him right away round the other side. And I stripped off.'

Virginia was stupefied. 'What did he do?'

'Played a blinder. He did. Credit where it's due.'

'What?'

'He was frozen for a second or two. I really had him. I did a few stretches and so on, just for devilment. He stepped back never took his eyes off me reached out and dimmed the lights, imagine that, hey, dimmer lights in the pool, and then he stood there with his head on one side like a kid.'

'The devious, calculating, old sod.'

111

Sarah waved Virginia's hissing cynicism aside. 'No, no. He was smiling all over his face. I dived in and he sat there with his drink, watching me. I had my swim, few lengths, ploughing up and down. Thought I might intimidate him a bit; some bloody chance. Anyway, I went over to where he was sitting and hauled myself out. You know, straight arm lift.' She showed Virginia what she meant, hands flat on the table, her shoulders like a Valkyrie's. 'All streaming and mermaidy. Then I left him sitting there, went and found his bed and got in it, put the hi-fi on, and off we went.'

'Yeah? Go on.'

'Go on what?'

'Go on.'

Sarah ate some salad, a bit of duck, an olive. 'You want details, go and get some for yourself.'

***

Virginia finished her last end of sausage. 'How's your fish?' she said.

Sarah looked up at her: 'It's all right,' she said, quietly. 'I knew that Richard had told you about Dan and me so I wanted to sit with you for a bit.'

'Oh well,' said Virginia.

'Did you see the pictures?'

'Of you?' Virginia grinned, 'Richard said they were pretty good.'

'I've burned them.'

'That bad were they?'

'Didn't Richard say? The sod seems to have said just about everything else.'

'What do you mean, you want to sit with me? What for?'

Sarah folded her arms and leaned forward onto the table. She looked away and then back at Virginia. 'I thought that if we were just together, you know, got into the way of talking to each other, then, well, it would make things normal. And then I thought you'd know how I felt about those two, bloody Dan and bloody Richard, the way they are. The way they make everything public. Anything you like and,

112

never mind how anyone might feel, whoof there it is up on the wall. It's a dirty game you know Ginny, all that not giving a toss.'

'Give him the sack.'

Sarah shook her head, sneering at herself.

'You've got Graham,' said Virginia, smiling spitefully.

'I don't want bloody Graham. What bloody good is Graham? I get a bit fed up of the way people carry on. I do you know. Get fed up of the way I carry on. But then most of the men, most of the women as well, that I meet, accountants, lawyers, business you know, they bore me shitless.' She sat up straight and sighed. 'And then there's the likes of Dan and Richard and Graham...'

'An accountant.'

'He's just a crook. I get with them and I'm suddenly doing all sorts. I'm like a bloody kid. I'm okay about almost everything when I'm at work. Work's fine. Work's good. But it seems like what it is and nothing else. It does to me anyway. You know, as if you're there because you're putting something else off.'

Virginia shook her head.

'I could get married couldn't I? I mean look at me, look.' She ran her finger tips across her bosom. 'I shouldn't have much trouble with that. Then four or five kids and bang goes the next twenty years. But that's just the same. I'll bet it is. Just the same. Just putting something else off.'

'Do what Dan did,' said Virginia.

Chapter 21

Claire was on her own, in the small blue dressing room. Sunshine poured in through a dirty window and all the white electric lights were on. There was hardly any space at all: one dressing table pushed up against a square wall mirror, a two-seater settee, an ironing board, the long metal rack of costumes.

'You look rotten,' Virginia said to her.

'I've just lost my breakfast,' Claire said.

'Listen, as long as we've got our story straight and we just stick to what we've worked out and do it then there's no problem is there, the job's done.'

Claire stared at her through the words. 'Smug bitch,' she said.

Virginia smiled, 'Come and have a bacon sandwich with me.'

Claire shook her head, 'I'd be sick,' she said.

'No you wouldn't. Come on, Dennis won't want us for another half an hour,' She got up. 'I'll go and tell him.' She went out of the bright light of the dressing room into the flat darkness of the theatre. The walls were black. There were yellow lights in the empty, girdered space above her. It was a big empty space with tiers of seats looking down onto the floor. Paul and John were on their hands and knees taping down the edges of the big black dance mats. They were ripping shiny lengths of gaffer tape from a big roll. John pulled back as if he were getting ready to throw a punch.

'Listen to that,' he said, 'you could do lightning with that.'

Paul knelt up and took the roll from him and they leaned away from each other pulling, tearing. 'Wonder what they did before gaffer tape?' Paul said.

'There was never a "before gaffer tape,"' said John. They were struggling to keep the shiny tape between them tight and smooth. She watched them smooth the long pull of tape into place and smooth it with the palms of their hands, bent double to the floor, shuffling. They leaned back. John looked at her. 'Done,' he said. He rolled over onto his side and sprang up. He reached down for Paul's hand and pulled him to his feet. They started to unroll the stage cloth, bending over, pattering at it with their hands.

Virginia shouted: 'Dennis,' making her voice raucous.

'Noisy cow,' John said. They had the cloth unrolled and were on their knees again starting to tape its edges tight.

'We'll be all right for half an hour won't we?' Virginia asked. She looked down and thought that they would walk over the sombre colours, dirty sprawled gold, scabbed dry blood, and show this ugly thing that they had made and be told that they were wonderful. Paul looked up at her. 'You look bloody awful,' she told him.

'Keep it tight will you,' John said. He had the roll at his teeth, biting.

'I've been sick,' Paul said.

'Don't be so silly,' she said. 'What the hell do you want to be sick for? We know what we're doing don't we?'

'I don't want to be sick.' Explaining to her as if she were soft. 'I get a bit wound up.'

'Well,' said Virginia, 'I've never understood all this carry on, all this first night stuff. If I was sick and wound up I'd get another job. Tell him John.' John sat back on his heels. She could see him breathing heavily. 'The three of you, you're all at it.' She shook her head. 'What a bloody crew.'

***

In the evening Virginia was early to the theatre. Well before the hour call, she was there and watched the house manager fixing the loose seats, a lovely jigsaw of new-seeming seats, red upholstered, rows and rows of them, blank and smart against the high black walls. The lanterns peeked out from the blackness, red and yellow. The technician, she had never seen him before, a fat man in small jeans, was standing on tiptoe near the top of a high, metal ladder, gaffer-taping dangling flex to a scaffolding bar. She watched him make things tidy, working slowly, carefully. He looked down, saw her, smiled and winked. She tried a smile herself but only managed to give him a big, blown out sigh. She turned away from the light and stood in the back-stage darkness behind the tall, black curtain. She turned into the light again, back to the dark. She heard Dennis saying: 'Don't look at it, don't hurt your eyes.' She turned and saw Dennis saying to Claire: 'Final position.' The technician was still up the ladder, shining the new taped lantern onto Claire's upturned face. Dennis held her hands. 'Don't look at it. Don't hurt your eyes.'

Paul lay down, star shaped, bright eyes. Claire went and knelt at his head. She picked his head from the floor, both hands reaching deep down, taking the nape gently in her palms, softening his neck, rolling his head, softly. He moved away from her, turning, cat-like onto his hands and knees, straightening his back and she lay under him. He leaned over her, whispering, touching her arms, sides, belly, centring her. He smiled at her as he got up, made her smile back and then, flat on the floor, she stretched.

Paul faced the empty, red seats. He started, a strong, grunting workout, stared like a fighter, pulled big shapes of air around himself, balancing, big stretching. Down onto his toe tips and fingers he cat-crawled into a sit-up, again and over again.

Claire avoided Virginia's eye. Virginia watched her, saw her street white face, frightened, made calm. Fear made her young, made her big eyed, opened her mouth with breath. She roared a bass, dense column of noise and beat it, flat palmed against her ribs, into a dark wave. Virginia saw her watching Paul. Paul stood still, eyes closed. Claire loves him, thought Virginia, loves him.

She dared the audience to come in. She did not want them. She wanted to go now, straight away and make this play. It did not matter who for, it was enough, much, much more than enough to go straight away, now and make this perfect thing. Like paintings unseen; enough, enough, being perfect.

Dennis whispered at them, they had a few minutes, standing them closely crammed in, touching each other's heads and shoulders, breathing each other's breath. They stood away from each other; John smiled, big toothed, white. Virginia wanted no-one else. No foolish lovers. She wanted the lovely cruelty of this, balancing it on the balls of her feet, feeling it poised in the line of muscle to her skull.

She stood, waiting, behind the black curtain, dark blue, darkening her skin. She heard the play streaming out. She stood and felt time slip smoothly towards her, turning her out into the light. There she was, not daring to be there. She heard the moist, bare soles of Claire's feet and the silence that ate up the two, three seconds and she walked into the light.

Chapter 22

'You two are looking a bit pally.' Virginia had spotted them standing together at the bar. Where's Sarah, she wondered. They turned to her.

'What a play,' Graham said. 'What a thing to be in. How can you put up with it? You frightened me to death.' He stood up straight, smiling at her, shaking his head. 'Is it you now or is it that horrible shit you were when you were on the stage. It's you, it is, isn't it?'

'Bloody good,' Richard said, softly. 'Bloody good Ginny.' He leaned back on the bar, staring at her. 'Bloody good,' he said. 'Bloody good.'

'Get her a drink, Richard,' said Graham. 'Is that what you've been doing every day, putting yourself through that? How the hell do you do that? I couldn't do it.' He was smiling at her all the time that he was speaking. 'I know I couldn't do it. I'd be crap at it, I know. But, I couldn't put myself through it that's what I mean.'

'We all put ourselves through it,' said Virginia, not rising to his smile.

'I don't,' said Graham. 'I've never felt anything like the stuff that those buggers in your play were going on about.'

'What will you drink?' Richard asked.

'No,' said Virginia, 'it's okay Richard, I'm with someone.'

'Why didn't they just go out for a drink with their friends,' said Graham, 'and have a bit of a laugh, bit of leg-over and a curry. There's no need for all that. People don't put themselves through all that.'

'You are a bloody simpleton,' said Virginia. 'A fizzy water and a large scotch,' she said to the girl behind the bar.

'I'm bloody right though,' said Graham. 'You all want too much. You're all greedy for the wrong things, all you clever buggers. There's nothing intelligent or, or sensitive or whatever about misery, any bloody fool can be miserable.'

'Greedy?' said Virginia, she pushed between the two of them to reach out for her change. 'You're a fine one to talk about greedy, Mr. Greedy you are, you could advertise for Greedy Incorporated you could.'

'I could, I could, of course I could. But, not greedy enough to eat my own liver; not greedy enough to gobble up more misery than my fair ration like you silly buggers. Yes, you as well.' He gave Richard a nasty jab on the shoulder. 'You both go in for it don't you? And this bloody play, well, it defeats me it really does. What's it for? What good does it do? What do you want us to do at the end of it, slip off home and slit our wrists?'

'You liked it then?' She smiled at him. 'I'm taking these drinks over to my friend; come over and join us.'

'No,' said Graham, suddenly made angry by the confidence in her smile, 'no I didn't bloody like it if you must know. I wish I'd not come. I'm not saying it wasn't good and that you weren't good, in fact you were bloody wonderful, but I don't want my nose rubbed in that sort of thing. I want sex and jokes and a bit of tension and sentimentality, that's what I want.'

'Sounds hard to beat,' said Richard.

'What friend anyway?' said Graham. He was puffing from losing his temper. 'Oh God now people are looking at me.'

'Shouldn't throw wobblers,' said Virginia. Anyway, it's me they're looking at, I'm the star here.' She turned away, hands full of bottles and glasses. 'Come on, come and meet my friend. I think he agrees with you.' She walked off and left them to each other and hoped that they would not come and meet Hank.

Hank took the bottle of water and a glass. They juggled about, trying not to spill things.

'Pour some of your water in my scotch,' she said.

'Don't worry about me,' Hank said, 'you go and have a wander if you like. There will be queues of people waiting to talk to you. I've seen it on the telly.' She scowled into his smile.

'It was terrific, Virginia,' said a large, handsome woman in black and scarlet. Her face was alight with sincerity. 'Come and meet Madelaine.'

'Hank?' said Virginia.

Hank slouched against the wall and sipped his glass of water. 'Go on,' he said, 'go and meet Madelaine. Go on, and for heaven's sake don't start introducing me to people. Introduce them to each other; they'll like that.'

She leaned forward as if to kiss him and whispered, 'Arseholes to you mate.'

She came back to him every ten minutes and he smiled at her and told her he was fine and no he didn't want another glass of water, fizzy though it might be.

'Who are those two at the bar?' he asked. 'Those two, Laurel and Hardy.'

'Oh God,' said Virginia, turning round to stare, 'they are, aren't they?' She had a gulp of whisky and laughed with her mouth open.

'Don't get drunk,' said Hank.

'Too late sweetie,' she said and kissed him. She undid one of the buttons on his shirt. He stopped her, covering her hand with his. 'They're my pals. Richard, he's the little one. He's only little when you see him at the side of Graham; on his own he's all right.'

'Is he?'

'He was Dan's pal really,' said Virginia. She stopped herself, stopped the words so deliberately, because she was into her fifth glass of whisky, that Hank said, 'You don't want to tell me about Dan do you?'

'No.' Saying 'no' made her heart jump.

'Why's that?'

'No,' she said. I know why, she thought. I know why I don't want to tell you anything.

'Don't pout,' said Hank, 'you look silly.'

120

'Nothing to do with you. It's none of your business.' She kissed him again. 'I'll just go and say goodbye to Stan and Ollie and then we can go.' She turned and walked away, knew that he was watching her and made her back straight for him, moved her hips. She smiled, laughed as she came up to Graham and Richard and reached between them to tap her glass down onto the bar. Graham turned, looking for the barmaid. 'No,' she said, 'no no no. I'm going now, just came over to say goodbye.'

'He's a big, tough looking chap,' said Graham.

'He's lovely,' said Virginia, smiling away so that they did not know how serious she was.

'More lovely than me?' Graham said, trying to look hurt and smiling back at her.

'More chaste,' said Virginia.

'Chaste?' said Richard, sneering. 'Chaste?'

'More than you two shaggers,' said Virginia. 'More than you two dick driven old shaggers.'

'How chaste is he then?' Richard said and Virginia thought how sardonic and rat-like Richard could be.

'You sardonic shitter,' she said.

'As chaste as you?' Richard was giggling.

'Chaster, much chaster than me. Anyway,' she turned away from them, 'goodnight.' She turned back and said, as if someone else were saying it, 'You're both shagging the same people. Did you know that? Did you? I'll bet you did. Bet you did.' She stepped away, went back to Hank blushing for herself. 'Come on,' she said to him, 'we'll just up and go. Make a dash for the door or we'll be half an hour saying goodbye to all this damn bunch.'

'Okay Boss,' he said.

She took his hand and pulled him behind her, stepping briskly away from what she had said.

They sat in Hank's car in the dark street. 'How are you doing?' he asked her.

'Doing fine,' said Virginia.

121

'I thought you were getting a bit excited in there.'

'Was I?'

'What with one thing and another.'

'I shouldn't drink.'

'Oh yes?'

'I get drunk you know. It happens all of a sudden and then I'm a bit overcome with it all.'

'Suddenly after five or six doubles in half an hour or so?'

'It's a mystery.'

Hank started the car and the dials and digits of the dash board lit up in the dark.

'Like an aeroplane,' she said. 'You need to read off all that information, do you, before you can pull away from the kerb?'

'Yes,' said Hank.

'It's a big car,' said Virginia. She watched him put the engine into gear, saw his hand, his shirt cuff folded back over his forearm. He twisted round to check the road. 'Hold hands,' she said. He turned back to her. 'Hold hands, come on just for a minute.'

He flicked the gear into neutral and turned over his hand, offering her the palm. She held two of his fingers tightly and lifted the weight of his hand onto her lap. He closed his hand on hers. 'You great soft mullock,' he said.

'What's a mullock?'

'It was Janice's word. Janice worked for us when I was little. Worked in the house, cooked and cleaned and so on.'

'Oh, so you had staff did you?' She lifted his hand and kissed the back of it. 'Posh git,' she said softly. 'Come on, get me home.'

'You're going to fall asleep aren't you? As soon as this car starts you'll be snoring.'

She stayed awake until the hump-backed bridge, but when the street lights ended and she had to watch the dark hedgerows and the headlights she closed her eyes and was gone.

Hank woke her up. 'Home,' he said and smiled at her. 'How do you feel?'

'Okay,' she said, 'not bad.'

'I'll pick you up tomorrow,' he said. 'About ten; will that be all right?'

'Come in for a drink. I'll make you some tea.' She really didn't want him to go, didn't want the red tail lights pausing at the bottom of the lane and vanishing.

'No,' he said, 'you need to sleep.'

She sat still, made no sign of ever moving out of the car. 'Did you like the play?'

He didn't hesitate, it was as if he had the words ready to burst out at her. 'I thought it was appalling, dreadful, a horrible depressing mess.'

The bastard. 'Yes, but apart from that?'

'There was no "apart from that." You know perfectly well that it was good, all the technical stuff, all the acting, all of that, of course it was good, damn good. But the play, the play was abusive, it abused the audience and made them indulge parts of themselves that ought to be kept in order. Not everything that can be said or thought should be said or thought.'

'This is the review we can expect from Farmers Weekly is it?' she heard herself sulking.

Hank spoke softly: 'Not what you want to hear on a first night,' he said. 'Sorry.'

'I'm sorry as well,' said Virginia.

'What are you sorry for?'

'For Farmer's Weekly,' she said and made him laugh. 'Come on, come in and have some tea.'

Hank shook his head, 'No,' he said.

She wanted to make him, make him turn off the engine and come and sit with her in the kitchen and then get into her bed with her and wake her up in the morning. She didn't want the empty house.

'No,' he said. 'Go on, push off and I'll be round tomorrow.'

She thought that she would not sleep, not after the half an hour in Hank's car. She drank a glass of water standing at the sink then splashed cold water on her face, already feeling a headache from the whisky. I don't mind him saying that about the play, she thought. He's right, it is dreadful. She splashed her face again and felt the wet material of her blouse on her cold skin. She wiped away some of the water with the flat of her hand. I wish Hank had stayed. I wish that he was up there now and I could get into that bed with him.

She left open the curtains in her mother's bedroom so that she could lie awake in the dark and see the sky high above the valley. She went to sleep straightaway and dreamed about Dan's pictures in the next room. She dreamed about them precisely, one by one in a single straight line and the dream vanished without any recollection of it left for her.

The light made her wake up. It was almost half past six and the sun made a bright light against the pale wallpaper and the oak wardrobe and glared against the tilted mirror on the dressing table. Go for a walk, she thought, get up now and go for a walk and get wet in the long grass at the bottom of Clay Lane. It'll be cool and damp down there. Get cold so that I'll have to hurry back up here and get in the bath. She went back to sleep in the sunlight and when she woke up again the room was hot and she thought she felt her whisky headache, just a small ache in her eyes and teeth. She went downstairs and telephoned Hank, but there was no reply.

***

That afternoon Hank drove her back to Bedford.

'This is nice of you,' said Virginia.

'There's nothing much to do at the moment,' Hank said.

'I thought that farming was dawn till dusk? It always is on the Archers.'

'Only with livestock and we haven't done that for years. It's pretty well just a case of watching the stuff grow for the next few weeks.'

'Don't you have to spray it or something.'

'Not all the time. In between sprayings I'm free to come and dote on you.' It should have been a joke, something with a saving measure of irony in it, but he spoke softly as though she were not supposed to hear. Virginia did not reply, they both sat quietly with the last words that he had spoken and looked through the windscreen at the empty, mid-morning road.

'Where do you go after Bedford?'

'Cambridge,' she said, 'Thursday, Friday, Saturday.'

'I'll drive you,' said Hank.

She turned in her seat, leaned across, pulling against the seat belt and kissed his cheek. It was as though she had struck him. She felt him flinch and his face fell. She kissed him again. 'The first few times are the worst,' she said. 'It gets better. You'll get used to it, honest you will.'

'I hope so,' he said. He glanced at her, frowning.

He drove along the small country roads and picked up the Bedford Road at Denton. What's the matter, she thought. What does he expect? 'Tell me about the fields,' she said. She pointed ahead. 'What's that purple stuff for instance?'

'No,' he said. 'You don't want to know all that rubbish.'

'I need to. I should do anyway, being a country-girl.'

'This isn't country; this is a big flat factory.'

'You cheerful bugger,' she said, letting herself be annoyed with him.

He turned his eyes from the road and smiled. 'I am aren't I?' he said. 'It used to be all forest, but we cut it down for ships. I'd like to plant it all again, bring back the dark and all that settled quietness you get in woodland. It would make England a mysterious place again. There's no depth to the place is there?'

Bloody hell, thought Virginia. She kissed him again. 'I never think about it,' she said, 'England. Not in that way anyway.'

'I do,' he said. 'A place to wander off into, lose yourself, shake off the dogs and keep on going into something that will always be going on in front of you.'

'That's what you want is it?'

'I want the thought of it.'

When they stopped outside the theatre Virginia said, 'I'll be a couple of hours.'

'I'll wait.'

'It's all right, I'll be fine. You can't wait around all that time.' She gave his hand a squeeze.

'I'll have a pot of tea somewhere, read the papers.'

'Then I'll have to be back here for six o'clock.'

'Come back with me to the house. Have a sleep on the settee and let me cook for you. Then you'll be really ready for this dreadful play.' He looked down at his hand held in both of hers. He smiled at her, 'It really is dreadful you know.'

'Are you sure?'

'About the play?' smiling his face into a knot.

'No you sod, about all this ferrying about.'

'Of course I'm sure.'

'There's no need to come to Cambridge; I'll get a bed and breakfast with the others.'

'No you won't, you'll let me drive you, then you can sleep in your own bed and be yourself.'

She almost said it, almost said, I'll stay with you, but had just the sense to keep her mouth shut. There was some slow, fastidious reserve about him, anchored, that would only move slowly and against its own intention. She got out of the car and stood on the pavement, watching him drive off. He stopped at the lights, moved on, turned right and was gone. He would find somewhere nice and sit back with his tea and the papers, she thought and wished herself with him. There was a narrow street down to the back door of the theatre and then, inside, it was still and empty. She went into the auditorium, pulled down a seat on the front row and waited.

The three of them came in together. She heard them talking then singing in the tiny dressing room and then in the short, black corridor.

'Hello beautiful,' John said when he saw her. He stood in the middle of the stage cloth and spread his arms wide. 'Were we in all the papers, have you seen?'

'No,' said Virginia.

126

'Well, with your celebrity, your TV cachet, I thought we'd be written about.'

'Maybe at the weekend.'

'Do you think so?' he dropped his arms, 'do you think so?'

Virginia shook her head. 'No, no, no. Don't even think about it. And if they do they'll say that we were crap or that one of us was and that will be even worse.'

John smiled and came and sat with her. He perched on the edge of the seat and turned to look into her face. 'We weren't though, were we?'

'Weren't what?' said Claire. She and Paul came and stood close up to them, holding hands.

'Holding hands now are we?' said Virginia.

'Crap,' said John, 'I don't care what anyone says.'

'It was brilliant,' said Paul.

'Yes it was,' said John, 'it was.'

'We only hold hands in public,' said Claire, 'for display.'

'What do you hold in private?' Virginia said.

'Everything,' said Claire, 'All the time, simultaneously.'

Then Dennis came in. 'Come on,' he said, 'let's get on with this.'

Chapter 23

Hank drove her backwards and forwards, sat in theatre bars, killed time in tea shops and cafes. She tried to stop him, but he told her that he liked it, said that it meant that he could sit and read. She really did stop him from driving to Colchester and High Wycomb and stayed with the others in digs, gobbling up the fried breakfasts. She had wanted him to say that he would stay with her, stay with her and find a hotel, like a holiday, but she could see him stepping back from that, even though he knew.

She sat in Graham's new bar and told Sadie about it.

'Where is he now then,' Sadie said, 'if he's as keen as all that?'

'I'm seeing him later.' She was feeling inept, transparent against Sadie's battering, common sense.

Sadie pursed her lips and squinted. 'You should just grab him,' she said, 'you know, don't take no for an answer, get right into him.'

'I can't do that.'

'Course you can.'

Virginia smirked and said: 'That's what you did to Richard is it?'

'Oh very likely; chance would have been a fine thing with that one. He fell on me like a wild beast. I'm telling you.'

Virginia was giggling, covering her face. 'Wild beast?'

'Wildest wild beast I've ever come across, I'm telling you.' Sadie leaned forward and took hold of Virginia's arm, she was trembling. 'Ripped the clothes off me.'

'Ripped?' Virginia was laughing out loud.

'Shush,' said Sadie, 'don't make a show of me.' She lowered her voice, 'He's a great big feller as well, scared me to bloody death at first.'

'What? Richard? You mean?'

'He's wearin' me out. I'm telling you, he is. I'll have to get somebody in to help me if it carries on like this.'

'What do you mean? Like a team?' Their heads were together, like conspirators.

'Yeah,' said Sadie, nodding and whispering.

'Sarah never let on about this.'

'Bloody Sarah.'

'It must be you. It must be the inflammatory effect you have.'

Sadie shook her head, puzzled. 'Anyway, she said, 'never mind about me, what do you think this one of yours is playing at? What are you messing about for? You want to get a grip of him that's what you want to do.'

'No,' said Virginia and she thought about the impossibility of grabbing Hank. She didn't want to grab him; she wanted to wait for him to finish whatever he was up to with her. She knew that something was going on.

'What does he do?' Sadie said.

'It's hard to tell you,' said Virginia. She paused, thinking about Hank. 'He's like Mr. Rochester.'

'Who?'

'In Jane Eyre.'

'I saw that on the telly, yeah I remember. Christ, I'm not sure he'd be worth waiting for.'

She made Virginia smile. 'You should read the book, well the Rochester bits at least. Get you all sexed up. It will.'

'What? Jane Eyre?'

'Never fails.'

Sadie sat back, took a drag on her cigarette and looked around the quiet bar. 'I'd better get on and look as if there's something to do. If Graham comes in he'll start huffing.'

'What about Graham?' Virginia asked, falsely.

Sadie gave her a squinty, hard look. 'What do you mean, "What about Graham?"'

'You know,' said Virginia nodding her on.

'Oh,' said Sadie, as if her penny had just dropped, 'you mean am I giving him one as well?'

'Well, are you?'

Sadie grinned. 'At first I thought it was a bit bad, you know, a bit unethical like. Then I thought, fuck it I'll have the two of them, why not.'

Virginia was delighted. 'A bit of a contrast.'

'Not bloody half.'

'Go on then,' said Virginia. 'Go on. What?'

Sadie looked prim. 'I'm not telling you. If you really want to find out you know what to do.'

'I can't. I can't do that.'

'Course you can.'

'I can't, not with Hank.' Virginia stopped laughing. 'He's too lovely. He is, Sadie, he's too lovely.'

'Aren't they all bloody lovely,' said Sadie, 'and then you get to know them.' She got up, squashed out her cigarette and walked around the tables picking up the few empty glasses that were there. She came back and put two handfuls of glasses on the bar top. 'Mind you,' she said, 'he is nice looking, for an old bloke.' She stood reflecting on it. 'And quiet, you know, dead still and quiet.' Virginia waited for her to say something else about Hank. 'And he's a bit of a giant isn't he? You'd know about it if he fell on you.'

'He's not old,' said Virginia, quietly.

'Not for you,' said Sadie.

'What a cow.'

'No, seriously, I'll bet he's older than my Dad is, a lot older.'

'Doesn't matter,' Virginia said.

'No, it doesn't matter does it?' Sadie grinned. 'Not if he's lovely, eh?'

She watched Sadie wash up the glasses and chop up bits of lemon on a saucer.

'Don't they mind, Sadie?'

'Don't who mind?'

'Graham and Richard, you know, going twos up?'

Sadie laughed, 'You just bloody watch it with your twos up. Them? They've no idea what's going on.'

'You sure?' said Virginia and she felt scared, remembering what she had said after the play.

'Well, they've not mentioned it and I don't think that I shall. Be a bad idea, don't you think?'

'They'll find out.'

Sadie turned back to cutting up the lemons and Virginia could see that she was giggling to herself.

Then there were people to serve and Virginia was left on her own. He is lovely, she thought and she could not help but think about Dan, about how he was lovely and that she had the same word for the two of them. She wondered why that was and why she was so captured by Hank. He was big, she thought, that was why. She thought about the thickness of his body. Not very tall, she thought, not like Dan, but when he came in he would stand a pace away from the bar and put out one hand flat on the shiny surface and she knew that if he closed his fist he would tear out a lump of the wood.

'What are you smiling at?' said Sadie.

'I'm not smiling.'

'You've got her smiling before she's seen you.' Sadie was calling across the room and when Virginia turned there was Hank. He wore a light grey jacket and a pink shirt open at the neck. Virginia stared. He smiled at Sadie, gave a little shrug and opened his arms, hands upturned.

Maulers, Virginia thought. She turned back to Sadie. 'Lovely,' she whispered, 'he's lovely.'

131

Chapter 24

I've got Hank, she thought, I've got him, and I can stop feeling angry with Dan. She had the two of them lumped together in her head, thinking of one and then the other, feeling the same desire. She was sitting up in bed, reading, with her mind sliding away from the page and then she thought that she would have another go at the paintings across the landing.

She stood in her nightie and looked around the room at them, there, leaning on her walls, waiting to be made something of. This is crap, she thought. I can't keep on coming in here for a look at all this like some half-baked wife making a shrine to the artist. There I am, lying on the sofa in my blue dressing gown. It had fallen open and there were her bare legs, crossed at the ankle. I used to lie there and watch the telly, all the sit-coms and soap operas while Dan cursed me for it.

'You can at least turn the sound down.' And she would. 'Christ, what shit it all is. Why the hell do you watch it?'

'All right, lovey,' she would say and then, when he was drawing her, looking up and down, she would ratchet up the sound one notch at a time so that he wouldn't notice. You wouldn't have thought that would you? Not much of the life of the artist about any of that; watching telly on the sofa and having a cup of tea.

I remember this one, she thought, I remember this. 'I'm going away for a few weeks,' she had told him and saw his face fall for an instant and then the smile come into his eyes and the struggle he had to keep on wearing his glum face. As soon as I'm gone he'll have the house full of scrubbers. She never told him that and went off to wherever her agent sent her, locking her room so that none of the little cows, or Dan himself for that matter, could rummage around in there. Or worse. What a way to live, she thought: a room at Dan's, sometimes here with Mum. I should have stayed in London, stayed there all the time. I should have married a bank Manager and had four kids. I would have been happier.

They drive Hank out that's what they do, these bloody pictures. They push me back into all that. I ought to have left them. It was greed that's all it was. And wanting to hang on. She couldn't remember what had become of that dressing gown. She used to lie around in it; it was one of those things where the cloth felt softer than it should. She would get up and have a bath and always lock the door. 'Keep your clothes on,' her mother had said. 'Never mind all the fancy talk, you stay dressed.' She didn't want Dan around with his camera or his sketch pad, sitting there with his legs crossed and a fag on, drawing her. No, not in the bath. What he remembered or made up was bad enough.

'You're not, you know,' she turned on him, angry, and he looked away from the easel.

'What?' he said as she pulled him out of what he was doing.

'I shall attack it. I shall. You can stop it there and save your time. I'll burn the bastard.'

'All right, all right.'

She didn't know why she was so vehement, but she wasn't having it. No. Final.

She turned the picture of her in the blue dressing gown to the wall. Held the top corners firmly in her hands and walked it out and round. The next one she remembered. She remembered liking it when Dan surprised her with it at his Christmas exhibition.

'Who've you invited?' she asked him. She was putting on her earrings and thought, that's a good picture, saw herself, in the mirror, touching the tender flesh of her earlobe, piercing it with gold. 'Paint this,' she said.

'What?'

'Paint this; me doing this.'

He was hardly listening, 'No,' he said.

'Why not?'

'Don't like it. Looks mean, you twisting like that to look at yourself,' not caring what she thought. 'It's a crap moment.'

She watched him stand up straight and smooth the front of his jacket, all buttoned up, with the flat of his white hand. He was laughing at her, all of his face lit with malice and vanity. She watched in the mirror as he sipped from a glass of whisky. Smiling in his good suit, sipping his whisky, waiting to go and lord it at his Private View. 'You smug bastard.' She had made him laugh again. He laughed, she saw it herself, because he knew that she meant it and would still stay with him for the bits of himself that he would offer her.

'Who've you invited?' she asked again.

'Every deadbeat in town.'

'After last time?'

'Especially after last time. It was bloody good wasn't it having to call the police to the Art Gallery.'

He didn't warn her, let her find it for herself. She lay asleep and her face was like a ten-year old's face turned innocently in upon itself and weighted with sleep. She went and took hold of his arm. He was standing with Richard and two tall girls, taller than her.

'When did you do that then?'

'What?'

'That,' she said and took a big fistful of his lapel and pulled him off balance. 'You spy, you fucking spy. Spying on me.'

He put his arm round her and walked with her back to the picture. 'Took ages,' he said. 'It's lovely isn't it?' Then, she saw that he was serious. 'You don't mind; you can't mind something like that.' But, she did not like the thought of him sitting quietly beside her, looking on, as her flesh thickened into sleep. 'It took weeks and weeks, catching you asleep and not waking you and then not letting you in on it.' He spoke quietly and she, quietly too, said:

134

'Why not?'

'You would have stopped it.'

'Would you have stopped?'

Dan had smiled at her and turned away. 'Don't stand there staring at yourself; it looks bad,' he said.

She sat down on the floor of the back bedroom so that she was level with the picture. She was cross-legged and her knees pulled tight the material of her night-dress. Big tears plopped onto the taut cotton as though some heartless cartoonist had drawn them in.

She saw later, in the catalogue, that he had marked it Not For Sale.

She thought of another one. I could do with a laugh, she thought and got up and started pulling the paintings back, one by one from the wall and peering over the tops, looking for the right one. Got it. She turned it round, struggling with it a little, a good four feet square. It was the cheek of it that she always smiled at first. He knew her clothes-on rule, her mother's clothes-on rule, and she could see him laughing and painting away, cheering himself up with her futile outrage.

'What makes you think it's you?'

'Who else is it then?'

'I made it up.'

'I know me when I see me.'

'From this angle?'

Then with a second breath she had smiled at how gently he had painted the dark pubic hair and the softly creasing flesh, the grain and texture of hair and skin, the sheen of light on her open thigh. Just that part of her, four feet square, and a creased, dark sheet beneath. Dan had painted with acrylic so that there was that false, enhanced reality of a French film about it.

Oh bugger, she thought, I can't go on like this.

Chapter 25

In the morning she saw Harry in the garden hanging out his washing. He was struggling a bit, getting short of breath with all the bending and stretching. He had on his gardening rags. She went out and called to him: 'I've made a pot of tea; do you want some?' He nodded to her, mutely, and she saw his shiny, false teeth biting on a clothes peg.

She climbed over the low wall balancing two big mugs of tea and sat on his weedy lawn, watching him. When he had put in his last peg she said, 'Can't you get someone in to do that?'

'Then what would I do? Sit and watch them? I'm not helpless yet.'

'I only asked. No need to scowl at me.' Virginia rested her weight back onto her elbows and stared at the valley. She looked up at Harry.

'Come indoors,' he said, 'I'll find you a biscuit.'

'I'm not a kid, Harry.'

'Course you are. Worse than a kid in fact.' He turned away and started for the house.

Virginia rolled over on the grass and began to get up. 'What do you mean?'

But he was off, half plodding, half shuffling, an old man's walk, his broad shoulders dipping and swaying, still strong. She caught up with him as he stood in the narrow hallway on the big square of coconut matting, struggling a little to step out of his loose garden shoes. He stood in his thick, grey socks and watched her up the three steps to his threshold.

'I've been watching you,' he said and she smiled at him as he claimed all the spurious privileges of age.

'Have you?' she said, cheekily, and stepped out of her own shoes. She knew the rules in Harry's house. In Harry's house she had to be a lady. When she was little she would come and sit with Jenny, Harry's wife, and Jenny would make sure that she sat up straight at the table and ate her cake nicely and did not slurp out of the china cup that even the little girl was given. Jenny had been in service and knew how things were and should be done. Now, years and years after her death, Harry kept her standards and polished and dusted, washed and shined. Except of course for his raggedy self, but these were workday clothes. At the weekend he would smarten himself: suit, collar and tie and good, local shoes from Barker's factory.

Virginia sat with Harry at his shiny formica table in the kitchen and said thank you, when he offered her a biscuit from a china plate. She sat with the biscuit in her hand and he put a smaller, matching plate in front of her. She remembered the feel of her school uniform, the blazer's not quite clean feel towards the end of term, Jenny's brown bread and butter on these plates, sitting here with bare legs and white ankle socks.

'You look tired,' said Harry.

'It's been hard work, this play.'

'You've had all the rest to cope with, though, haven't you? Your Mother and then that chap of yours, Dan. And now there's this other one that you've taken up with, the one with the big car. You look buggered.'

'Just a couple more nights of the play, then we'll be done with it.'

'Hasn't it gone well?'

'It's been terrific.' She sat and thought and Harry watched her fiddle with her biscuit as though it were a domino. 'It's a terrible play though, Harry, miserable, harrowing.'

'I only ever go to the pantomime in the village,' Harry said. 'I watch you on the telly. I shall have to keep a lookout myself, now that your mother's gone.'

'I'll ring you up when something's on.'

'No,' he smiled at her, 'You'll forget.'

'I shan't you know.'

'They'll let you back on will they?'

'Back on what?'

'On the telly.' He gave her his old fool's smile and she tumbled into it as she always did.

'Of course they will you daft devil. I've just had a break for a few weeks that's all.'

Harry paused, stared at her and licked his lips nervously as if he were concentrating on getting his words just right. 'Now look,' he said, 'here's a silly question for you. Why then if it's such a, what did you say, a harrowing play, why did you do it? All these weeks of rehearsals and putting it on every night. It can't do you much good can it, going through all that over and over, if it's as bad as that?' He was out of breath with his question.

'Starting with the easy questions are we?'

'That's right,' he said, head on one side looking as though he were eager for her reply. 'Is it, what do they call it, realistic?'

'It's that all right.'

'I thought it might be.' He kept on staring at her. 'Eat your biscuit,' he said. He waited until she had the biscuit in her mouth. 'It's nice is it, that biscuit?'

'Lovely.'

'Realistic?'

She started to laugh. 'You sneaky old bugger. Nobody ever really likes a smartarse, Harry, do you know that?'

She couldn't put him off; there he was, puzzled and intent. 'I would reckon,' he said, slowly, half-wittedly, 'that nice things were just as realistic as nasty things, wouldn't you?'

'But not so interesting.'

'A smack in the chops never seemed that fascinating to me.'

'I'm not arguing with you, with your watery, simpleton's eyes; you're just a devious old pest.' He sat quietly and watched her smiling at him.

138

'Don't hum,' she said. He looked hurt. 'Yes you were, you were drifting off.'

He sat back and closed his eyes as if he were concentrating for some great effort. He took a deep breath and said: 'Look, you want to look after yourself a bit more. You're not a kid, you're a middle-aged woman. It's no good looking like that, like you are. You've had a couple of knocks and you can expect it to take a while before you're yourself again.'

'I've hardly thought about my Mum.'

'You will.'

'It's Dan, you see, coming just after. I think that being here for him dying, you know watching it happen, it sort of pushed my Mum out of it.'

'She'll be back,' said Harry.

'Then there's Hank.'

'That's the big feller is it?'

'You've seen him have you?'

'I peek through the curtains.'

'I wish he'd come along a bit later. Next year say.'

'Well, just take your time.'

'Yes.'

Chapter 26

In the afternoon it started to rain and made the air heavy. Virginia was doing beans on toast for her tea when Sadie phoned.

'Graham's been arrested,' Sadie didn't soften the blow. Virginia stood dumbly, feeling herself breathe, not knowing what to say. 'Arrested,' Sadie said, voice raised. 'Are you there?'

'Yes, I'm here,' said Virginia, irritated. 'Give me a second, I'm just going to turn off the cooker.' She put down the phone and went into the kitchen and turned off the gas. She watched her beans bubbling for a moment. Now what, she thought. She went back and sat down on the settee with the phone. 'Right then, go on.'

'Joe, you know Joe..?'

'Yes, I know Joe.'

'This lunch-time, Joe calls me at the pub, warning me, the cheeky git, to keep my mouth shut. What does he think I am? I told him: you're born with your mouth shut where I come from.'

'You're telling me all about it.'

'Joe told me to. Bloody hell, don't you start.'

'Sorry. Go on then, tell me. Tell me what he's done.'

'Joe said to tell you to keep your head down. Stay away.'

'Why me?'

'I don't know do I? I'm just the messenger. You were only an afterthought. "Oh yes," he says to me, "You might give that pal of yours, the actress, a ring." Just as if he'd never hardly heard of you. So, anyway, there we are, Graham's in the lockup.'

'You sound pleased.'

'Do him good won't it? He was really pissing me off. You know the way he is, all that smarmy confidence.'

Virginia could not help laughing. 'What's he done though?' she said.

'I don't know.'

'I'll ring Joe.'

'Christ no, don't do that. Just do what he says and stay away.'

'That's your advice is it?'

'It bloody is. You're the last thing that anybody needs. Can you imagine it in the papers, can you? TV Star in Police Drama.'

Virginia put the phone down and sat back into the settee. Brilliant, she thought, bloody brilliant. Anyway why phone me? What's the sod done for me to worry about? She went into the kitchen and shook her pan of beans. They looked hot enough.

She sat in the kitchen, reading the paper, waiting for Hank to come and drive her to Milton Keynes. Through the rain flecked window she heard Harry's voice and then a car door closing. She picked up her bag and checked that all her stuff was there. The gas was turned off. She reached over the sink and pulled the window shut. Hank saw her as he came level and ducked down to smile in at her.

She slammed the door shut behind her and said: 'He collared you then did he?'

'What,' said Hank, mildly, 'the old chap from next door?'

'That's the one, Wurzel Gummidge with Brylcream.'

'What's the matter?'

'Nothing, nothing at all. What did the old bugger have to say?' She took Hank's arm and walked him over the yard and onto the pavement. 'I see he's made himself scarce.'

'What's he done? Seemed a nice old boy.'

'Was he asking you things?'

'No. What things?'

'Thank God for that then.' She waved her hand at the car. 'Are we going then or what?'

141

They drove along, wipers flicking on and off. She said to Hank, 'I've just had Sadie on the phone.'

'Sadie?'

'From Graham's pub.'

'Oh yes, isn't that the rather pleasant girl with the curves?'

'You noticed, did you?' and smiled at how polite he was.

'Of course I did,' smiling back at her. 'Well tell me then, what did she want?'

'Nothing to do with me really. Graham's in trouble with the police. Overdue I would have thought.'

'Never met the chap,' said Hank. 'Has it made you feel fed up?' And then he shut up and let her sit.

They were through Stoney Stratford and into the driving by numbers traffic system in Milton Keynes before she said: 'I can't help wondering if he's all right though. I'll give Sadie a ring from the theatre.'

'Be careful,' said Hank, quietly.

'What about?'

'If the police are involved it would be a silly thing to do to have them think that you were connected with some crime or other.'

'Me?'

'Well, you're quite well known. The papers would stick their noses in I'm sure.' He sounded a bit prim, she thought.

'I'm not bothered about all that nonsense.' She laughed and turned to look at him. He was looking ahead, frowning at the road.

When he parked outside the theatre she kissed him. She could see that he was worrying and so she kissed him twice, got hold of his arm and bit her fingers into the soft flesh inside his biceps, pulling herself over to him.

'Ouch,' he said it slowly. 'What bony fingers you have.'

'What's up with you then?' she asked him.

'I'll see you afterwards, in the bar,' he said. 'We could go for a curry.'

***

142

They sat on the front row, eating crisps.

'Just look at that will you,' she said to Claire. She leaned back and stretched out her arms along the back of the seats. Dennis stood in the middle of the stage cloth in the acid light from the scaffolding above, the only light in the big blackness of the theatre. Virginia watched him stand up closely to Paul and John, whispering. They stood away from each other. Paul smiled, big toothed, white. She cupped her hand over Claire's shoulder. 'He won't leave it alone will he? We're almost at the end and there he is, still arguing the toss about how to do something or other. He's not like that with you and me is he?'

Claire smiled, 'Boys together,' she said and they laughed across the room at Dennis putting his hand on Paul's shoulder and then laughing, hand on his nape, pulling him in and speaking quickly and seriously, his other hand a raised fist, their heads close together.

I don't want anything else, Virginia thought. No more foolishness with lovers. 'People talk shit about actors,' she said. 'They talk such shit.'

'Sure do,' said Claire, becoming Texan.

'Nobody works as hard as we do.'

'Sure don't,' said Claire, she rustled her crisp packet, filled her mouth with crisps and crunched them all around the bare, empty air of the auditorium and set Virginia giggling.

'What a bloody noise, how do you do it?' Then, she sighed and said: 'Nobody else has to get things perfect do they, but we do though, don't we?'

'Sure as shit,' said Claire.

'And we help each other,' said Virginia. 'We do don't we, we help each other to make it all bloody perfect.'

'Bet your ass,' said Claire.

'Not like all the other buggers, not like all the tricky sods you meet.'

'Steady on,' said Claire, suddenly English again. She put her crisps down. 'What's up? Don't cry. Your Hank, he's nice, isn't he? He's a nice bloke.'

Virginia nodded, agreeing. 'But, nobody's like us though,' tears rolling down her face, 'nobody's like us.' Paul and Dennis were walking towards them wide eyed. 'And after tomorrow that's it isn't it? That's bloody it, finished.'

Dennis sat beside her and she let her arm fall onto his shoulder, 'What's up?' he said.

'Don't encourage her,' said Claire. Virginia pulled her hair.

***

She was becoming used to her dark drives with Hank. She gave him a kiss on the cheek as they sat in the car outside her house. 'You don't flinch anymore,' she said and made him hold hands with her.

He made himself not smile. 'It's not so bad. Not now that I'm becoming accustomed to it.'

'What excuse will we have for meeting after tomorrow when the play's finished?'

'Do you want to?' he asked and because she thought he was serious she snapped back at him:

'Of course I do you fool.'

'Good,' he said quietly.

'But you can't sit there like Buddha. Something's got to happen. All this stolid mysterious stuff, it's a burden.'

'Lots of things have happened.'

'Shut up. If you keep on coming round here I'm going to jump on you.'

It made him smile. 'Are you?' he asked her.

'Sooner rather than later,' she said and did not smile back. She let go of his hand and opened the car door; the night sighed in on her. 'Come for lunch tomorrow. Come early and I'll cook lunch for you.' She was out of the car, bending to look in at him.

'What about your sleep?' he said.

'I'll sleep on the settee and you can watch.' She shut the door before he could reply and turned away. She walked a couple of paces across the pavement and into her yard, turned back and saw him looking at her still. She waved and he drove away.

The lane was gloomy in the half-hearted street lamps and she could see, above her, patchy, moonlit clouds. The air was still and quiet. She turned to the house and stood in its deep shadow, fiddling with her keys.

'Virginia, Virginia.'

'Oh dear God, you made me jump.'

'Where've you been? Where?' Sadie stood up close to her and shook her arm. 'Do you know what the time is?' She was whispering, urgently, into Virginia's face.

'What are you doing here? What do you want?' whispering back into Sadie's breath in the darkness.

'Just open the door, will you?'

Virginia scratched at the keyhole, found it and pushed open the door into the warm house. 'Go and sit down and I'll make some coffee.'

Sadie shook her head, 'No I'll stay here and watch you.' She sat down at the kitchen table and leaned her weight forward onto her folded arms. Virginia could see that she was agitated.

'Sadie, you scared me to death.' The blue flame whoofed under the kettle.

'You want to get an electric one.'

'Yes. Right. I'll get one. Now, tell me what you're doing here.'

'Don't get snotty. No need for that.'

'What?'

'Hey now listen. Right? It's not just Graham in the bridewell, they lifted Richard at the same time.'

It took her breath away: 'Richard? Why Richard, what would he do with Graham.'

Sadie nodded, 'Yeah, Richard.'

'What for, Sadie?' Virginia stopped herself. Then she said: 'If you don't tell me and stop messing about,' she picked up the breadknife from the draining board, 'I'll bloody well knife you.'

145

Sadie went big eyed, thrilled with the bad news. 'They were round at your Dan's, loading his paintings and stuff into a van and the bailiffs or the Social Services or somebody came and caught them at it.' Virginia covered her eyes with her hand. 'For the Crown,' said Sadie, 'they come and take everything for the Crown when there's no will and no family.'

'Bloody Graham,' said Virginia, 'bloody, bloody Graham, the sticky fingered fat bastard.'

'Hard to disagree,' said Sadie.

'I can just see him talking silly bloody Richard into it.'

'It's worse than that,' said Sadie.

'Well, I'm glad that you're so pleased.'

'There's forgeries,' Sadie was whispering.

'What forgeries?'

'Your Dan's forgeries. His and Richard's forgeries.' Virginia sat and stared at her. 'That's shut you up hasn't it?' Sadie said.

'It bloody well has,' said Virginia. 'What were they of? The forgeries, what were they forgeries of?'

Sadie pulled her face into a grimace. 'Don't ask me,' she said. 'I thought to myself that would be a good thing not to know. Know what I mean?'

They sat on the settee drinking the coffee that Sadie didn't want. The closed curtains made the room tiny. Sadie looked around the room. 'Your Mum's stuff?' she asked.

'I don't know what to do with it,' said Virginia. 'It seems a dirty trick just to get rid of it.'

'Give it to her mates. Tell yourself it's gone to a good home. That's what we did with my Gran's stuff.'

Virginia wasn't listening. 'Where are they now?' she asked.

'Oh they let them go on bail. The cops don't want their cells cluttered up with respectable criminals when they've got drunks and smackheads queuing up round the block. The streets are full of people vomiting and bleeding, every gutter you look in; they don't want those two taking up space do they?'

146

'Did they send you?'

'Well,' said Sadie, hesitating as she felt Virginia's anger, 'yeah, they did.'

'The bastards have dropped me in it haven't they?'

'Well, yeah, they thought they might have.'

'Might have? Did they tell you about my roomful of stolen bloody art treasures?'

Sadie nodded, 'Richard did.'

'Bastards,' said Virginia and spilled her coffee.

'Richard said that...'

'Richard said, did he? And how likely am I to take the advice of the intellectually crippled?'

'That you should just keep your head down.'

'Oh, it's as sophisticated as that is it, his advice?'

'Well,' said Sadie, lamely, 'they've made up a good story.'

'Oh good, well, come on then don't keep me in suspense.'

Sadie had had enough of her. 'Hey pal,' she said, 'you can stop slearing and carrying on at me you know. I'm the silly bugger who traipsed all the way out here into the leafy sodding countryside to warn you. You're the thief not me. You're the one with all the bent gear upstairs. Me, I'm just the chest behind the bar, that's all I am. I'll bloody well push off now if you like.' She put her feet up on the coffee table and crossed her arms and sniffed.

'Go on then,' said Virginia, quietly, 'tell me properly what they did.'

'Yeah, well,' said Sadie and told her.

Later she walked with Sadie back to her car. It was parked under the overhang of a neglected hedge at the bottom of the lane.

'You could stay,' she said.

'No,' Sadie said, 'best not.' She smiled, then looked away and pulled open the car door.

'Oh yes, I see,' said Virginia, 'reporting back are you? Which of them is it tonight or are they both tucked up in the one bed waiting for you to drop into the middle?'

'Knock it off.'

'I can just see it: the three of you in your wyncyette; you making the Horlicks and those two buffoons comparing willy sizes.'

'Have you done? Have you?' Virginia knew when to shut up. Sadie spoke more softly: 'Tell you the truth, Virginia, I've given Graham the elbow. Not that he knows it yet, but I'm going to focus on the young feller.'

Virginia whispered back: 'Keep your clothes on then.'

'What?'

'Keep your clothes on. Don't let him be photographing and sketching and painting and God knows what.'

'What are you on about?'

Virginia shook her finger, 'You've been warned.'

Sadie got in the car and started the engine. Virginia held on to the open door; she almost pushed it closed, but then said: 'Go on then, tell me, why does Graham get the elbow and not Richard?'

'There's nothing to him is there? He's just a bit of a laugh, but Richard's got something about him. He's a pain in the arse, I know he is, and awkward as buggery, but I don't mind that.' She got the car going and Virginia slammed the door. Sadie rolled the window down. 'And I'll tell you what, if he wants my clothes off he can have them off. Anytime.'

Walking in the dark, back to the house, Virginia thought about that: about the accusation in what Sadie had said.

Chapter 27

She thought about buying fish and chips rather than cook lunch for Hank, but she drove to Sainsbury's and bought some real fish to poach and salad and a piece of cheese. It'll only take ten minutes, she thought, the chip shop queue would have been longer than that.

She had the kitchen window open, listening for his car and she was standing in the open door when he walked down the yard.

'Sure you want to risk coming in?' she said.

'It's daylight,' Hank said, 'I'll probably be safeish.'

She sat him down on her mother's big three-seater settee. 'See the view,' she said and watched him look through the bay window across the miles of wide valley. 'Brilliant isn't it?'

'Lovely,' he said and looked away from the window to smile at her. He was staring at her, sitting there in the middle of the settee, pink and blonde, his big body filling out his summer suit, big thick hands folded in his lap.

'We can eat in ten minutes,' she said.

'Good.' Just the one word again and he made her feel awkward.

He always makes me feel awkward, she thought. He makes me think that I'm being too deliberate, makes me watch myself, that's what he does. When she got up he got up with her.

'I'll come and watch,' he said.

'I'll break the dishes.'

'What, if I watch you?'

'Yes, if you watch me.'

He put his hand on her shoulder and kissed her. She turned her face up into his and stood absolutely still, doing nothing, letting him kiss her.

'Go on,' he said, 'your turn in a kitchen.'

They ate at the kitchen table.

'What's for pudding?' he asked.

'You've had cheese.'

He pouted. 'Pudding's always nice.'

'I'll try to remember,' she said. She smiled and thought about kissing him. No, she thought, I'll just sit here and let myself tremble for a bit.

***

It was night again; another clear summer's night being driven through the moonlit black fields.

'I was ready for a party tonight,' Hank said.

'Sometimes there is,' said Virginia, 'but I think that we were all quite pleased to get to the end of this one.' There were tall hedges, ragged against the navy blue sky, and the long lit road in front of the car. 'We do terrible things don't we?'

Hank nodded, 'They certainly look it.'

'By the time we do it, you know do the performance, it doesn't seem terrible at all. I don't think that it is anyway. I just know exactly what I'm doing and going to do and I do it. Night after night, no problem.'

'You make fools of people.'

'No I don't.'

'Yes you do. You say to yourself, this is how to manipulate the silly devils who've paid good money to be made miserable and then you watch for the effect that you've had. It's a smug, superior business this acting lark. I'd never thought of it like that before, but it is isn't it? At least all the woe is me stuff is. It's manipulative, cold hearted.'

She waited to be angry, but it wasn't there. 'It's because we rehearse stuff, go over it again and again.' She spoke quietly. 'When you start on something, something tough like this one we've just done, it's a difficult thing to do. You keep on coming on things for the first time

150

and it gets you, it does, it gets you. Then, you do it again and again and you wear it out and then you can do it.'

'It's no way to live,' said Hank.

'Oh no, you can't live like that,' said Virginia, 'of course you can't live like that.' But I do, she thought. I do. I go over things over and over them in my head and then I think, Yes, that's what I'll do. I do it with Hank. I don't want to get it wrong with Hank and so I put it all into rehearsal, so that I can do it, so that I make it possible. It's not cold hearted. It's not, not by a mile.

'What will you do now?' Hank said.

'I'll go to London and kiss and make up with my agent.'

'Have you fallen out?'

'Not really. But he was right, I shouldn't have done this. It wasn't worth it.'

'That's not what you said.'

'I know.'

It would have been better, she thought if I had stayed away and never watched Dan dying. I could have missed him sneering at me, making me a fool. I could have come up for the funeral, had a weep, and then pushed off for a few months of feeling miserable. This sod of a play pinned me down, all ready, like a biology lesson rat, to be picked over. A bit of telly, a couple of voice overs, that would have been better for me than all this bloody anguish. Anguish, she thought, what a word. Has it been that? Yes it has, she thought, off and on.

'What are you smiling at?' said Hank.

'Just dreaming.'

'I could see that. Was it a good dream?'

'No,' she said, 'it was a crap dream. I was just thinking that I could do with a bit of reality. Not crap reality, though, good reality.'

'No problem,' said Hank.

***

'I don't know how he's managed it,' said Virginia, 'but Dan's causing more trouble dead than alive.' She was sitting on the floor resting her back against the settee. She drank some more whisky and then put her head right back to look at Hank who was sitting on the soggy cushions. She rested her head against his knee. 'He's dropped Richard in it and Graham too I suppose, although Graham was a late volunteer and probably deserves a lot more than he's going to get.'

She looked at Hank, big and crumpled, sinking further into the settee. 'Are you listening?' she said.

'You know I am.'

'Good, because I'm a bit worried myself.'

'Surely not.'

'Listen will you? Graham...'

'That's the big fat one is it?'

'That's the one. And Richard. They were caught by someone, bailiffs or somesuch when they were round at Dan's nicking his paintings and loading them into the back of a van. Then the cops locked them up for a while.' Suddenly loving the story, telling it spitefully.

'Did they charge them?' said Hank, quietly.

'Then for a bonus, Sadie tells me that there's a pile of forgeries that Dan and Richard had produced.' She spoke carelessly as though it was all silliness and what could you expect from such a bunch of clowns.

'Keep out of it,' said Hank.

His sharpness made her stretch to look at him again. 'What's the matter? I'm just telling you.' When she saw his expression she scrambled round to face him and knelt up straight, in front of him. 'Don't look like that.'

'Sorry. Didn't mean to snarl.'

She put her hands on his knees and shook them. 'Listen then,' she said, 'it's got me worried.'

'What forgeries?' Hank said. 'Do you know about these forgeries?' Virginia shook her head, bewildered by his anger. 'Have they used them? Have they actually defrauded anyone?' She shrugged and shook her head again. 'You keep well away then, well away. People get serious bird for fraud.'

She sat back on her heels. 'There's no need to get excited,' she said, gently, 'I was only telling you.'

'Sorry,' said Hank, curtly. 'I didn't mean to sound angry.'

'That was angry was it?'

'Yes, sorry.'

'It's not what I call angry. Slashed suits and pots whizzing round the kitchen, a few black eyes and smashed windows, a sauce bottle up your bum, that's what I call angry.'

He tried to smile at her, 'Oh I couldn't do that.'

'I could though, so you'd better behave yourself mister.' She was smiling, trying to bring him back. 'Don't worry,' she said. 'Come on, for goodness sake.'

'They're a pair of fools,' he said, 'doing something like that.'

'Sadie told me that Richard had been making forgeries, you know art forgeries, with Dan. Bloody typical Dan-type move that, taking the piss you see. Anyway, I'll bet that Richard wanted what there was of that.' She stopped babbling. She did not care what they did. She had had enough of them, enough of her half life with Dan, of dropping in and out and being careful enough to keep a good guard on her self-preserving distance. I'll have Hank, she thought, and shocked herself with the deliberate words. I'll stand in his kitchen and cook dinners and go to church on Sunday morning. I'll do that. It's what I want.

'I'd better be off,' Hank said.

'What?'

'It's getting late. Best make a move.' He stood up, awkward at first because she was kneeling so closely. Then he was at the door and she was looking up at him.

'It's late,' he said, and she could see that he was aching to leave and struggling to be polite. He held out his hands, 'Starting to be busy, you know. Have to be up early in the morning.' The lie made him look away from her. She did not try to go with him to the street; she stayed there on the floor and heard the door close behind him.

What have I done, she thought, what have I done? Nothing, I've done bloody well nothing.

Chapter 28

Time passed. She waited for Hank to call her and he didn't. She watched herself waiting until she was embarrassed. She telephoned him and there was only the answering machine. She telephoned her agent and agreed with everything that he said. Yes, she said, no more arty nonsense and agreed to make some money and be rich and famous.

Harry came and looked at her mother's furniture and said the same thing as Sadie. 'Get shut of it, get shut of the lot of it.' And she had a brief flurry of half-remembered friends of her mother's collecting bits and pieces from the house. Harry's pal had a pick-up truck and took the three-piece suite and the carpets to the tip. She was down to the floorboards and some favourite bits of crockery and silver and all the tapes and photos. Harry said his cousin's granddaughter would rent the place. Can't she buy it, Virginia asked him? I'll see, he promised.

In the evenings Harry cooked for her and she sat and watched television with him and then went back to sleep on her futon on the floor of the back bedroom with Dan's paintings leaning on the walls. Every evening she telephoned Hank. Sometimes she phoned him during the day as well. If she were sitting in the garden or sitting reading, perhaps, with Harry, she would think about Hank and then go and telephone him. He was never there. One evening at the end of a week of this she said to the answer-phone, 'You're never there and I love you.' She banged the phone down. 'Oh shit,' she said out loud. 'Why say that? Why say it?'

The next day she drove on the twisted, hump-backed lanes across the valley and onto the Bedford road. She drove quickly, stupidly, so that there would not be time to think again, nor time to think about what she would say to him. The last thing I need for this is rehearsal, she thought. I'm having one go at this or I shan't do it at all.

It seemed always to be hot in Hank's village. A village of square Georgian stone soaking up sunshine from the pavement. She turned off the main street, passed the stone walls that belonged to Hank and turned fast right into the open square of the farmyard. It was still. He's not here, she thought. He's hiding, a foot behind one of those windows, holding his breath and watching me. She slammed the car door as hard as she could, half spinning on her heels in sudden fury. She banged on his door with the side of her fist then picked up the heavy ball of the knocker and made the noise clap itself around the empty house. She bent and picked up two big handfuls of gravel, closing her fists around the tiny stones so that they hurt her and she felt the sharpness of them under her nails. She swung, right hand, left hand, recklessly, almost falling with the momentum, spraying the upstairs windows. She stumbled, caught her balance, her breath. Her face was tight with anger. She stood and looked at the placid house with its rough weathered honey-stone and old black-wood sills, the dark, reflecting glass.

She left the car and walked back down the narrow half-sunken road to the main street. Fuck it, she thought, fuck it, I'll just go in the pub and ask where he is. I don't care what the bastards think. Think what they like, the bastards.

She stood at the bar. 'Half of bitter,' she said to the fat landlord.

'Good morning to you too,' he said.

'Yes,' said Virginia.

He put the beer down on the bar and stood, looking at her.

'I've no money,' she said, still snapping at him. 'You'll have to trust me. Bag's in the car outside Hank's. Where is he anyway? Do you know?'

'Wouldn't tell you if I did,' said the landlord, casually, 'wouldn't tell anybody.'

She looked away and then said quietly, 'When will he be back?'

The landlord hesitated, weighing her up. 'Well,' he said, 'he's got to be back soon. Got to be, this time of year.'

Virginia drank some beer and the landlord watched her. 'Is he all right?' she said in a small voice.

'Course he is. Why shouldn't he be?'

'Good,' she said. She looked away from him, but she knew that he was still watching her. 'Quite a few in for a lunch-time,' she said and felt foolish. She stepped back from the bar. 'Excuse me.'

In the white, shiny room she washed her hands in hot water to get rid of the dust from the gravel and rinsed the grit from under her nails. She ran cold water over her hands and forearms and splashed the water up onto her face. She pulled out three lengths of the roller towel and dried herself. She looked in the mirror at her rubbed face, shook her hair.

There was a row going on in the bar. She stood in the low doorway, in shadow and heard the rapid voice of the landlord, high and angry. Someone laughed, an open-mouthed snarl of a laugh. She stood listening, knowing that she should wait to hear about herself.

'You keep your trap shut. While you're in my pub, you keep it shut.'

'Poor girl,' a sneer in the voice.

'Go on,' said the landlord, 'push off and don't come back.'

But the voice went on, derisively, 'Imagine how you'd feel if she went the same way as the other one. More than one for all we know.'

There was a crash of glasses and Virginia stepped through the door. The landlord had a tall, dark man by the hair, had grabbed him by the top handful of his hair and was holding him, arm's length across the bar. She saw his big, white fist and the other fist coming back to his shoulder. The man's checked shirt and dog-tooth jacket were wet. The landlord shook him, pulling the skin up from his face. Then he stopped and looked around the bar, saw everyone staring. He let go of the man's hair, let the hand fall to the man's shoulder. 'Go on,' he said

156

and slapped him, an open-handed, upwards scutch that made his mouth bleed. 'Go on, go on,' as if driving an animal away. The tall man stepped back, half turned, spat on the floor and then banged out through the door.

Virginia slipped into being Mae West in a saloon brawl. She watched herself do it, swing her hips across the room and sit on the bar stool where the counter was running with spilled beer and there was broken glass. She picked up a beer mat and pushed the mess away from her.

'Where is he?' she said.

The landlord was staring across the room. When she spoke he dropped his gaze to look at her. He bent down and came up with a dust pan and brush.

'Where's my drink?' said Virginia. What's going on? she thought.

He brushed the glass towards him, over the edge of the bar and into the dust pan. 'Me and Hank. We were pals when we were little, at the nursery and then at the school in the village here.' He was panting with anger.

'I thought he was sent away to school,' she leaned forward, whispering, so that her quiet words were not caught up in the tight silence of the bar.

'That was after. He was about nine or ten when they parcelled him off. Stupid bastards. He was all right with us.'

'You stayed friends?'

'Too right we did. He's a good lad your Hank. Always came back to us. Always. He's back now.'

My Hank, she thought, feeling it suddenly in her throat. 'Back?' she asked. 'Back from where?'

The landlord shook his head. 'Go and wait up at the farm, he's out doing the combining.' He smiled at her and pointed into her face, 'Keep me out of it, don't say I said.'

'What was all this about?' said Virginia, still whispering. 'What's going on?'

'Go and wait up at the farm,' he said. 'If he's got sandwiches for his lunch you'll have a long wait. He'll be back before dark though.'

Chapter 29

She waited all through the afternoon, sat in her car in Hank's farmyard and tried to wonder what it all might be about. But she couldn't; her mind wandered off into what her agent would find for her to do, how much the house might go for, Dan's pictures, Dan, Dan's house and Richard and Graham in the lockup. Then there was a play on the radio and then some eager man talking about films, the news.

The sky clouded over and hurried the evening on and there Hank was, walking through the high, wide gateway in the old stone walls. He was wearing shabby grey trousers and a dirty white shirt. She watched him through the windscreen just for seconds, then got out of the car, slammed the door and waited.

'Did you get my message on your answering machine?' she said, surprising herself with anger.

He nodded. Up close to her she could see that he was tired; the breath was coming up into his chest, panting, as though he had been running. 'Yes,' he said.

'You heard what I said, did you and you just left it at that?'

He nodded.

'Bastard,' she said, 'bastard.' She could hear him breathing. 'Did you know that I was here? Did that bastard from the pub tell you?'

Hank nodded. 'On my mobile,' he said, quietly. 'He wasn't going to but he thought better of it. I stayed away so that you could have time to get fed up and go.'

'Bastard,' she said. She opened the car door, 'Well I'll bugger off now then.'

Hank took hold of her arm. He looked away from her and they stood there, fools, not knowing what to do.

***

'They were talking about me in the pub,' she said. 'Having a bloody good row about me. He drew blood that landlord pal of yours.'

'George,' said Hank.

'That's his name is it? Seems to think the world of you.' She was angry still and it made her words seem spiteful.

'Yes, he does,' said Hank.

'So, come on then, why am I being talked about? What's the big secret. Did your pal tell you what was going on in that pub? Did he?'

Hank nodded, 'Yes, he told me.'

'Well, I wish he'd told me.'

'He's not your pal, he's mine.' Hank spoke quietly into her anger. 'One or two people have passed comments.' Virginia turned to him, almost said, What, comments about me? but stopped when she saw him, head down breathing hard. 'I've been out of prison now for nearly three years,' he said.

'What?' she could not get the sharpness out of her voice.

'On licence,' he said. 'If anything goes wrong, they'll lock me up again.' He looked up at her, his face pale, stubborn with fear. 'Can't do that again,' he said.

***

She took him inside the house. 'You look terrible,' she told him and then, stupidly, 'I'll cook you something. You sit down.'

'You can't cook,' he said, 'not properly.'

'Sit down and tell me while I'm doing something.' That's my mother she thought, that's what she did and she could feel her mother bustling round her. She took hold of his face and held it tightly between her

159

palms. She could feel his jaw, the stubble on his skin against her hands, her finger tips touched the curl of his ears.

He took her hands away and kissed one of them. 'There's not much in the fridge,' he said. 'It might have to be tins.' He opened the fridge door and its light was bright and clean in the muted light of the low kitchen.

Virginia picked out a tall can of lager. 'I'll share this with you,' she said. 'Go on get two glasses and pour it. And sit down will you? Let me get on and do this. I'll ask if I can't find anything.'

***

Hank sat at the kitchen table, his arms folded in front of him, taking his weight. Two glasses of lager were going flat in front of him. 'I did eight years,' he said. She felt it like a slap, remembered what the man in the pub had said, that thin vindictive bastard, glad for his split lip. She had two forks in her hands and carefully turned the sausages, one after the other. She pushed them to the edge of the pan. Then she peeled off a rasher of bacon from its pack and laid it in the pan, then two more so that the pan was full.

'What for?' she said, 'what had you done?'

'I killed someone,' he said.

'Who?' she said. She turned over the bacon. The pan was hot and it was cooking quickly.

'My wife,' he said.

***

'No, not Kate's mother. Not her; she buggered off years before all of this. Kate was three. I'd just come out of the army and she couldn't stand having me around every day. Couldn't stand me at all, so she just pushed off and left the two of us.'

Virginia put the bacon and sausage onto two plates. She got the frozen chips out from under the grill. 'This is a really nasty dinner for you,' she said. She put the plates on the table and sat down facing Hank. 'Go on,' she said, quietly.

'I was inside all the time she was doing her GCSEs. She brought the results slip in and I cried my eyes out. They were all As. Same with her A Levels, except she messed them up a bit: only two As, a B and a C.' He looked up at Virginia. 'More damn tears.'

'Eat your chips,' said Virginia.

'She lived with my cousins.' He picked up his knife and fork. 'Do you want me to tell you about Paula?'

'Tell me what happened.'

'My second wife was called Paula,' said Hank; his face was flat as a stone. 'We made each other miserable. The first few months were okay and then we were damned miserable. It was a classic really. I came home when she didn't expect me and caught her with a man. I opened the kitchen door. Saw. Then closed it and stood in the hall. I thought that I was going to be sick, just the shock you see. I stood for a few minutes, seemed a long time. I opened the door again and she had got rid of him. She was standing at the sink, drinking a glass of water. She was still naked and she couldn't have cared less. She turned and grinned at me and there was a look in her eyes. I hit her, hit her like you hit a man. Broke her jaw, broke her neck, cracked her skull on the quarry tiles. I knew straight away. So, I phoned my cousin to head Kate off from school. Then, I phoned the police. Couldn't even say that I didn't mean to do it. Couldn't say it. They lifed me off.'

'Did you love her?' said Virginia.

'Yes.'

***

'You don't have to eat it,' Virginia said.

'I know,' said Hank. 'Sorry, put it in the microwave. I'll eat it. Really, I'm hungry.'

Virginia looked at Hank's congealed plate. 'You'll need to be,' she said.

'I can always eat,' he told her. 'No matter what happens it never keeps me from eating.'

She stood in front of the microwave, trying to make sense of the dials. She heard Hank's chair scrape and she stood, doing nothing, waiting for him to come up behind her. She felt his hand on her left shoulder and he reached over her and turned the dial with his right hand. She caught hold of his wrist and pulled his arm across her, leaned back into him. 'You should have told me about all of this.'

'How could I do that?'

'Instead of running off and hiding.'

'Yes, I know that. I panicked a bit.'

'There was no need, was there? Why did you jump the way you did? You were up and off like a shot.'

'I'm serving a life sentence, sweetie.'

'I'm your sweetie am I?' She held up his hand to her face and kissed it, touched the palm with her tongue. 'Anyway you're out now; it's over with.'

'It's never over. It's life.' She could feel his breath as he spoke softly into her hand.

She was startled and turned to face him, the palms of both hands on his chest. 'They've let you go.'

'On licence. That's why I ran off the other night. If they even think that I'm associating with anyone unsuitable they'll revoke my licence and I'll be back in jug.'

She shook her head, 'They can't. Not just like that.'

'They can and then you're in the system again. And it's quite a system.'

Virginia stared at him, not understanding. 'I'm not unsuitable,' she said.

'Your friends are.'

'What?'

'Your art thief friends.'

Oh shit, she thought and thought about Dan's pictures in her back bedroom.

The microwave beeped and Hank smiled at her. 'My dinner's ready,' he said.

When she put it down in front of him he put his knife and fork under the chips and fluffed them up. 'Perfect,' he said. 'Why don't you do the same with yours?' She pulled a face. 'Go on,' he said, 'give it a quick blast, I'll eat it.'

**

She sat and watched Hank eat. He was so neat. He held his knife and fork in just the right way in his thick hands and touched his lips with the square of kitchen towel before he sipped his glass of beer. He cleared his plate and they sat waiting for the micro-wave to beep again. 'Sorry,' she said, looking at the warmed-up dinner and made him smile. 'What are you smiling at?' she asked him, and it kept the smile on his face.

She sat down at the table and drank her beer.

'Be careful,' said Hank, pointing at the glass, 'you have to drive.'

'No, I don't,' she said. That's shut him up, she thought, and stared at him so that the weight of her attention, focused on him, kept his eyes down, on his plate, in the synthetic chips and sausage.

He shook his head, 'I can't eat it after all,' he said.

Virginia looked at him sitting there perplexed and thought about him hitting his wife. She ran through it in her head, building it up into something that would work, positioning them, seeing her, Paula, with the glass of clear water catching the light from the window, her grinning bitch teeth. Hank's blow, the way he would have moved, one two steps across the kitchen and the sudden, fractured movement of her twisting and stretching against the force of it. No, she thought, pinned with guilt as she made a scene of it that she could rehearse over and over in her head so that she could get it just right. So that she could make it play as though it were real. That's what I do, she thought, that's what I always do.

'I haven't slept with anyone for twelve years,' said Hank.

'Good,' said Virginia.

**

163

Virginia turned on the television in Hank's bedroom. 'I've got just about my entire telly career on videotape.'

'Oh yes?' said Hank.

'My mother recorded everything. What do you think I should do with it all? There's boxes of it.'

'Save it for your grandchildren,' he said. His words caught her nicely and she turned to him, halfway between anger and tears, but he was in the doorway and gone. 'I'll get us a drink, shall I?' she heard him say.

Why feel like that then, she asked herself. She knew and saw the picture of herself and her mother, being two women even when she had been a little girl. She could hear him on the stairs and then the stolid house swallowed up the sound of him.

On the television there was a repeat of a drama about people leading very complicated lives where no-one had any idea of why they behaved as they did. This is dreadful, she thought. I haven't lived like this have I?

'What are you watching?' said Hank. She didn't turn round.

'It's about what happens when people don't behave themselves,' she said.

'Isn't there any football.'

'No.'

'Or a pop concert.'

'A pop concert?' It turned her round. 'You, a pop concert?'

'Oh yes, I like all that stuff; fireworks and melodrama, love it. Country and Western's the best. I've had many a good cry to that, sitting on my bed after bang-up.' She saw that he was carrying a bottle of whisky and two glasses.

She shook her head. 'No more crying after bang-up, sweetie,' she said, crying herself.

***

'I'd better go to sleep,' said Hank.

'Okay,' said Virginia.

'I leave the curtains open so that the early light wakes me up. Doesn't make me jump like the alarm clock does.'

Virginia had the duvet up to her chin. 'That's all right,' she said. 'I do that myself. How early is early?'

'Sixish,' Hank said. 'I'll turn the telly off, shall I?' He got out of bed and went across the room, clicked off the television and the room was quiet.

'I like your blue pyjamas,' said Virginia. 'You look very dressed up in them.'

'Shut up,' said Hank. 'This isn't a joke. Go to sleep.'

He was lying on his back. Virginia took hold of his arm and held it tight. 'Night night,' she said.

'Yes.' Hank said.

Chapter 30

When she woke up in the sunlit room Hank had gone. There was a note on his pillow. "Gone to work. I'll ring and give you half an hour's notice for lunch. Could go to pub?" Bloody cheek, she thought, "half an hour's notice."

There was a long, Victorian bath in the bathroom. It stood in the middle of the big, open room and the pipes came up to it from the sun-darkened floorboards. She slipped underwater, full length, and there was still plenty of room. The towels, folded neatly on a chair, were as big as main sails.

She drove back to Barton and let herself into the bare house. The end of this; it is really, now, the end of this, she thought. She thought of Harry, clinging on to his wife's ways. No he's not, she thought, that's the way he is himself. He's taken her on hasn't he, rehearsed himself into her? That's the way he really is.

She packed her hold-all; threw things in and went and knocked on Harry's door with the bag in her hand.

'You're early,' he said.

She looked down, knowing what she would say and awkward over it. 'Harvest time,' she said. 'Hank's up at first light this time of the year.' She looked up at him.

'I only ever had one woman,' he said and she could see that he was angry, 'and that was the right thing to do and I was happy with that, see? How many men have you had then?'

'Harry?'

'And it's made you very bloody happy hasn't it?'

'There's no need to swear at me.'

'Yes, there is.' They stood in his yard staring at each other and then he spoke quietly as though he were ashamed of himself. 'You've never been happy, not since you were little, have you? You've been running round like a blue-arsed fly; what for God alone knows.'

Oh God, she thought, I'm having a talking to.

'If you set up with this chap, Hank is it, then make your mind up to him. Don't balance him off against other things that you might like to do. You've got to take him on board properly.'

'Where does that leave the other things?' she said.

'Nowhere,' said Harry.

After that he got her into the kitchen and made her a bacon sandwich for her breakfast and they talked about selling her mother's house. She told him to say to his cousin's granddaughter that she could have the house. She could rent it first if she liked and buy it later. 'She is from Barton is she Harry?'

'Course she is. Born and bred.'

Harry put a white cloth on the table and cut her bacon sandwich nicely into quarters.

'It looks lovely all this,' said Virginia.

'I was a rough devil, you know, until my Jenny got hold of me. Shy with girls, but a bit on the rough side.'

'You had a real romance with her didn't you?'

'I did,' said Harry, his voice big with pride.

She smiled at him, 'You are a soft thing, aren't you?'

'I am,' he said.

***

Hank sat in the cab of the combine with the ear defenders pressing mutely over his head. The following wind pushed dust past him into the sunlight and over the cloud shadows on the waiting field. What I should do, he thought, is stop all this and just whip her off into bed. Imagine that. Adrian had told him, told him in the showers, about this

167

course that he was doing where they had to write down the names, 'Made us try to remember the names see, of all the women we'd fucked. There were stacks of them I couldn't remember. Made me feel a right slut it did. There was this kid though, about twenty-two, three, only a kid, who remembered everything. He went back for more paper. Know how many names? Over a hundred and sixty. Dirty bastard.'

'Christ,' Hank had said, impressed. 'I'm not even into double figures.'

'Trouble with girls nowadays,' Adrian said, 'is that they think they're lads.'

Not lads like me though, thought Hank.

I can do all of this, he thought, this whole field. And after this I could just carry on. There's days of it. Then there's putting the combine away and cleaning and making sure that everything's okay around the barn. I'll try and find out where the cats are. And she will be gone. When it's dark I can go back to the house and see what there is in the fridge and the fridge light will make my shadow in the kitchen when I open the door and rummage in the cold sour smell for whatever there is for me to eat.

***

When she got back to the farm it was still only mid-morning. She sat in the kitchen and thought about having a quick look through the house, but it seemed a bit paltry. I'll wait for Hank to show me round, she thought, I'll try to hang on until he offers. She made a pot of tea and pushed back a space on the table so that she could spread Hank's Independent out flat. She read for a while, then put her head on her arms and went to sleep.

Hank woke her up when he rattled open the door. She opened her eyes, head still down, and watched him trying not to make a noise.

'You're not asleep, are you?' he said accusingly.

'No.'

'What are you doing?'

'Waiting for you, watching you.' She screwed up her face to see him better. Her cheek was squashed on her bare arm and her skin felt hot and sticky.

'Why me?' It was a funny question, but she knew what he meant. 'Why watch me?'

'No good reason,' she said. 'It's only physical anyway; it's because you're a big blond farm-boy.'

She made him smile and he said: 'What's in the hold-all then?' He nodded at the hold-all that she had left on the kitchen floor.

'I thought I'd move in.'

The smile had gone, falling from him in sudden panic. 'No,' he said. 'You can't do that. You can't just do it like that with a bit of cleverness.' There was more that he was going to say, but his breath got in the way. He bent and picked up her bag from the floor, stood holding it, looking at her, his breath shallow with fright.

She sat up, frightened herself. 'There's nothing clever going on here Hank. Honest there isn't. I think you're lovely.' There were the silly words thrown out at him, a plea.

'I thought we could go out for the afternoon,' he said, stiffly.

'What about all the work you've got to do.'

'I've rearranged things.' He pulled back a chair and sat down close to her, his hand flat on the table. She pushed herself up, touched her face.

'I've dribbled,' she said. 'Just let me get straightened up and we can go.' She ran upstairs to the bathroom. She was muttering to herself: 'Bloody, bloody hell, what a fool.' She washed her face and looked in the mirror. 'Good idea to keep your mouth shut,' she said.

***

Hank sat quietly at the table. He looked around the stillness of the kitchen and saw the narrow sunlight that came in through the old windows and lit up all the room. There was his wife, but by now he did not know whether he saw her or any of the thousand visions of her he had remade over and over in his mind. Killing her now was vivid and

169

fleeting, just as the moment had been and however it had really been he felt, as he always felt, its intimacy somehow in his flesh. I could have turned away and shut the kitchen door. He thought it again as he always thought it. He thought, I could have got into the car; I could have driven away. But it was irresistible; such intimacy it had been, to join her in that moment of loss and complicity and leap into her across the room. He felt it again. He tried to think of her eyes, her face, but all of that had gone and there was only the feeling of her nakedness in the light of the window. How can I tell, and for a few blank seconds he had forgotten Virginia's name, how can I tell Virginia this? I never shall, he thought. This is something for me, a bit of old loving from another life.

***

Then they sat on the lawn at the back of the house.

'I thought that we were going out,' said Virginia, not knowing what to make of him.

'Yes, I know,' said Hank, 'but this is fine, isn't it. You don't really want to go out do you?' He stretched in his plastic chair and folded his hands in his lap.

'Am I going to watch you fall asleep?'

'No, no, I promise,' he said and closed his eyes.

They sat in the shadow cast by the house. Going up the slope, away from them, was sixty feet of lawn, dark green, sunlit.

'The lawn's nice,' said Virginia, feeling clumsy with him.

'Hundreds of years old,' said Hank, without opening his eyes.

'Who does the veg garden?'

'I do.'

'Oh yes?'

'I like a bit of gardening.' He opened his eyes. 'Do you garden?' he asked, sounding hopeful.

'If you like,' said Virginia, ready to do anything at all. I'll do what Harry said, she thought. 'Come on, get up and walk me round it; tell me the names of all the things.'

'What, here are the carrots, here are the onions, here are the beans?'

'Don't get clever pal,' she said and pulled a face at him.

'You'll stay like that if you're not careful.' He spoke softly, half way into being asleep.

Virginia stood up and walked across the lawn, out of the shadow, and felt the sun on her back. There was a path of trodden earth through the vegetables. Everything was in lines, weeded, tied up, everything growing away with all its regimented might. She thought of Dan throwing the wildflower seeds up, scattering, into the air. She heard Hank calling her and she looked round, squinting into the sun. He was standing, holding up her bag and pointing at it.

'Your phone,' he shouted.

'Answer it.'

As she walked back to him she could see him fumbling to open the metal catch. Then he stopped and shrugged.

'Ring them back,' he said.

She kissed him. 'God you're lovely,' she said and kissed him again. 'Made you smile,' she said. She sat down with the bag on her lap and fiddled with the phone. 'Don't know who that is,' she said and fiddled again. She looked up at Hank. 'It's Sarah, she's in the car park at work.' She sat and listened, 'Oh sweetheart, don't,' and then she gave her directions to the farm and rang off. 'It's okay isn't it?' she said to Hank.

'Have I met this one?'

'No, I don't think so.'

'And this will make up the entire Asylum set will it? I've told you about pulling faces.'

***

'Do you mind,' Sarah asked, 'you know, about me and Dan?'

Virginia shook her head. 'I would have done at the time I suppose, but not now.'

'Should I go?' said Hank.

171

Sarah looked up at him with her face full of tears and shook her head. 'I'm really sorry. You don't know me at all and look what I'm doing in front of you.'

Hank smiled. 'You have a jolly good cry if you want. It always does me a world of good.'

He made her laugh and made her cry. Then she got her breath back. 'Anyway,' she said, 'that's the lot, that's what's wrong with me.'

'Dan's died, and Richard's run off with a barmaid,' said Hank, heartlessly.

'Hey you,' said Virginia.

'Two giant strokes of luck if you ask me.'

'Yes, you should go,' said Virginia. 'Go on, bugger off and make some tea.'

He took no notice. 'Were either of them a single bit of good to you? Were they? Pair of tossers, if you ask me.' They stared at him. 'Were they ever going to stay with you through thick and thin; were they ever going to be a good father for someone; were they going to worry about making you happy; well, were they?'

'They were a laugh, said Sarah, 'they…'

'Rubbish,' said Hank, derisively. 'I've met mass murderers who were a bloody scream, but I'd still have had them topped. I'll tell you what you should do,' he waved Virginia silent, 'you should find a nice farmer, a nice, simple country boy and have a house full of kids and a dog and a pony.' He fell silent and watched Virginia. 'That's what Virginia's going to do,' he said, staring at her.

'Now I really do want you to bugger off and make some tea,' said Virginia.

'Are you?' said Sarah, picking up a smile from somewhere.

'He won't,' said Virginia. She made an angry, flat face for Hank.

They made him get up to make tea.

'Do you want a real tea,' he asked them, still angry himself.

'Don't be angry,' Virginia said, trying to show him how sorry she was.

'With cake and sandwiches and so on? Yes, I can see that you do.'

172

'Is that really what you're going to do?' Sarah asked, as soon as Hank had gone.

'I don't want to talk about this,' said Virginia.

'You've left it a bit late haven't you?'

'What?'

'To have babies.'

'Oh thanks. What a wonderful thing to say.'

'Well, haven't you?'

'Not if I get pregnant within the next couple of weeks. That should just about do it. You'll have to be going soon, I expect. And in any case I only invited you here in the old chap's recovery time. Unless you'd like to watch of course? Nosy cow.'

Sarah laughed, a dirty shout of a laugh. 'Oh I am glad I phoned. Oh sod Richard then, sod him,' and she laughed again.

Chapter 31

When she had kissed him and cried and called him sweetie and held his arm she had set all of it running and it came at him again and again. At first in sickly, lucid, half sleep and then between the words of his reading and then into the noise of the tractor and the football on the television and the mouthfuls of his dinner eaten alone at the kitchen table. Seeing the upstretched arm of the photographer and the light slashing into the darkened window of the turning prison van. When he first came out he would stand at George's bar and blink at the television set, his glass frozen in his hand or find himself driving slowly in the middle lane. When his cousin Charley had picked him up from the prison, 'You drive,' he had said. Charley had a massive car that soared and Charley had talked him into it and then onto the motorway, forgetting the prison for an hour in the outside lane as if he had never been away. He was thinking, now, about that and staring at his newspaper and sipping beer, one thing leading him onto another as it had done in the prison until he learned to think about today and only write down in his letters what he would do, what he would plan and then seal up the wishing and send it away. He let himself think ahead a couple of days to his canteen on Friday and sometimes to dates he had, two weeks, no more than that, firm dates in official print: a visit and getting his C Cat, town visit, his D. I miss that, getting my canteen on Friday. The new things in their wrappers: deodorant and soap, a couple of bananas, chocolate. He kept it all in the plastic bag it came in so that he could rummage through a jumble of things. When he set it

174

out on his shelf or on his blanket it was a forlorn workhouse
Christmas. Once, he had swept it all away and stamped it in rage into
the floor of his cell. 'Silly cunt,' Taff had said in the morning and made
him laugh.

He wished that he could talk to Taff now. 'I don't fuckin care.'
That's what Taff said. 'I don't give a fuck man. Fuck the lot of them.
Yeah, well, fuck it.' Speaking quietly, shrugging and turning away and
into himself so that Hank, who never shouted through his window,
would get up in the night and stand on his chair and shout for Taff
through the tiny casement, trying to twist his voice in Taff's direction.
'What the fuck do you want. Of course I'm fuckin all right. What are
you fuckin on about. Wake me up again and you'll get a fuckin slap in
the morning you fuckin cretin.' Nobody could call you a fucking cretin
like Taff could through his tight-lipped Glamorganshire teeth.

Must tell him about Virginia, must do. They had sat on Taff's bed
watching a cops and robbers series on the tiny television that filled
Taff's cell. 'I'd tell her everything,' Taff said, pointing at Virginia. 'You
ever seen a detective looking like her in real life? Course you fuckin
haven't. I'd just tell her everything. I'd make fuckin stuff up just to
please her. I fuckin would. What a fuckin babe.'

'Say fucking babe again Taff. Go on say it in Welsh.' Hank was
laughing again, now, remembering.

'She fuckin is a fuckin babe, you posh cunt.'

He thought about Taff having a wank for Virginia. 'What a fuckin
babe.' I can't tell her that can I? How would I say that to her? He
turned away from the thought, laughing, and the sound of his laugh
brought him up short. I was past all of this. I dropped all of this
behind me and now here we are again in and out of the obsessive talk
in those tiny rooms. He told his army stories about chasing Arabs
around the desert and the guy from the Foreign Legion got onto Chad
and guys being dragged behind jeeps for not cleaning their rifles.
People were comparing stab wounds and Adrian would show how the
knife went upwards into his lung, 'never felt it, I never,' and his lung
went down and never came up.

'I was on the street when I was twelve,' Taff said. 'There was this girl, she was a prostitute, yeah, I was twelve and she took me under her wing. When you live like that there's a bond, really close, like a family. You say to each other, "You don't want to go with him. You want to watch him you do, he's a right bastard." Fourteen she was, Hank, and she was my big sister. When you live on the street. When you live on the street. I said to her, right, would she give me some of her blood and I got this syringe and filled up the barrel of it with her blood. She had everything man, she was dying of everything. This bastard met me at the station, right, dirty bastard was going to take me home and go through the fuckin card with me, really make a fuckin mess of me, fuckin right up for it he was. In the station man I just stabbed him with the syringe, on fuckin tiptoe man to reach him, cunt thought I was going to snog him or something, right deep into his neck, two handed, squeezed her rotten dirty blood into his neck. Fucked him man.' Taking Hank's breath away. 'Think I'm a fuckin nutter now don't you?' Taff smiled at Hank and slipped away behind the smile.

I have to do this all over again, thought Hank. There was no one left in the pub. Outside it was sunny and the door was wedged open so that the intermittent noise of the road came into them. George stood across the table from him; he had a white apron creased tightly around the barrel of his torso. 'Just let me clear this lot away and we'll have a drink.' He walked backwards and forwards picking up the mess of someone's meal. Level with Hank again with a pile of dishes held tight against his front, 'I thought you'd have a lot on,' he said, 'this time of year.'

Hank picked up his newspaper and started to read. 'You'd think so wouldn't you,' he said, without looking up, 'but I haven't.' he sat and read the paper, read it without choosing, read the lot of it just as it came up on the page. When George came back with two pints of beer Hank said, 'What a life,' and laughed and looked up over his glasses at him.

George sat with him sipping beer and watching him read. 'I bloody envy you,' he said.

'Oh yes,' said Hank.

'You've had a really adventurous life haven't you?' George was looking around, it looked shiny and polished in the dusty afternoon sunshine. There was the piled mess on the bar, waiting for him.

Hank put down his paper and looked with him, saw what he saw. 'It's been wretched,' he said. 'Really it has, wretched.'

'Thought I'd travel and have lurid sexual adventures,' said George.

'Good idea, have a couple for me,' said Hank and looked at the newspaper again.

'I'm serious you know.'

'Good. It's a good idea. Good. Go and do it.'

'Come with me.'

Hank banged the paper down. 'You what?'

'Not for ever. Just for a few months.'

'Me? I don't want that George. All I'm ever going to do is stay here.' Hank leaned forward and covered George's hand with his own and felt George start with surprise at his touch. Then, because they were there in his head, he said: 'My friends in the jail, guys doing life, they're the ones I listen to now. I see what they see. They talk about going fishing and being able to keep a dog, doing a bit of cooking. Nothing fancy George. You want to watch out for the fancy stuff.'

George got up and closed the doors, shot the bolts and turned the deadlock. 'Still know people inside then do you? You never say.'

'One or two.'

George went behind the bar and started on the washing up. Hank watched him, read a bit more of the paper and watched him again. The room was silent, empty chairs and stillness and the sunlight on the carpet. Half past four nearly and Hank thought about bang-up: an hour and a half while the screws counted and had their tea. For God's sake don't start that again, he thought. Even Taff was out of that now in his Cat D. Open Prison, it made him smile. Put a foot wrong and see how open any of it would be.

'I'll give you a hand shall I George?'

'No, it's okay.'

Chapter 32

Richard and Sadie were sitting in faded deck chairs on the first terrace of lawn in Richard's enormous garden.

'I've been knocking on that door like someone demented,' said Virginia. She could see the shapes of them shifting around, trying to turn to see her. She walked across the lawn and faced them. They were both naked except for their sunglasses.

'I'm not talking to you,' said Richard, 'unless you take off all your clothes.'

'Yeah,' said Sadie.

Virginia stared at her. 'Terrific tits,' she said.

'Yeah,' said Sadie.

'Shame about your friend.'

'He's the father of my children and the man I adore,' said Sadie.

'That'll be nice for you,' said Virginia. She sat down on the grass and leaned back on her elbows. She was wearing a cotton dress that covered her legs. She squinted in the sunlight and looked across the valley. 'You're not in jail then?'

'Nope, I'm in the nude.'

'How come?' She spoke without looking at him, trying to find Barton and then the church and then her mother's house across the bright valley. She heard him say:

'Well, it was a sunny day and Sadie was out here sunbathing and I thought…'

'No,' said Virginia, resenting the casual smile in his face. 'I want to know about this, Richard.'

'Oh be serious Virginia, there's nothing to be upset about. I hadn't done anything wrong, not really. They could see that I was worried about Dan's pictures. I mean, the hi-fi and the video were untouched so I wasn't an uncouth burglar was I?'

'What about Fatso,' said Virginia and enjoyed the sudden malice that she felt for all of them.

'Same went for him,' said Richard in the same careless way. 'They all knew him anyway, the cops. It all got quite matey after a while.'

'Sadie made it sound like a real problem when you sent her round in the dead of night to warn me.'

'It was,' said Sadie, slowly, as if she were getting ready for a row. 'For a few days, Virginia, it was.'

Virginia saw herself sitting on a lawn with naked people. She crossed her legs at the ankle and then, with her toe, pushed off one of her espadrilles. She let them sit quietly for a while and thought about what to say.

'And nothing else was mentioned was it?'

'Such as?' said Richard.

'My pictures for instance; your forgeries for instance.' I'm having a quarrel here, she thought. 'We're having a row aren't we? How have we managed that?'

'Now that you know Sadie you'll be having lots of rows,' said Richard. 'I've had a lifetime's supply in two weeks.'

'What did he say?'

'What do you mean?'

'Graham. What did fat Graham say to persuade you?'

'Oh that.'

'That.'

'He made me think of all Dan's pictures lying there in that empty house, holding their breath, wondering who was going to come along.'

'Graham said that?'

'Yes, yes he did. Why not?'

179

'Go on.'

'I thought about it.'

'You thought about it did you?'

'I thought about it and I saw them being picked over by some scrubbed up office boy. Somebody from Social Services or, I don't know, the Coroner's Office.'

'So, you had a few drinks.'

'Don't be snotty.'

'Got pissed and burgled the place. What did Graham do?'

'He stood outside.'

'While you broke in.'

'And watched the van. What do you mean, broke in?'

'Have you got a key?'

'Had one for a while.'

'You stole it out of his stuff at the hospital, didn't you?'

'Me?'

'You little rat.'

'Graham shat himself actually.'

'What?'

'He'd been thinking of a few paintings. He'd no idea, none at all. There's so much stuff, a houseful.'

'I know.'

'Good stuff.'

'I suppose it is. But, Richard, honestly, who cares, who gives a toss.'

'Do you want a drink?' said Sadie.

'I'll make it,' Virginia said.

'No, you're all right.' Sadie was struggling to get out of the deck chair, one arm across her breasts to stop the wobbling. Virginia laughed out and turned her head so that she did not miss any of it. Sadie rolled out onto her hands and knees and then stood up straight and brushed herself down with the palms of her hands.

'Can I come and watch you quivering around the kitchen?' asked Virginia.

In the kitchen Sadie said: 'Pass me that apron will you? Kitchens always make me feel a bit vulnerable when I've got all me bits out.'

'Have you seen anything of Graham?'

'No we bloody well haven't,' said Sadie. 'I mean, obviously I haven't have I, what with one thing and another? And Richard,' she shook her head, 'don't mention him to Richard.'

'I thought he sounded a bit cool.'

'Cool? Not half. He reckons Graham's a manipulative greedy gobshite.'

'No, he's not,' said Virginia. She paused, 'Is he?'

'He'll stand watching,' said Sadie. She smiled and Virginia thought, I'll give him a ring. She thought about how he had danced with her and waited, gently, until she had stopped crying.

'How's the big feller?' said Sadie. 'Never mind smiling at me, have you jumped him yet?'

'Hank?' said Virginia. 'No, no I haven't jumped him yet.'

'What a bloody carry-on,' said Sadie.

'He's not that sort of a man,' said Virginia, quietly.

'Oh yeah?' Sadie's voice narrowed into a sneer. She turned away to pick up the kettle and Virginia leaned forward, reached out and gave her a smart slap on her bare bum.

'You cow,' said Sadie, laughing, wriggling away.

'You have to wait for Hank,' said Virginia.

'I wouldn't.'

'Yes you would; anyone would.'

'Christ, he's only a feller. You'll have to manage him better than this. This bugger I've got here, I'm going to have to get him trained.'

I could never manage anybody, thought Virginia. Dan turned me inside out. Did what he liked. Hank, she thought, he'll do the same, I know he will. And she wanted him to. When he came into Graham's pub, when she saw him standing on his own at some theatre bar, she wanted to stand by him, close to him, so that by leaning just slightly, just shifting her weight to the other foot, she could feel the weight of his body. And then one day she would feel his hand pressing against the very bottom of her spine and she would turn to face him.

'You do know how soft you look?' said Sadie.

'I don't care,' said Virginia, not caring at all and smiling at the pleasure of it. 'Why him though?' she said, bemused.

'What do you mean?' said Sadie.

'Well,' said Virginia, 'I mean, why him? Look at him, Farmer Giles for God's sake?'

Sadie put down the tea tray, rattling the cups and saucers in anger. 'Look at him, look at him?' she said, 'What are you talking about, look at him? He's a great big strapping blond feller with blue eyes, built like a brick shithouse. Christ, I'll have him if you don't want him. And he's rich. He's a bloody landowner, got the accent and everything.' She picked up the tray, 'I like big fellers,' she said, a faraway look in her eye.

'Richard's not big,' said Virginia, feeling a bit tentative.

'Yeah, well,' said Sadie, smiling again, 'I like little fellers an' all.' She picked up the tray again. 'Come on, tea's up.'

'Listen Sadie,' Virginia said, 'I've got a real problem with these pictures.'

'What pictures?'

'Don't you know? Haven't you been listening?'

'Know what?' Then she turned and grinned, 'Oh of course, that's right, you were at it as well weren't you?'

Virginia couldn't smile back. 'I suppose so,' she said. 'but they were mine, you know. Of me. They were pictures of me.'

'Don't be daft Virginia. Look, go and talk to Richard about all this; he's the one who knows.'

She didn't want to talk to Richard. Richard was Dan's friend, more than that, much more, and she didn't want him raking it up again. It was hard enough for her, on her own, to keep Dan out of her mind. There he still was, rolling in when she was pouring tea or having a glass of whisky. He always came with that first sip, half taste, half scent as she got her nose in a glass. And flowers, she thought, bloody flowers

182

of all things. It was that garden she always thought of, that mist of colour, crammed into Dan's tiny garden.

She went back to Richard with her mind full of Dan. As she came up behind his deck chair she touched his head. He looked up at her and she brushed his hair across his forehead. 'I'm sorry you're upset about Dan,' she said.

'I shouldn't carry on about it should I?'

'Are you doing?'

'A bit.'

'Give it a little while and then he'll come back to you without being dead. He'll be normal again.'

'Who says that?'

She looked down into his face, almost kissed him. 'Harry, my friend Harry. He lives next door to my mother; he's a thousand years old and I suppose that all of his mates are dead so this is something that I'm taking his word on.' She sat down on the grass. 'Is everything okay, you know, with the cops and everything?'

'There's no problem, really there isn't.'

'Even these forgeries of yours?'

'I don't think anybody knows what they are, not yet. To tell you the truth I panicked a bit when I told Sadie about it.'

'She claims not to know.'

'Ancient code of the scousers isn't it?' He smiled at her. 'I'll tell you what though, Ginny, we could have made a fortune. We had a few Samuel Palmers done, etchings you know, dead easy to do, black and white sketches with a nice ink wash. Not Dan's cup of tea at all, all those lowering starlit nights, but easy, dead easy. I was going to get him to do some Constables.'

'Did you sell any of this stuff?'

'Never got round to it, which is why we're in the clear.' His voice fell. 'He never really had his heart in it, Ginny. I thought it would appeal to him, you know, a bit of mischief.'

'Is that what you were trying to do?'

183

'He wouldn't have it. Of course he wouldn't, I was only a pest in the end.'

'Well, you just put that to one side, the way it all ended up, just edit that out and have the other bits.'

'Is that what you're doing?'

'Not really.'

'He'd have been good at the Constables.'

'Would he?'

'Oh yes, the oil sketches, very easy to do, very loose, use a big brush. There's nothing difficult about copying. A nice twelve by nine sketch could get maybe three or four grand at auction. Turner, he's another good one, Cecil Collins, John Piper, it's endless.'

'Yeah well, you can forget it pal,' said Sadie. She knelt down awkwardly, keeping the tea tray level.

'This looks good,' said Virginia, surprised. And then, thinking again of Harry, she smiled at the cups and saucers, milk jug, biscuits on a plate. There was even a cloth.

'I'm being gentrified,' said Sadie.

She sat with them with her old life, but could not believe herself to be sitting in the sunlight on Richard's lawn. There, instead, is Hank, still in jail, waiting for her to take him out of it.

Chapter 33

Then he had followed her out of the pub and had started talking to her about being on the telly. She had turned his heart over, just like that. It had taken him back to the shock of all that romantic talk, all the faith in it, the respect that Taff and Adrian had when Big Larry talked about his wife. My Missis, he called her and just the thought of her caught Larry on the raw, you could see him lost in her like a child and so Hank had told Larry about killing Paula. 'Fuckin hell,' Larry had said. 'Fuckin hell mate.'

I'll go and look Larry up, thought Hank, he only lives in Northampton. This is what happens to you when you follow women out of pubs to catch them on their own and be shy and clumsy with desire again. Larry had put his arm on Hank's shoulder and, even for Hank, Larry had seemed big. He had brought Hank's head up.

'My Missis would never do that. I told her, when I came in here, when they sat me down for nine years, I said she could piss off if she wanted to, but she wouldn't have it. So, I said it was ridiculous and if she was getting, you know, her womanly urges, it was all right by me whatever she did. Nah, she said, she didn't reckon that. So she keeps coming to see me and she keeps on bringing my kids, my little girls. They're not little now. When I get out they'll be women won't they? Little women. What am I going to do, they'll think I'm a right old sod. I won't know what to do will I? I don't know what to do with kids, with girls. Know what they've done? They've kept all my Christmas presents and all my birthday presents, all the Christmases and birthdays that I've missed, they're all waiting for me to open them when I get out. My Missis she started them off with that when they were babies and they've kept it up. They have. They go out and buy my presents and wrap them up with everybody else's stuff under the tree and then they put them away for me to open later. Silly cow, my wife.

Visits, I really get it on visits. They sit and weigh me up, the three of them. They see how I look and then it's, why don't I look better? Don't get a belly dad, look after your skin, can't I get a better haircut? I had me head shaved last year, a number one. My missis went apeshit and my eldest cried. She saw it then you see, saw she had a convict for a dad. I borrowed a hat, baseball cap, for the next few times I saw them. They don't give me a minute's peace, I'm telling you. Always writing letters: make sure I go down the gym, no smoking, keep up my Open University. Bloody OU, that's a laugh. I only started it to encourage them with their homework, now I'm bloody stuck with it aren't I? And drugs, don't take drugs, that's their mother that is, setting them onto me. They're bloody clever my girls; you wanna see the GCSEs my eldest got last summer. If I don't pass my OU I'm gonna look a right dick. I'm not really up to it, but I've got to do it now haven't I?'

He pulled Hank into his family and Hank told him about his own daughter.

'Yeah, that's what it's like,' Larry said. 'Women are fuckin marvellous aren't they? You got a bit of a renegade with your wife, what else could you do? You did fuckin right Hank. Should never have phoned the Old Bill. Should've said a burglar did it.' Just like that, Big Larry telling him that he had done the right thing.

Virginia had touched his face. When she held his hands and kissed him, like a slap to wake you up from a dream, it had set his wife whirling in his head. I remember, I remember feeling like this. She kissed him and he remembered his wife's flesh, her wide eyed, open face, her teeth behind her opening lips.

'They make me remember it', Adrian had said. 'Every fucking time that fucking psychologist talks to me she's making me go through it and go through it again. Do I feel remorse she wants to know? The silly cow, what does she expect me to say? I wish I hadn't done it, obvious I do. Not what she means though is it? She wants me to go off on one about how evil a thing it was, how evil I am. Oh the poor man I killed. Poor my arse, he was a nasty vicious scumbag. So, I give her all that don't I? Course I do. Not like this poor cunt.' He pointed at Hank.

'What?' said Hank.

Adrian was laughing. 'I'm gonna watch him and I'm gonna do what he does. Like in Drama, so I can put a fuckin good act on next time I see the psychologist.'

Nobody makes me remember, thought Hank. Adrian's ugly face grinned, eyes slitted in a scowl of laughter. I remember Paula. He thought it sitting in Taff's cell watching the six o'clock news with Adrian leaning in the doorway with his squashed troll's face, mocking his accent as he always did. He thought it again, now, his heart beating in his throat as he put his hand on Paula's shoulder and she turned to him, when she had loved him, sipped her whisky and turned, stepped closer to him and let him touch her. Her eye curved, the line of it a sombre shadow in her flesh and then she licked her lips, sticky with colour, a soft ripping apart and the tip of her tongue touching and vanishing.

Taff said: 'When they locked me up I didn't speak. I didn't speak for nearly three years. What was that then? I don't know. When I look now and say, "I didn't speak for three years," I don't know what to make of it. I don't. How did I do it? It wasn't an effort, it was just never in my mind to speak. Did I speak to myself? I wonder if I did? Never thought of that before. Other people said things, that's right, they did. I remember that. I was only a kid. I was a savage. Worse than that; worse than that, Stab a guy up? Okay, two bags. See it all the time. See it, do it. Like a little animal. When an animal eats another animal, I've seen it on telly, it doesn't care if it's dead or not it just eats it. See a

187

lion with something, doesn't occur to the lion does it? Just tears into its dinner. Like that. That's what I mean. That's what I was like. What you've done mate, I'm telling you, it's fuckin nothing.'

Chapter 34

'They sound nice,' said Hank.

'Nice isn't the word for them,' said Virginia, 'They've driven each other potty. Don't laugh, it's true. There they are sitting naked on the lawn with the Earl Grey and the Spode tea set. You can meet them in the winter when they're dressed. I wouldn't trust any man in a confrontation with Sadie's bosom.'

'I'm beyond bosoms,' said Hank.

'Oh no you're not,' said Virginia. She squeezed his hand and as they walked she swung his arm as though she were twelve years old. 'Show me this village of yours,' she said, 'I only know your house and the pub.'

'And the church. What more do you need.'

'Come on,' she said, insisting, and she pulled him along, past the pub and down the shady street. They waited for a string of cars and crossed the road into the sunshine. There was a triangular green and two large chestnut trees.

'That's the other pub,' said Hank and pointed to an older, lower building of crumbling stone with heavy ornate lintels. 'It's pretty old, I suppose; all this bit of the village is. You can see where people have slated rather than renew the thatch. Can't blame them can you, it's a terribly dear do, thatch. It's all a bit small scale and pushed up together round here I always think. Still, people seem to like it.'

'It's lovely,' said Virginia.

'If you like this sort of thing.' They will all see me, he thought, holding hands with this woman. They will all see another woman and think that: another woman. It came upon him like a sudden shiver of fever. He felt as he had in the army on a street where someone might have wanted to shoot him, when his skin would crawl against his shirt. When everyone knows the inside of you, he thought, and you have to account for your nakedness. 'I went to school here,' he said.

'I know,' said Virginia. She swung his hand again and he could feel her happiness pulling at his arm and remembered the happiness of running across the black tarmacked yard to his mother and the happiness of the space he made by running quickly and then being in the crowd of tall women in amongst their skirts and the smaller children and the push-chairs and school bags. Standing close to his mother who would only rest her hand on his shoulder exactly as he wished her to. All of them would know now that there was another woman, another, and there in their minds, alongside, would be Paula lying naked, with her neck broken, on the kitchen floor.

'Tell me about all this,' said Virginia.

'It's only what you can see,' he said.

There was no pavement and the grassy verge at the roadside was uneven and awkward underfoot. They were out of the village now and across the road was an open field where huge trees grew like specimens in a park and a gang of black and white cows lay huddled. They were walking beside a hawthorn hedge that bristled with green light. 'Down here,' Hank said and they stepped around the corner of the hedge and onto a rough bridleway, tractor rutted. Underfoot, loose chippings, bits of broken brick and stones were trodden in. The middle tongue of grass bent around a far corner and out of sight. There were bigger trees in the hedge now and deep drainage ditches either side. On their right there was a wood, a shaded mass of thick darkening green, layer on layer of it falling back into its own shadows. Hank turned to go into the trees where tall stems of grass, bent over a softer, narrower path. Virginia could see, this way and that, glimpses of sunlight floating in the shadows, picking out the still, undulating green.

He went ahead of her and she stopped so that she could watch him walk. He said something, but she was too far away to make it out. Then he ran one or two steps and was gone. She ran herself and felt the grass whipping at her legs like a child feels it.

There was a steep bank down to a thin strip of metalled road. Beyond the road a thin, wire, cattle fence and more of the pasture that looked like parkland with its massive, abandoned trees. Hank stood on the road staring up at her. 'Two cars a month,' he said and laughed. She ran down to him, awkward on the grassy slope, digging in her heels, feeling the air for balance and stepped solidly, relieved, onto the road. 'Come on,' he said, briskly, and she had to skip after him before she caught his pace.

'Hold on,' she had hold of his arm, 'where are we going?'

'Doing the tour,' he said, 'first the charming old village, then the leafy wood and that's your lot.'

'You've made me run through it all. I've hardly seen a thing.' She looked at him, held onto him and made him stop. 'Are you angry?'

'Not very,' he said.

She could feel him pulling away, wanting to be off. She held onto him, pulled back with all her strength so that he had to step towards her.

'Stop it,' he said. His voice made her panic. She pulled him more, three, four steps until she felt the strength go out of him and he let her walk him away, let her pull him where she wanted to.

'Stop it will you, Virginia. You can't just pull me about like this.'

'Yes,' she said, 'yes I can.' She stopped and they stood still.

It was as if he were accusing her. 'You can't come and take me over like this,' he said.

'You started it.'

'Don't say childish things like that.'

'You did,' she said, softly, 'you started it. You followed me around and now I love you.'

'Be quiet,' he said.

'Fuck you,' she said. 'Fuck you.'

191

Hank shook his head, 'Be quiet Virginia, don't do this, you're making me afraid.'

'Afraid, why are you afraid?' With each word she tugged at his arm.

'I don't know, but that's how it feels. I don't know why it should,' I'm lying, he thought, 'but it does.'

'I'm not going Hank. I'm not. I'm just going to stay and wait till you're okay.'

'You're going to wait till I'm okay are you?'

'Yes.'

'Well, I don't think I'm going to be.'

'Pretend to be.'

'What?'

'Pretend to be, just act okay. Ask yourself what an okay person would do and do that. Then say to yourself what would some ordinary son of a bitch who hadn't murdered his wife think and then think that and then feel that and do it a few times over and over so that you get it right and you can make yourself o-fucking-kay. And while you're doing that I can have you and feed you all the lines you need. And what makes you so fucking special, you cunt.' And she stepped up and tried to hit him, a lovely swinging haymaker that he swayed away from so that she lost her balance and staggered a step and a half into the slope. She sat down on the grass. 'Stay there,' she said. 'Don't you walk off, stay there.'

He sat on the grassy bank, just below her, so that his feet were on the black tarmac of the narrow road. He said: 'Love me do you?'

'Not from choice,' said Virginia and heard herself sounding nasty and silly all at once.

'Why's that?'

'Because I didn't choose it.' I bet I did though, she thought to herself.

'No, not the choice bit,' said Hank, still not looking at her, still gazing at the air, 'the other, the love.'

'How about you?' said Virginia not wanting to say it again, feeling stupid enough saying it at all.

'No,' he said, 'no I don't. I'm not having any more love.'

She pushed belief away. I'm not having that, she thought. She felt sick and then she heard herself being Lauren Bacall. She spoke slowly, 'You damn well will,' she said.

They sat on the grass for a while, saying nothing again. Virginia had her chin on her knees. She kept her eyes on Hank; he was staring away from her as though the fields and specimen trees had him fascinated.

'It's damp,' said Virginia. She stood up. 'I'm cold and damp from this grass.' She bent down and kissed the top of his head, then she took hold of his arm and pretended that she could lift him to his feet and he pretended that she could take his weight. He was on his feet and let her pull him towards her. She stood close up to him, still holding his arm. 'You're so big,' she said and leaned against him.

'I'm not like you,' he said, 'not a bit. I know that I plod around a bit, but I know where I am.'

'No you don't,' said Virginia.

'I don't go blundering about mislaying the truth like some self-deluding kid.'

'Oh don't start all this truth nonsense with me. How happy is truth going to make you, whatever truth might be?'

He wanted to tell her about Paula lying naked on the kitchen floor.

'You're a liar then?' he said.

'You know where you are with a good lie,' Virginia told him and she smiled. 'It's something you can shape and work on a lie is. You can make it just right and fit it in nicely to what you want it to do.' She stopped herself, not really wanting to have said this.

'And what's that?' said Hank.

'To make you happy,' she said. She stopped herself again and they walked on. 'Now we're into the truth, okay? I get round to it every now and again.' She pulled his arm and smiled up into his unsmiling face. 'I don't avoid it deliberately, you know. It's there to be used.'

'But you need to be cautious with it?' Hank said.

'This isn't a seminar, Hank, there's no need for cleverness.'

'What should I be then, stupid?'

193

'You should be quiet.'

'Thank you.'

'And accept the illusion.'

'I don't have illusions. I have the farmyard and the accounts. I wring the chickens' necks and shoot the old dog and telephone the knacker's man and the slaughterhouse.' And Paula, he thought. His head was down; he spread his arms and turned the palms of his hands upwards showing her the strong flesh of his fingers, the dark, thick strength in his palms. He looked up and saw her calm face, how confident she was of him.

'You've mixed me up,' said Virginia.

'Have I? Good, I hope you like it. You'll have to work it out for yourself.'

'Oh,' she said, 'shall I? I'll make up something for you and you'll just have to have what I give you, won't you?'

Chapter 35

That night they lay in bed together drinking whisky and watching more football on television.

'Are you sure that you like football?' Hank asked.

'I like the Arsenal,' she said.

He turned his head so that he could stare at her. 'Arsenal,' he said, 'you like Arsenal?'

'Why shouldn't I?'

'You should support Northampton Town.'

'Why should I when Arsenal are just around the corner from me.'

'Are they? You never said.'

'What did you think I did in London? I live there. I only come up here for deaths and to make myself miserable. I could have done the play from London. I wish I bloody well had, then I wouldn't have found Dan the way he was.'

'Where do you live then.' He was abrupt, sounded as though he didn't believe her and didn't want this bigger life she had thrown casually at him.

'Told you, just near to the Arsenal, in a house.' She sipped her whisky and pretended to concentrate on the television.

'A house?'

'Yes, a house. Where did you think I'd live,' she said, managing to sound annoyed and she pointed at the screen as if to say, don't interrupt.

'When are you going back?'

'When the phone rings, I suppose,' as if only half listening.

She knew he was staring at her. 'What do you mean?'

'When my agent finds something for me.'

'And will he?'

'Any time now,' she said, very matter of fact.

'Are you really going back?'

'Why not?' she said. 'Dan's dead, I've sold mum's house, you don't love me,' she turned to him and shrugged, 'so sod it, I'll go back.'

'If you have to work in London you could commute from here.'

'What for if you don't love me?' she asked him, stony faced and false.

'A weekly commute would be less stressful,' he was starting to grumble.

She sighed, 'If I'm not loved there'd be no point.'

'Please your bloody self then,' he muttered.

'I shall,' she said, 'and mind your language.' She went back to the football.

Hank said: 'Did you come back up here so that you could take up with Dan again?'

'You sound as if you know him,' said Virginia.

'I'm getting to.'

'You wouldn't have liked each other.'

'Might have.'

'No, Dan would have seen how much I was in love with you and he would have turned nasty.' She said it with malice, matter-of-factly, so that he would be guilty and awkward in his buttoned up, asexual, blue pyjamas. 'Do you stay chained to Paula because you loved her?' Oh shit, she thought, that's done it. Why say that? Why say it? She kept her eyes fixed on the television.

'I thought that you would have gone after this afternoon,' said Hank, calmly.

'No, not me,' said Virginia. 'What brought all that on anyway.'

He nearly told her about Larry's wife. About listening to Larry going on about his wife. 'Being in the village. I could tell you the name of just about everybody who lives here and put the names into the right houses. I know who's related to whom; I know about marriages, births and deaths and everybody knows everything about me.'

'Do they know that I'm in bed with you?'

'Yes, they know that.'

'And they all knew Paula?

'They knew her a bit. We didn't live here.'

'You sod, you could have said. I've been imagining that it all happened in this kitchen, the kitchen in this house.'

'Well, it didn't.'

Virginia got out of bed and turned off the television. She got back into bed and pulled the duvet up to her chin. 'You don't want to talk about this do you?' she said.

'No I don't.'

'Well, I think you were right.'

'What?'

'I do, I think that you were right when you hit her. There was no other way you could have reacted.'

'Shut up will you?' said Hank. After a few seconds he turned out the light and lay down beside her. 'You don't have any clothes on,' he said.

'I know.'

'It was a bit of a shock when you got up just now. I thought that you would have a nightie or something.'

'You never look at me.'

'I can't do this Virginia.'

'What?'

'You know damn well.'

'It's not compulsory,' she said, trying to sound hurt.

'Isn't it?' Hank said. 'It's like being a kid again. That's prison, it makes a child of you; It takes away…' he stopped.

'What?' she said.

'Nothing,' said Hank, 'I'm sorry, I was just getting started on a bit of a rant there.'

'I've never heard you rant, sweetie. Go on, you have your rant if you want to. I might like it.' She whispered it to him gently, but he was too far from her.

'No you wouldn't. I should be over all this by now. Thought I was and now I've let you stir it all up again.'

'I'm glad,' she said.

'What do you have in your head,' Hank asked her. She felt him turn over, away from her. She reached out and touched him, feeling for his shoulder with the tips of her fingers. 'The big bright images for me, you know, the ones you go back to, they begin with seeing Paula smile at me at that damned kitchen window and then I go on through things from there.' He spoke softly, his lips against the pillow, muffling the words.

'Do you do that a lot?'

'I used to. Two years into my sentence I fell apart a bit. Then I was okay.'

'Why was that then? How did you get to be okay?' She wanted him to tell her and knew that if he did then he would have drawn her in and she would never be free of him. And then she thought, not like Dan and realised that she had always wanted to be free of Dan. Perhaps he wanted me to stay, all those times that I went away and the guilt of it caught her. No, she told herself, don't make up what wasn't there. She rubbed her hand on Hank's back as if she could rub the pain away.

'I think that it was the ordinariness of it, the prison, the tiny constricted routine of it all, that's what let me get myself back together again. The other guys as well; they were all in bigger shit than me, at least in B Cat they were, deep, deep shit. Not bad men, you know, not bad men at all.'

'Weren't they?' he could hardly hear her.

'Not as many as you might think.'

'What did they do?'

'They got on with it that's what they did. They did the next thing and then the thing after that. No whining. And they were a bit brisk

198

with me, I can tell you.' He turned to her, suddenly. 'We watched you on the telly, you know. A bit of a babe we reckoned.'

'Did you?' she said, pleased as a child.

'We did. I'll write to my pal Taff and tell him about having you here starkers.'

'Will you?' she said, more pleased than ever.

'He'd want to know.'

'What will you tell him?'

'He'll think I'm barmy.'

'Will he?'

'I know what he'll say, "Fuckin give her one why don't you" that's what he'll say.'

'Why don't you?' said Virginia. Hank didn't reply to her. He turned over again. 'I think you're making a bit of a song and dance about this Hank.' Still he didn't reply. 'Your mate Taff's got the right idea,' she said, softly.

Chapter 36

'This is a nice tea you're giving me.'

'Yes,' said Graham, 'I like tea; it's such a good idea isn't it, to slip in an extra meal?' He smiled at her, pleased with himself. 'It's a way of extending the eating day: fill up on cakes now and push back dinner to nine o'clock.' He bit the end off an eclair.

'Wipe your mouth,' said Virginia.

'And it's always the nicest things to eat. It's a treat meal, and it's innocent. Don't you think? How can anything be nasty at tea time?' He finished off the eclair.

Virginia sipped her tea. 'I've never been here before.' She looked around.

'It's new,' said Graham.

'I like the plants.'

'Full of snakes and spiders,' said Graham. 'Are you going to eat any of this?' He lifted the cake stand an inch or two nearer to Virginia.

'I'll have this chocolaty thing,' she said. 'It's very colonial this place, isn't it? Very Singapore and up the peninsula.'

'Are we meeting here in secret?' Graham asked.

'Sort of.'

'Bad as that is it?' He tried to look glum, but she could see that he didn't give a toss. He tried to be sympathetic with some bad news of his own: 'Sadie's packed in her job at the pub.'

'And the rest,' said Virginia, suddenly pleased.

'Sadly,' Graham shook his head. He picked up another eclair. 'I liked to watch her trying to deceive me.'

'I thought that was mine,' said Virginia. He bit off half of it. 'You've still got Sarah though?'

'I have, haven't I?' And he pushed the rest of the eclair into his smile.

I'll bet that you haven't, she thought, not for much longer anyway. 'Don't smile,' she said, 'don't sit there thinking God knows what and guzzling eclairs.' She took a very obvious good look at him. 'How do you do it?' she asked.

'Do what?' He drank some tea, leaned forward and turned the cake stand round, choosing.

'How do you get all this sex?'

'Do I?'

'You're up to your ears in it and to be frank, Graham, you're hardly a heart throb now are you?'

He picked up the other chocolate cake and smiled at it. 'I ask,' he said.

'Just like that?'

'Of course, just like that. I asked you didn't I?'

'I turned you down.'

'Most do.'

'You sod.'

'But many don't.' He swallowed some of the cake. 'It's just a question of taking a bit of stick.'

'You make it sound simple.'

'It is.' He put the rest of the cake into his mouth and licked his finger and thumb.

No it's not, she thought, I can't make myself make it simple. She said: 'How do you separate them out?'

'Separate what out?'

'The women, how do you keep them distinct?' She could see he was puzzled. 'You know, how do you deal with them one by one? Come on, you know what I mean.'

He pulled a face, shrugged. 'I don't know. I don't see what your problem is.'

'Don't they all shade into each other,' she was making herself angry, 'don't you think sometimes that you're with one and it's not, it's another one?'

'Oh yes, that.' He grinned. 'Calling Sadie Sarah for instance?'

'Yes,' Virginia scowled at him, not liking this at all. 'Yes, that for instance.'

'Can be difficult.' He nodded, conceding.

'Doesn't it worry you?'

'Only if they get angry.'

'What about you? Doesn't it worry you, you yourself.'

'Not really.' He put his hand on hers and stared at her until she looked back at him. 'What's the matter love?' he said. 'Why are you going on about this? You're upset aren't you?'

'Do you think that I'm going to tell an old shagger like you?'

She couldn't offend him. 'Tell me,' he said, 'come on, you're my pal.'

'I get Dan mixed up with Hank,' she made herself sound angry so that she could get the words out.

'So what?' he said, mildly.

'So what. Is that it? Is that all you've got to say?'

Graham shrugged, 'Well, yes. It's hardly unique is it, getting people mixed up?'

'Yes it is,' she felt silly as she said it, but she knew that he had missed her point. 'Yes, it is,' she said again, 'it is.'

'Love is it?' said Graham. Virginia kept her mouth shut. She could feel herself sulking. 'Don't worry,' said Graham, 'it'll wear off.'

'Stop fiddling with that bloody cake stand,' she said.

'It always does,' said Graham, keeping on at her. 'Dan will wear off because you're with this Hank chap and he's there and Dan's not, so Dan will fade out and the other chap will fade in.'

'I don't want that.'

'Said you did.'

She leaned forward over the table and spoke into her tea cup. 'Well, I don't. I don't want him to fade away, I want him gone, now. I don't want him walking around with me and Hank. I don't want to be loving him and loving Hank. I can't do it.'

'Don't be foolish,' said Graham. He leaned forward so that he could speak softly to her. 'Don't you think that Hank's got a headful of someone? We've all got someone: lovers, old pals, favourite dogs, fantasies. At our age we've all got a headful, you, me, Hank as well.'

'I suppose he has,' said Virginia. I'll tell him that, she thought, I'll tell him that about Paula. Then she thought that she wouldn't. 'The bloody paintings don't help,' she said.

'What paintings?' said Graham and then, alarmed, 'No don't tell me.' He sat back and put up his hands in self-defence. 'I've had a gutful of that bugger's paintings.'

'I'll tell you anyway,' she said, cheering up. And she told him about her roomful of paintings and her stack of drawings and how they were round the walls so that she could stand in the middle of the bare floor and knock herself about.

'Give them to the Art Gallery. From what I can see they don't have much in there. They'd snatch your hand off.'

'What, just like that?

'Go and do it now.'

'What, just go down there?'

'Why not? No, don't ask, I'm not going with you. I'm not, no bloody fear.'

***

'I had a talk with Graham,' she said to Hank.

'That's the fat one?'

They were standing at the bar. It was early evening and there were the same men she had seen when she had first stepped into the pub on her way home from rehearsing the play.

'Evening Gorgeous,' the grey haired man said to Hank.

'You do see what you've done, Virginia, don't you?' Hank said and he blushed.

'That's him,' said Virginia, 'yes, the big fat one. 'You'll like him. He's a very sensible man.' She paused and, as the thought struck her, she said, 'Not like you at all.'

'What?'

'No, you're like me aren't you?'

'I certainly am not.'

'Yes you are. You stand around paralysed; no idea what to do. Head full of this that and the other, forever tossing up the odds, going over and over stuff. You're just a bloody fool Hank. You want to spend a bit of time with Graham; he just gets on with what he wants and doesn't brood. Listen, if it worries you living here where they all know about you, well sod it, sell up and move in with me next to the Arsenal.'

'I don't own the farm.'

'You what?'

'No, it's my cousin's.'

'Well, I don't care about that. Listen,' she put her hand on his breast, 'I want you to come and see Dan's pictures.'

'Okay.' He smiled at her and covered her hand with his.

'Of me.'

***

They sat in Hank's car outside her mother's house.

'I want you to see them because they've been worrying me.'

'So, I'm looking at them for you. You don't care then if I get upset?'

'Don't mess me about Hank,' she looked at him, hard, turning in her seat to stare. 'You're taking the mick now aren't you? You are aren't you?'

'You'll never know.'

'Come on,' she said, 'come on we're going to start doing stuff.'

'Like Graham?'

'Yes, like Graham. We're going to do stuff. Stuff like happiness for instance. I've had enough of this.'

'Of what?'

'Of ferreting around inside. And you can stop it as well.' She was out of the car and slammed the door with all her might.

Hank got out himself. 'Will you stop doing that?'

'Come on,' she said.

She got him through the empty house, banging up the bare stairs. 'There they are, see.'

He stood in the middle of the room and turned, glancing at them, one after the other. 'You look lovely,' he said.

'Thanks,' she said, curtly.

'They're real pictures of you,' he was delighted, 'not some clever mucked about stuff. Your house will have to be big to take this lot.'

'What?' she said. 'What? You've missed the point of all this haven't you? I'm showing you this lot before I get rid of them.'

'What point?'

'I'm having a clear out.'

Hank shook his head, bemused. 'Okay, have a clear out,' he said.

'You have a clear out,' she was shouting at him, 'you have a bloody sodding clear out.'

He stood, tongue-tied.

'And if you can't, well, that doesn't matter either, just put a bloody act on can't you? I can show you how to bloody act.'

'This is all right,' he said, gently, 'what are you worrying about?' He turned round and round, looking. 'I like the muff,' he said.

'You like what?'

He pointed to the big picture of her groin. 'It is you, isn't it?'

'I didn't pose for it.' She turned away, pouting with embarrassment.

'You would say that, wouldn't you?' said Hank. 'Can I have it?' She turned back, but before she could spit something at him he went on, musing, as if he had been struck, quite suddenly, by a good idea. '"Oh yes, I thought it would be the best place for Virginia's muff, over the

205

mantelpiece. It sort of flickers in the firelight don't you think?"' He cracked into a laugh, 'Go on let me have it.'

She couldn't help herself. 'If this is what they teach you in that prison,' she was laughing, hands on hips, 'then you're not going anymore. Muff? What sort of talk is that? I'll give you muff,' she said and set him off laughing again.

Chapter 37

They parked outside her mother's house half on the narrow pavement so as not to block the street. Virginia stood fiddling with her keys and Hank stood up close to her trying to get into the lea of the wall and out of the rain. Then they were in the empty hollow of the house. Hank picked his wet shirt away from his skin and shivered.

'Take it off,' said Virginia, 'and I'll put it next to the oven to dry.' She pulled her sweater up over her head and ran her fingers through her hair, shook it back from her face. He held out the shirt for her to take. 'What's that?' she said, her voice rising with shock.

'What's what?' he said. She stepped up to him and put her hand over the scar. Hank put his hand over hers. 'Oh that's from donkey's years ago. Some chap shot me'

'Shot,' she said. 'You've been shot.'

'Years ago,' he said and gave her a smile, but she was crying. He put his arms around her. 'You don't half cry a lot,' he said.

'No I don't,' said Virginia. 'It's just everything. And now, on top of it all, you've been shot.'

'I was only a kid.'

'Who did it?' She snuffled up her tears.

'Oh some Arab lad. I was seconded, you know, the Middle East, with one of the Sultanate armies.

'Did it hurt?' she said.

He laughed at her. 'Of course it hurt.' And suddenly he remembered. 'We were in the street, waiting for a truck to pick us up.'

'Did they get him?' She was wide eyed.

'No, he vanished. I'm glad he did; wouldn't want him on my conscience.'

She kept her hand over the scar and kissed his chest. 'You're lovely,' she said.

'So you keep saying.'

'Lovely and pink,' and she kissed him again.

'Worth being shot,' he said.

She pushed away from him, opened the oven door and pressed the button that made the gas pop into flame. She took the shirt and draped it over the oven door.

'What do we have to do?' Hank asked.

'Oh, the Art Gallery people will do everything.'

'Here's your neighbour,' said Hank and pointed through the window at Harry. Harry was awkward not knowing, now that he was with them, what to make of the two of them together. Virginia didn't help him. If he wants to be nosy, she thought, then he can suffer a bit for it. She could see him wondering what to say about her tear-filled eyes and Hank stripped to the waist. She watched them. They shook hands. Hank patted his chest and said: 'I'm just drying off,' and nodded at his shirt.

'Caught you did it?' said Harry. 'It'll not last.'

'Hope not, we're harvesting. I don't want the contractors held up, it'll cost me a fortune.'

'No, it's clearing up all right,' said Harry. 'You're down Bedford way then?'

'Not quite Bedford,' said Hank. 'Getting on that way.'

Virginia had started up the stairs; the sound of her feet on the bare treads made them both turn.

'Have you seen the pictures?' Hank asked. 'They're damned good. Come and have a quick look now.' He saw Harry's reluctance and jollied him up. 'Come on.'

'Best not,' said Harry but he had taken two steps into the house.

'Virginia,' Hank shouted, 'I can't get Harry to come and have a look at the pictures.'

'Yes,' she called back, 'come and see.'

They went up the stairs, Harry slowing them down with his dot and carry. He paused twice on the stairs, straightened his back, blowing for breath then stretching to find the balance he needed to start himself off again. Hank waited for him. 'Would you like a push,' he said.

'No, I'm used to it.'

They could hear her banging around. 'I've just put the better ones out for you,' said Virginia when Harry came into the room. He looked at the pictures, turned from one to another, his face blank with the effort of taking them in.

'You don't mind all this then?' he said to Hank.

'It's not my world at all to tell you the truth,' said Hank and turned to move one of the paintings aside.

'By God,' said Harry, 'that's a nasty mark.'

'They shot him,' said Virginia.

'Who did?'

'Some Arabs.'

'Years ago,' said Hank, 'in the army.'

'What were you in then?' said Harry and he bent to look more closely at the white star of flesh.

'Anglians.' Hank twisted so that he could join in looking at his scar.

'I was in when it was the Northamptonshire Regiment; that's when it was the real army. When there was a war, a proper one. If it had been the bloody Jerries that had shot you you'd be dead now. They didn't bugger about. Lost half the battalion we did.' He stood up straight. 'Marvellous,' he said.

'What is?' Hank asked.

'These pictures. Makes you wonder how he did it.' He put his head close to Hank's in a parody of confidence. 'Did you know him, this painter chap?'

'Never met him, Harry.'

'Well, he was a right basket.'

209

'Oh Harry, don't start.' Virginia knew what was coming. She knew that Harry would make her feel a fool. I am a fool, she thought.

'People like that,' said Harry, 'they have to have a bit of a screw loose, if you see what I mean. Not right in the head.'

'It's always seemed so to me,' said Hank, delighted, smiling so that it hurt his face.

'By God, that's a good likeness.' It was a portrait of Virginia, staring, almost angry. 'It's you and your mother both.'

'Would you like it?'

'You sure it won't be missed?' His face lit and she could see how much he wanted it.

'They don't know what there is.'

'Better look slippy,' said Hank, bullying Harry into it before he could change his mind. 'Go and open the doors, look sharp.' He picked up the picture, a stretched, three by four canvas.

'Leave it back to me in your will,' said Virginia.

'Right, I shall.'

'Don't forget.'

'I shan't.'

They went after Hank. Virginia pushed past Harry. She turned back and looked up at him, 'And mind these stairs.' Hank was waiting at the kitchen door. She held it open for him and saw him through, raced him up the narrow yard, onto the street and down again to Harry's door. It was unlocked and she nodded Hank in.

'Where should I put it?'

'Hang on, wait for Harry.'

'In the living room,' Harry said, 'where it'll be seen.'

***

They were sitting in Harry's kitchen, drinking coffee.

'Van's here,' said Harry. Outside there was a tall white van. They heard the doors bang and the three of them went out into the yard.

'You found us,' said Virginia. It was sunny and the sheen was drying from the road.

'Yes,' said the young woman, 'we missed it at first and went into the village.' She turned and pointed to a squat, dark haired man who had a big nose. 'This is Lesley.' He nodded at them.

'Morning.'

Virginia took them into the house.

'Who's she then?' Harry asked.

'She's from the Art Gallery,' Hank told him. 'Sandra Vauxhall, she looks after the pictures.'

'Do they need much looking after?'

Upstairs Virginia watched Sandra Vauxhall put on a pair of white cotton gloves and take the picture of her in the pub, it was a chaos of mess and noise, and lay it down flat and cover it with layers of soft tissue paper and over that layers of plastic bubble wrap. 'I just chucked them in the car,' she said.

Squat Leslie stood and watched the careful wrapping and carried the paintings one by one down the stairs and stacked them in the van. It struck her, shockingly, from nowhere, what Dan had done with all the racket of his life: he had not meant any of it. All of it was just what he happened to be doing. She hardly noticed the first three or four paintings going, but then she saw that the room was emptying and that soon there would be nothing there. Not again, she thought, I don't want to feel this again, and she went downstairs on the bare treads and then there was the empty sitting room, no table and chairs in the kitchen. She stood with Hank and Harry.

'It's like the funeral again,' she said.

'Oh shush,' said Hank and held her hand.

'Are these things worth a few bob then?' Harry asked. He lowered his voice, a conspirator. 'That one you've given me, what would it fetch?'

'Do you mind if we go back to your house, Harry?' said Virginia.

'If you like.'

She sat and listened to Harry telling Hank about the regiment during the war. How old can he be, she thought? It shocked her to think of Harry doing all that, having people shoot at him. 'It was bloody terrible, it was,' she heard him say. She got up and they looked at her, both their faces turning to her.

'I can't sit still,' she said and left them talking.

She had two suitcases in her mother's empty bedroom. She brought them downstairs one by one and then, one by one, out onto the pavement and put them into the boot of Hank's car. She left the boot open and went to find Hank. He and Harry were laughing.

'Would you carry some boxes for me? There are only two, but they're too heavy for me,' she said, lying. 'It's just some things of my mother's. Family stuff I suppose. And some linen.' Hank was staring. 'Would you?' she said. I've nowhere else to go, so you'll have to put me up. Unless you want me to go back to London.'

'No, don't do that.'

Chapter 38

No, don't do that, he had said and she had sat quietly in his car, looking away from him, watching the fields and the sky. He had made lunch for her in the kitchen: scrambled eggs and a thick slice of ham.

Virginia sat and watched the sunshine on the lawn behind the house. She had carried her bag upstairs and then dressed herself up for the garden: a long, light dress that buttoned up the front and made her wish that she had a straw hat. She sat in the shade that the house made and looked up from her newspaper. There were the ragged colours of hollyhocks reaching up into an old, sinuous apple tree. She could see the apples. There were the violet pink spheres of hydrangeas moving in the air. Shadows came and went in the sunshine on the grass. She sat through the afternoon: her mother, the house, village, lover, play, all done with, gone. There was a thrush on the lawn, hopping into a ragged border of raspberry and nettle, gone. Hank made tea for her, made her sit still and wait for him. He came and went, wandering about in the garden, poking and clipping then settling to the vegetables at the far end. She sat and watched him bending and shaking something free of the earth. Then standing up, straight and ponderous. She saw him in the sunshine: his shoulders and the looseness of his shirt, unbuttoned at the cuffs. It was as if he could lean over her and turn the wind and the weather away. In the lea of the world, as if some bluff of land were taking the weight of the air away from her. As Dan had done, she thought, and surprised herself on this old, familiar ground. She wanted Hank to touch her, in a moment panicking, flurried with fear. I only pretend, she thought, but there he is with the marks on his body, never pretending. She had wanted him to touch her when he took her by surprise, standing in that bar with the other men. Surprise again when he followed her onto the street. She had wanted him to touch her straight away; when he had first spoken to her she had wanted him to take her hand and laugh and stroke her arm like an Italian in Paris would. She had wanted him to touch her, it was as simple as that. She imagined, now, being touched by his hand, doing that violence to him, yes, touch me, let him. Then, a heartbeat and being still and looking at him.

Hank was hoeing between the rows of beans and leaks; the peas were starting to jungle up. He flicked the long handled Dutch hoe into the earth, working for a couple of minutes at a time then looking up at the sky and the lawn and the old stones of the house. He picked a handful of radishes and brushed the earth from them with his hand. There were a few early potatoes and he made a pouch for them with the front of his jumper. Quite enough, he thought, enough to get by with, living alone in the old house where lives tumbled over themselves in memory and imagination. Fear seals him in. There is nothing to be done. He half runs the farm, he gardens, cleans the church, goes to the pub because George fetches him if he misses a day. His cousin checks up on him, his daughter checks and worries and nearly kills him with his sorrow for her. He sends her away with his tough smile and gossip from the pub and choir practice and stories about Taff. She writes to Taff. Uncle Taff she calls him. Ridiculous. None of it was any good.

What I should do, he thought, as he stood at the sink running cold water over the potatoes rubbing away their filmy skin, is put my hands on her hips and pull her into me. Stop buggering about Hank. If she were to come in now, just get hold of her with your cold wet hands; mess her up a bit. It could all happen again. He thought this and thought the words as if someone were saying them to him, not knowing if they were true. Being the stolid man in the pub and the church, going on George's trips to the races, working the farm, these

214

things let him have his life. Virginia kissed him, as though this version of himself were worthless, brushing aside the raw stoicism that he had made for himself in the jail, teasing his shyness as she might a boy's. He had heard her, across the bar, whispering to Sadie at the top of her voice, 'He's lovely.' What was she doing making him stand there delighted with his foolishness and hers. What does she imagine, he wonders, in the world that she is conjuring. Does she imagine a blow. Imagine him doing that to her? He imagines it. He imagines taking two torn strides into the kitchen and bringing his fist down upon her. He turned off the tap and put the potatoes into a saucepan.

They will say, 'Well, he's done it once.' And then someone else will reply, 'It shows he must be capable of it.' And, 'It must be in him, mustn't it?' Holding their shopping bags by the freezer cabinet or drinking tea in front of the television.

Hank is an open book that any simpleton might read and he, still appalled, breathless, colludes with any simpleton.

Hank watches her. When she is in the car, he watches her rummaging for sweets in the dashboard, fiddling with the radio, pulling a Bloomsbury face at his Country and Western tapes. 'There's Dusty Springfield as well,' he told her, 'you'd like Dusty.' She burst out laughing and started saying, 'Dusty, Dusty,' in his public-school voice and inventing silly hoity-toity gestures to go with it. He drove on absent-mindedly through the summer fields, dawdling behind lorries, smiling as she roughed him up. Living in the car would be fine.

He tipped the switch on the kettle and took two cups and saucers from the cupboard. He dropped two tea bags into the pot and waited for the water to boil.

'I did have a couple of fights.' He had told her this as she sat on the settee with him worrying and worrying as if he were still there in the prison. 'Not bad, two in nine years. Had to. This lad, big bloke from up north somewhere, don't know what became of him, it was early on and I was getting it, you know, being a posh bastard, bit of a toff, officer. This lad, from Leeds I think it was, he said to me: "Next time, Hank son, you just want to get hold of that bastard and paste him." He gave me a knife. "Use this, plunge him up." He meant it kindly, but I couldn't. I did make a mess of him though.'

'Did you?'

'Yes I did.' She had been still for him. 'I was always good like that. even at school. Made a terrible mess of him. I know all about that: school, army, prison.' He had wanted to say to her: I shall never let you down; I shall always keep faith; always. But he knew how odd it would sound and, anyway, there she was, frightened enough without having the melodrama of some blood loyalty oath forced onto her. 'I should have been a Zulu,' he had said, failing to make a joke, 'or a Red Indian. You should know all of this Ginny, that I can do all this. That I've had it done to me.'

He poured boiling water into the pot. Sometimes when Virginia touched him she made him afraid and he would shrink from her, still recoiling from Paula. The way his hand had stiffened, two knuckles that he could not bend, as he waited with her on the kitchen floor for the police to arrive. He sat with her with his back against the fridge; she was curled away from him and he could see the ridge of her spine, the changing flesh, the back of her thigh and the soft skin behind her knee. He had rolled onto his hands and knees, head down like a dog, onto his feet and found the duvet crumpled on the bedroom floor and covered Paula with it and never saw her again.

Virginia touched him. She took his hand and when she turned to him, to face him, she put her hands flat against his chest and he knew how he felt to her, there, under the palms of her hands. She took his hand and curled it into hers. She came back for him, two, three times, catching him in the pub, stopping for him in the street. He fell into her and into Paula; the same shock of being singled. He saw his hand against her cheek, felt the light shape of the flesh under her eye, masking the bone. He stood still, holding the tray of tea things. What does she see when she looks at me? He saw himself, the heavy torso, the fighter's shoulders.

He sat in the garden with Virginia, poured tea and stared at her. When she looked up from the newspaper he smiled at her. He tried to

216

run through in his head all the fights that he had been in. He remembered a boy called Philip slapping him in the face. They were in the yard at the village school and Hank had torn into him and discovered the celebrity of being a scrapper. Two older boys had plagued him in his first year away at boarding school. They had seemed giants to him and they had picked out his indifference to knock about. He had watched one of them playing tennis and afterwards tracked him to the showers and when he was soaped up had lashed him with a cricket bat. He had broken the boy's shoulder and had sat on his bed waiting to be sent home, but the boy never snitched. Hank had always liked him for that. The army slowed him down. Whenever people were killed it was in the desert fighting with Arabs or, once, with the French in Chad. He stopped the fights in his head, fearing them and brought himself back to the garden, a cup of tea in the shadow cast by the house and the old lawn. He had fought in prison. Taff had seen both. 'You mad bastard, you're fucking demented.' And he had felt leprous and had taken the medication and was out of things for a while. He stopped himself again and watched the sun on the lawn.

Virginia watched him. He sat thinking these things and she watched him drink his tea and stretch out his legs. She watched him put down his cup and saucer on the grass beneath his white plastic chair. Will the chair hold him, she wondered? How can it, he is so heavy? He rubbed the flesh beneath his shirt and she saw him feel the thickness of muscle in his arm and close his eyes, holding himself.

She thought how it was that he dare hardly touch her as if there were some interdict that exiled him. He lets himself be touched, she thought, allows it, but in acquiescence he was shocked, recoiling, feral. She liked to sit with him on the settee and pretend to fall asleep and feel him subside as she breathed quietly against him and then she would sleep and when she woke up he would be waiting for her and she would begin again. Each time that he tells his terrible secrets to her she steps into him and into him again and again and she always knows how it is to have her hand pressing against his chest, the thickness of his body to which there is no end.

Chapter 38

'Do you do this on purpose,' Virginia asked. She shuffled herself up close to him on the settee and took hold of his arm.

'Do what on purpose?' said Hank.

'All of this, this Christian gentleman routine. All of this sexual reticence.'

He looked away from the television. 'Of course I do it on purpose. Does it seem accidental?'

'Don't get smart,' she said, but he was back with the television. 'Don't just sit there, tell me.'

'Tell you what? Tell you about a string of bucolic girlfriends in green wellies and whipcord. How can I remember that far back? Tell you about knee tremblers at the point to point? Is that the sort of thing?'

'Ah,' she said, 'Now we're getting to it.'

'I'm going to have a bath,' Hank said. He sat back into the sofa and put his stocking feet up on the coffee table. She changed the television channel and made him scowl at her.

'Go and have a bath,' she said and drove him out. She sat on the sofa with her knees pulled up to her chin, watching a game show. The audience squealed and laughed.

I could go upstairs, just matter of fact, just a bit of domestic commonplace, and go into the bathroom and have a quick word with him. Give his back a rub perhaps. Could just get into the bloody bath with him. Yes, that would do it, wash his back and then get in with him. Keep my dress on and just get in with him. Make him sit up a bit, wouldn't it? She ran it through in her head. No, it wouldn't do. How would it finish? Nice shot to begin with, a wet dress clinging and billowing in the suds, but where do you go with it?

I shall though, she thought, I'm going to be in that bath with him one way or another. She thought about the bathroom, how the big bath was plonked there in the middle of the of the stark white light. I'm okay, she thought, of course I am, her courage failing. Nobody's that okay, not with that light, not standing there in the white light and getting everything off and into the bath. Could tell him to close his eyes, make him take sly glances on the blink.

How's he going to look anyway? Fine, she thought, he'll look fine, great big sod he is with his wet blond hair and peachy skin. Freckles, I'll bet on freckles, she thought and tried to remember.

I'll strip off in the bedroom and rush him; through the door, slosh, in the bath, Hello gorgeous.

She got up from the sofa and went up the stairs, running so that she would have no time to think again. Naked, in the bedroom, she had a quick look in the mirror, turned away, back again, quickly and again trying to leave herself with just an impression. She was okay, but the sun tan was anyhow, half way up her arms and down her bosom; there was her white arse. And it's only okay, she thought. Just about.

She turned off the big light and tried with the bedside lamp lit behind her. Dear God fancy doing this in rehearsal with a room full of people. People do. She had watched them do it. Be even better if it's steamy, she thought, it's bound to be in a bathroom. She did a couple of stretches, her arms pulling her out as far as she would go and then she found her balance and let her breath trickle out so that she slowed down and thought about how she felt and thought then about Hank's polished candelabra on the kitchen table. She went out of the bedroom, onto the bright landing and down the stairs.

She heard the television laughing. The matches were in one of the drawers. She remembered him lighting the candles and pushing a drawer closed. She found the box and lit the half-burned candles.

In the bedroom she turned off the lamp and saw herself and the candle flames in the mirror. She held up the candelabra in one hand. It was heavy and trembled so that the light wavered. She stuck her chin out, ready to spit. That'll do it, she thought, and ruffled back her hair.

She turned off the landing light and the old house flew back in time with a naked mad woman on the candle lit floorboards. She put the candelabra down on the floor, opened the bathroom door and let out a split of light. She reached around the door jamb, just her arm waving around in the bathroom until she found the light cord and then the room was dark and there were the candle flames again.

'Hank,' she said. She heard nothing. 'Hank?'

'Whose asking?' he said.

Which end were the taps, she thought. Which way would he be facing with the bloody bath stuck there in the middle of the room? She had the candelabra, trembling, in front of her, both hands because it was so heavy. She stepped into the bathroom and there was Hank, pink and wet in the hot water. His big shoulders were hunched so that he could fit in the bath.

'What's your game then?' he asked her, softly. 'Don't burn yourself you twerp. You'll set your hair on fire if you're not careful.'

'Are you angry?' she said. She had had it straight in her head, fixed, that she was going to go straight up to his big, wide eyes, put down the candelabra, kneel down with it to the floor, then stand, just for a second, in the yellow, wavering light, step over him into the bath and then down into the suds with her face full of smiles. 'Are you angry? You're not are you?' She knelt at the side of the bath, her chin almost resting on its rim.

'You've come to wash my back have you?' Hank said.

'I'll wash anything you like,' said Virginia.

'You're not mucky are you?' he asked, looking right down his nose.

'Mucky?' The silly double-edged word made her smile.

'I'm not having a mucky woman in my bath,' said Hank, 'and I'm keeping my end, you can have the taps.'

'Close your eyes.'

'What for?'

'There's no reasonable way to get into a bath and I don't want to look a fool.'

When she was in the water filled the bath to its brim. 'Open your eyes,' she said.

'Are you sure?'

'Did you peep?'

'Certainly not.'

'Come on Hank open your eyes. But no sudden moves.'

'Why not?'

'Because the water will spill.'

He opened his eyes. 'It's right at the top.'

'Keep still,' she said, 'and I'll find the plug.' She twisted around. 'Don't move, will you? Not before the water level goes down. There,' she said, 'no chance of a flood now.'

She stopped and stared. She put a look of astonishment, admiration, onto her face.

'I was a bit worried,' said Hank.

'Dear God,' she said. She crossed herself and looked up, into his face, getting a bit of wonder up there in her eyes. She made him grin, proud and daft. 'Bloody hell,' she said. She leaned forward and took hold of him in both hands.

Acknowledgements

I would like to thank everyone at Stairwell Books especially Alan Gillott and Rose Drew for their endless, sustaining enthusiasm.

Thank you to Dr. David Jones for his generosity in letting me follow him through rehearsals and performances and for his advice about actors.

Thank you once again to Dr. Amy Gotfried for her detailed commentary on the text and for her confidence.

Other novels, novellas and short story collections available from
Stairwell Books

Carol's Christmas	N.E. David
Feria	N.E. David
A Day at the Races	N.E. David
Running With Butterflies	John Walford
Poison Pen	P J Quinn
Wine Dark, Sea Blue	A.L. Michael
Skydive	Andrew Brown
Close Disharmony	P J Quinn
When the Crow Cries	Maxine Ridge
The Geology of Desire	Clint Wastling
Homelands	Shaunna Harper
Border 7	Pauline Kirk
Tales from a Prairie Journal	Rita Jerram
Here in the Cull Valley	John Wheatcroft
How to be a Man	Alan Smith
A Multitude of Things	David Clegg
Know Thyself	Lance Clarke
Thinking of You Always	Lewis Hill
Rapeseed	Alwyn Marriage
A Shadow in My Life	Rita Jerram
Tyrants Rex	Clint Wastling
Abernathy	Claire Patel-Campbell
The Go-to Guy	Neal Hardin
The Martyrdoms at Clifford's Tower 1190 and 1537	John Rayne-Davis
Return of the Mantra	Susie Williamson
Poetic Justice	PJ Quinn
Something I Need to Tell You	William Thirsk-Gaskill
On Suicide Bridge	Tom Dixon
Looking for Githa	Pat Riley
Connecting North	Thelma Laycock
Rocket Boy	John Wheatcroft

For further information please contact rose@stairwellbooks.com

www.stairwellbooks.co.uk
@stairwellbooks